Mr. Gilhooley

To Pegeen

Books by Liam O'Flaherty
published by
WOLFHOUND PRESS

Fiction

FAMINE

SHORT STORIES
(*The Pedlar's Revenge and other stories*)

THE WILDERNESS

SKERRETT

INSURRECTION

THE ASSASSIN

MR. GILHOOLEY

THE ECSTASY OF ANGUS

THE BLACK SOUL

Autobiography

SHAME THE DEVIL

Children's

ALL THINGS COME OF AGE AND THE TEST OF COURAGE

Forthcoming

THE TOURIST GUIDE TO IRELAND

LIAM O'FLAHERTY
A descriptive bibliography
(Edited by George Jefferson)

LETTERS OF LIAM O'FLAHERTY
(Edited by A. A. Kelly)

Mr. Gilhooley

Liam O'Flaherty

M. Wessel-Felter
March 1991
Auburn

WOLFHOUND PRESS

First paperback edition 1991
WOLFHOUND PRESS
68 Mountjoy Square,
Dublin 1.

© 1991, 1926 Liam O'Flaherty

First edition: London 1926

All rights reserved. No part of this book may be reproduced or utilised in any form or by any means electronic or mechanical, including filming, photography, recording, video recording, photocopying or by any information storage and retrieval system, or shall not by way of trade or otherwise be lent, resold, or otherwise circulated in any form of binding or cover other than that in which it is published without prior permission in writing from the publisher. The moral rights of the author have been asserted.

Wolfhound Press receives financial assistance from The Arts Council (An Chomhairle Ealaíon), Dublin, Ireland.

British Library Cataloguing in Publication Data

O'Flaherty, Liam *1896-1984*
Mr. Gilhooley
I. Title
823.912 [F]

ISBN 0-86327-289-4

Cover design: Jan de Fouw
Printed by the Guernsey Press Co. Ltd., Guernsey.

Mr. GILHOOLEY

CHAPTER I

Mr. Laurence Gilhooley emerged from The Bailey restaurant in Duke Street, Dublin. He was slightly drunk, having eaten a heavy dinner and finished two bottles of red wine. He stood in front of the door, swaying gently. His eyes were half closed. His head was thrust backwards. He looked from side to side, wondering whither he was going to turn for his night's amusement.

He was a large man, six feet in height, with broad shoulders, lean hips, muscular thighs, a prominent chest, strong jaws and a thick neck that was red at the nape. His face was fair and slightly wrinkled. His eyes were blue, soft and gentle. His eyebrows were white. Around the sides of his head the hair was grey. At the back it was still fair, while on the crown there was a bald patch, which he always tried to keep concealed by combing long strands over it from the sides.

He was a handsome man without a blemish of any sort, excepting some sort of pockmarks on the tip of his nose, the result of a disease he contracted in Valparaiso.

Yet, it was obvious from his dress, the pose of his body and the sullen expression of his countenance, that he was unhappy in his normal life, that he was getting old and that he would soon go to pieces like a disused hulk, unless something forced him to change the course of his life. He had a hangdog look about him; like a large, indolent, animal, confined in a cage, soured by confinement.

His clothes were of good material but they looked as if they did not belong to him. He might have borrowed them. Or he might just be sheltering under them from a shower of rain; presently to walk forth quite naked as soon as the sun reappeared. A whitish, soft felt hat with a light grey band was perched rakishly at the back of his head. His grey tweed overcoat was unbuttoned. Beneath it he wore a pepper-and-salt suit of Donegal tweed, muddy at the leg and baggy at the knees. His boots appeared not to have been polished for at least two days. His necktie was frayed.

He was a retired civil engineer, living in a boarding-house on the north side of the city, a bachelor with an income of seven hundred pounds a year, without any incumbrances. He had been in South America for twenty years in pursuit of his profession. Three years ago he returned, suffering from some slight affection of the heart, which he contracted while working in the Andes at a high altitude. Shortly after coming to Ireland the affection entirely disappeared but he never returned to South America. The natural indolence of the last generation of Irishmen overcame him. So that he became 'retired', at the age of forty-nine, although still a strong man, in full possession of all his faculties and of all his lusts. As of course, at that time there was no possibility for a man of his capacity to find any employment here that would be worthy of him, he just went on living in his boarding-house in absolute idleness. He began to consort with others like himself in character and age. Like them, he became soured, disgruntled and miserable. He developed the fixed habits of an old man. His energy, for he was a very powerful man, finding no outlet in healthy work, turned first to the pleasure of tippling and then even to other habits. At first he had thoughts of marriage but owing to his lack of family connections he failed to meet a suitable woman. Among the tipplers with whom he came in contact, he could meet only crude, stupid or shallow women who were ignorant of refined love and only regarded marriage as a form of cupidity. So that, failing marriage, he became a voluptuary as well as a tippler.

After considering for some moments whether he should go towards Dawson Street, or towards Grafton Street, he finally turned to the right towards Grafton Street. He wanted to fool around among the women of the town. Not with the intention of dissipating himself with them, for he was long since bored with crude adventures of that sort, but merely to pass away the time and digest his dinner by casual walking.

He set off slowly with his hands in his pockets, taking his steps with that curious languorous grace of an idle man about town.

There was a heavy mist falling. It smelt of charcoal. There was no rain. Yet the pavements were quite wet and water trickled down the shop windows. The gas-lamps looked like yellow moons. It was difficult to imagine that they were fixed on tall black posts. In the strange mist-wrought gloom, they seemed to be transfixed in empty space. Gloomy yellow moons. A number of business people were hurrying home, though it was twenty minutes past seven o'clock and business establishments had been closed for some time. They went past with lowered heads, gripping their raised coat-collars around their throats and coughing out the mist. Other people sauntered along, coming from their homes, seeking amusement.

Hither and thither, beneath the yellow lamps, they moved, hurrying, sauntering.

He halted when he entered Grafton Street. He surveyed the street. In spite of the mist, the gloomy yellow lamps, the wet pavements and the dull, hurried business men, the street appeared very gay to him. The gloomy appearance of the street merely enhanced the feeling of romantic sin that lurked there at that time of day. And for a bored man, gloom, under certain conditions, is more attractive than light and healthy gaiety. He watched the courtesans, swaying their full haunches as they ambled past, arching their shoulders and beckoning with their eyes. He recognized them all by their gay stockings, their rakish hats and by the peculiar look in their never-smiling eyes. That look of mingled avarice, suspicion and fear, which the eyes of courtesans share with the eyes of peasants who have come to the fair to sell something.

He felt a thrill of pleasure permeate his body. He shuddered slightly. He settled his hat at a respectable angle. He lit a cigarette slowly. Then he buttoned up his overcoat carefully.

'Doesn't do to attract attention,' he muttered.

While he was buttoning his overcoat he turned inwards to examine the contents of a shop window. But after he had buttoned it and it became necessary for him again to decide what he was going to do, the feeling of boredom returned in an aggravated state. With the cigarette suspended from his lower lip, he stared at the shop window listlessly.

'What on earth am I going to do?' he asked himself helplessly.

Ding-dong, came the uncouth sound of a tram driver's bell through the gloom. Like a monster with a blazing belly, a Terenure tram-car appeared from Nassau Street, rounded the corner of Trinity College and rattled down to College Green along rusty iron rails. It rattled. The feet of the courtesans, of the loiterers, of the hurrying business people shuffled. Street boys cried. A man was singing to the queue outside the Grafton Cinema. Yet there seemed to be no sound beneath the yellow lamps that shone through the gloom like sinister yellow moons.

'Anything good in yer mind, dearie?' said a hard voice close to Mr. Gilhooley's ear.

Mr. Gilhooley started. A rush of blood went to

his head and his brain whirred. He swallowed his breath, turned his head slightly and saw a woman standing beside him, staring into the window. She turned towards him slowly and winked one eye. Mr. Gilhooley shuddered. His face hardened.

'Who d'ye think you're talking to?' he said harshly.

The woman was a ghastly old harpy with a shrivelled face and a padded body. She glared at him malignantly. Then she made a noise with her lips and turned away, muttering obscenities rapidly. He raised his shoulders and kept them raised rigidly while her insults continued to reach his ears. Then he relaxed.

'God, it's awful!' he said. 'Women! Ough!'

He walked rapidly up the street towards Stephen's Green. At the top of Grafton Street, he crossed over to King Street and entered a public-house which was a favourite resort of his. Outside the public-house door he noticed two or three street urchins looking in. They were laughing excitedly. When he entered, he learned the cause of their excitement. Two of his own friends were in the bar causing a scene. They were Sean Macaward, a dissolute poet, and Shemus Hanrahan, an army officer who had recently been dismissed from the army, owing to some political intrigue in which he had taken part.

The public-house bar was a long narrow room, with a sawdust-covered floor and a bar counter formed of a broad deal board, three feet wide, unpainted, four inches thick, with a wainscotting of the same colour and material. Behind the counter, at regular intervals, stood the fat proprietor, with his enormous bare arms crossed on his chest, and two other attendants. There were several customers scattered at intervals in groups along the counter, and near the door, perched on his customary high stool, sat a drunken old racing tout with three yellow teeth in his upper jaw, who was always to be seen there from six o'clock in the evening until closing time. At the far end of the room, where the bar counter curved inwards, Mr. Gilhooley's two friends were standing. They were drunk and creating a scene, at which the customers, the proprietor and his attendants were looking with a sort of restrained amusement. The proprietor watched them without smiling, his red face like an old poultice, glancing at the clock opposite him now and again, as if he were waiting for the exact moment to intervene and hurl them out into the street.

Mr. Gilhooley paused within the door, nodded intimately to the proprietor, who returned the nod with the same intimacy. The proprietor nodded in the direction of the two drunken men, raising his indistinct eyebrows as he did so. Mr. Gilhooley smiled faintly with his thin, sallow lips, shook his head disapprovingly and walked up the bar. His friends did not notice him until he was upon them. He stood watching them for a few moments unobserved.

They were baptizing a small stray pup which they had picked up somewhere. Hanrahan, the ex-officer, was holding the dog and Macaward, standing a little apart and swaying heavily, was performing the ceremony with a glass of port wine.

Hanrahan was a man who looked fifty although he was not within ten years of that age. His body was rather short, and it looked like a closely-filled sack containing something soft. His face was bloated and red, and he had bright-red thick lips. His face smiled fixedly, manifesting no emotion. He might smile that way killing a man or giving a beggar the price of a bed or listening to a judge passing sentence of death on him. A man without any evil in his nature and yet without a capacity for making any effective use of the good in his nature. A man to be pitied by artists and women and looked upon with suspicion by all efficient citizens, who used him on occasion for rough work like warfare, but cast him aside when there was nothing of the sort needed. Beneath the ends of his thick, soiled, belted burberry coat, the legs of his black-spotted brown trousers were frayed, threadbare and muddy. Yet in spite of his shabbiness, his dissipated face and his hopeless expression, he had a military cut about him, that curious air of desperate gallantry which the born soldier of fortune retains even to the end of his career.

Macaward was an entirely different fellow. He was much older, probably about fifty. But it was impossible to say how old he was. He was a very small fellow, with a triangularly-shaped head, an enormous skull and a chin which, although it was not pointed, was very narrow compared to his broad forehead. His face was probably not sallow originally, but owing to drink and lack of washing, looked quite dark. His little extraordinary eyes had hardly any lashes. They were red around the rims and within the red rims there was a white line right around them. They were of a dim blue colour. His face was wrinkled like that of an old man. It continually changed its expression, at one moment having an ecstatic look of extreme and exalted intelligence, at the next moment looking devilish, at the next moment looking quite stupid and innocent, like the face of a peasant who is asked a question by a police officer.

This extraordinary man was dressed from head to foot in a woman's bath-robe, which was the colour of unwashed linen, with black and yellow vertical stripes. From the ends of the robe, the toes of two heavy army boots appeared, twisted and yellowish, as if they had been thrown on some refuse heap for a long time. His head was bare, still with all its hair, of a darkish colour. A small grey cloth hat, such as lunatics in asylums and children at the seaside wear, was stuck on a blackthorn stick against the counter. Both the stick and the hat belonged to Macaward.

Bending backwards, with his head cocked to one side, Macaward was baptizing the dog, tremulously pouring drops of wine over its shivering snout, while he chanted drunkenly, through his nose and through his clenched teeth intermittently.

'I baptize thee, mangy cur, fleabitten, lop-eared

cur, homeless, destitute cur, fatherless, manyfathered cur, bleareyed, cowardly cur, whining, grovelling cur, symbol of servitude. I call thee all the names of pot-bellied, yellowlivered publicans, shopkeepers, gombeen men and plaster saints, of which O Lord, our unfortunate country has a multitude.'

Every second word caused Hanrahan to utter a loud guffaw in which there was no mirth. As soon as Macaward paused to take breath, Hanrahan wheezed through his nose:

'Call it something it can understand. "Sailor" or something.'

'Don't interrupt,' cried Macaward, with an imperious, though buffoonish gesture. 'It's sacrilegious to interrupt.'

Then he eyed the cur seriously, with his head cocked to one side and a very melancholy expression in his eyes.

'Let the poor devil go,' he said at length. 'Let him die a pagan. He'd be unhappy in Heaven maybe. He'd be in bad company. Let him go to hell with us.'

Suddenly his whole body shook with laughter, but he uttered no sound. His mouth opened, showing discoloured teeth. He looked all around him, leering like a satyr, with a gleam of extraordinary intelligence in his fine eyes, fine at that moment. He looked at everybody with the same curious glance of mocking, extraordinary intelligence, despising both them and himself. Them for their low intelligence. Himself for being a buffoon.

Hanrahan dropped the cur clumsily and looked very serious, suddenly realizing that the situation had become ridiculous. He rubbed his palms and laughed uncomfortably. The cur, with its head turned to one side, its tail under its belly, dragging its haunches, crawled very slowly until it was near the door. Then somebody made a kick at it. It yelped and dashed out with extraordinary rapidity, going goodness knows where, yelping little sharp yelps.

Macaward tossed off the remains of the port at a gulp and then looked at Mr. Gilhooley. He gazed at him stupidly for a few moments before he recognized him. Then he uttered some sort of exclamation and came forward with outstretched hand. Mr. Gilhooley, smiling faintly, did not offer his hand, but Macaward took it, shook it vigorously and, pretending to be very drunk indeed, became maudlin, thrusting out his lower lip and bringing tears into his eyes.

'You're a man,' he said violently. 'A gentleman.' He looked around him with his underlip pushed out and a stupid expression in his eyes. Hanrahan, taking a cigarette from a packet, came a little closer, smiling. 'A man. I like you. See here. There's divinity in everything. Do you know that? Even in a cur. Do you know that?' He suddenly let go the hand and waved both arms in the direction of the others, the customers, the proprietor and the attendants. 'There's no divinity in them. Their souls are dark. Dark. In him,' he added, pointing to Hanrahan with his right forefinger, 'there's a little divinity but not much. He has a half-soul. But you and I have full souls. I, an artist, you, a voluptuary.'

'What are ye talking about?' said Mr. Gilhooley nervously, pulling away his hand.

Macaward staggered back a pace, looked at Mr. Gilhooley malignantly and then blinked his eyes that had hardly any eyelashes.

'Do you know the meaning of the word,' he said slowly and softly, 'the word "voluptuary"? No, you don't know the meaning.' He shook again with laughter, but made no sound. His eyes gleamed with the same light of extraordinary though buffoonish intelligence. Giggling, he said: 'No, he doesn't know the meaning of the word. He is something and he doesn't know he is it. That is funny. He has to buy a drink so. No, I'll buy a drink. I'll buy one for the voluptuary too.'

'Good man, Sean,' said Hanrahan seriously. 'Bit of a fog outside, Larry,' he said respectfully to Mr. Gilhooley.

'Yes,' said Mr. Gilhooley, still a bit nervous and flushing slightly, though he was trying to tell himself that it was ridiculous to pay any attention to the ravings of Macaward. 'Yes, a bit of a fog.'

'See here,' cried Macaward at the counter, pulling out a bundle of banknotes and fluttering them. 'You know me, all of you. Let everybody know me. I'm Sean Macaward. I order three drinks. Three drinks of whiskey. One for myself, one for Hanrahan, and one for the voluptuary. He doesn't know it, but he's a voluptuary. That's why he's a gentleman. A voluptuary.'

'Old Sean is flush to-night,' whispered Hanrahan in Mr. Gilhooley's ear. 'He got paid for a book he did for Greeley's, the publishers. A school book. It's a bloody shame. They pay him so much, knowing he's hard up. So much down, d'ye see? Then they make a fortune on it afterwards. Irish book, ye see. Everybody has to buy,' he hiccoughed, 'cause they must learn Irish for the Free State. D'ye see? Everybody has to buy but he only gets so much down. 'Tud be different ye see – up – if he got, ye see, so much a book, ye see —'

'I know. I know,' said Mr. Gilhooley irritably.

Hanrahan, who had recently, since his dismissal, constituted himself a sort of attendant for Macaward, told this story to everybody many times. He worshipped Macaward, but at the same time played terrible pranks on him, accordingly as the whim seized him.

Mr. Gilhooley accepted the drink with a good grace, although he was anxious to get away from them. At times, he enjoyed this company, but lately he was becoming more and more bored with it. To-night especially, he had a sour feeling within him. He felt a sort of remorse and a desire for something indefinite, which made him feel very miserable. He swallowed that drink in silence. Then he himself ordered a round. Macaward, leering, swaying, changing his moods with lightning rapidity, kept talking and staggering about.

'There are thirty-seven summonses against me,' he said knowingly. 'For pulling the alarm signal on trains. But they can't serve them. The superintendant held me up the other day in Dawson Street. You know him, Shemus, a bright young lad. But I know by the cut of him, he'll be a martinet in a few years. Power. Power. They begin to feel the joy of it after a few years. Then they become sour. Just now he's a gay young fellow. He has a good heart. Fine motor he's got. "Look here," he said to me. "I have to arrest you, Sean." "What for?" says I, though I knew very well what for. "Thirty-five charges," he said, "for pulling the alarm signal." "That's bad," said I. "Do you know why?" "Why?" said he. "Thirty-five is an odd number." And off I went. So that evening I made it thirty-six. Then I went next day and made it thirty-seven. So I must make it thirty-eight to-night. There's bad luck in odd numbers.'

'Better be careful or they'll lock you up,' said Mr. Gilhooley.

'No,' said Macaward resolutely. 'When I think they're going to arrest me I'll go down the country. Country jails are better. Better company there. Tinkers and tramps. There's divinity in tramps, you understand.'

'You're a hell of a fine specimen for a national bard,' said Hanrahan, suddenly becoming angry and melancholy for some reason or other.

The two drunken men looked at one another for a moment. Then they began to wrestle. Suddenly the proprietor, with a face like a poultice, unclasped his arms and approached, heavily striding.

'Now, men,' he said threateningly, in a great bass voice. 'Now, men.'

They had several more drinks. Mr. Gilhooley's brain began to get muddled, and he became more and more unhappy. Then a further disturbance was caused by the arrival outside of a jaunting car, on which there was a large man, cursing violently in a rasping, heavy, aristocratic voice.

'Hello,' said Hanrahan. 'Here's Culbertson. Look out now. You better be going somewhere, Sean.'

'I'll stand my ground,' said Macaward aggressively. 'I'm not afraid of him.'

Culberston advanced up the bar, bringing another man with him. Culbertson was a large man, with overdeveloped shoulders, hips, feet and head. He had a red face, splendidly featured, but with a brutal expression about the firm lips, like the lips of an army officer of a crack regiment on parade. He was a man-about-town, who was drinking some property that had been left him. Behind him walked a disreputable-looking fellow, with a fat old face and a baldish head. This man had no shirt and no overcoat, even though it was a cold February day. His toes were sticking out through his boots and he held the collar of his tattered coat about his throat. That however, did not prevent his wrinkled yellowish chest from being exposed a little.

'You hound,' yelled Culbertson, when he saw Macaward.

He halted and glared about him, exactly like an army officer on parade. Macaward had a short pipe in his puckered lips. He took his hat off the stick and lobbed it on to his head. He took up the stick and spat on it.

'Keep back,' he said malignantly. 'I'm ready for him.'

The proprietor leaned out over the counter.

'That's all right,' said Culbertson to the proprietor. 'No disorder in my company. I have a car waiting. However, I'll see to this worthy fellow first,' he said, touching the shabby man on the shoulder.

'Unfortunate circumstances, gentlemen,' said the shabby man, touching his temple with a palsied white fat hand. 'Unfortunate circumstances.'

'A bloody bum,' said Hanrahan aside.

'Not a bum, you hound,' yelled Culbertson, 'but a worthy fellow. Give him a cigarette, Gilhooley. Listen,' he said to the proprietor. 'On my account give him some money. I'm short, but you know me, Culbertson. It will be all right. Afterwards I'll settle with the other hound. I have a car waiting. I'll settle to-morrow. Give him some money. Some, but not much. He's a worthy fellow. His son, according to his own evidence, was an officer in the Canadian army.'

'An officer with an excellent record. Excellent war record,' babbled the shabby fellow, again touching his right temple.

'He refuses to drink,' said Culbertson, 'and he has no shirt, but that does not prevent him from being a worthy fellow. Charge it to my account. He wants to eat. Look at his feet. Show them your feet, damn it," he yelled to the shabby man.

The shabby man showed his feet, raising first one and then the other. 'Unfortunate circumstances, gentlemen,' he said, 'unfortunate circumstances.'

The proprietor thought a little. Then he gave the shabby man half-a-crown. Culbertson nodded. The shabby man began to retreat towards the door, bowing, touching his temple and murmuring. Culbertson then turned to Macaward. Breathing heavily through his nostrils, he surveyed him in silence for several moments.

'Ante up,' he said at last.

'What about?' said Macaward.

'That cheque,' said Culbertson.

They began an interminable argument about a cheque, talking very loudly and swearing. Mr. Gilhooley seized this opportunity of getting away from them. He moved over to the far end of the counter and whispered to an attendant. The attendant brought him a pint of whiskey, which Mr. Gilhooley secretly put in his hip pocket. He paid and while he was waiting for his change he noticed that the three men were leaving the place still talking very loudly. They were going to settle the matter, whatever it was, at the rooms of a student who belonged to their set.

When Mr. Gilhooley was coming out, they were all getting on the jaunting car. Macaward pretended to be so drunk that they had to strap him on with a belt which the driver used for luggage. A group of loiterers gathered, attracted by the extraordinary spectacle of Macaward in a woman's bath-robe with black and yellow vertical stripes in it. The jaunting car went off. Macaward kept gesticulating with his stick.

Then Mr. Gilhooley left the public-house.

CHAPTER II

IT was now a little after nine o'clock. Outside the Gaiety Theatre there was a ragged, thin loafer, a destitute one, watching the bright lights greedily, hoping to abstract from the lights some of the joy of the interior, where there was music and gay figures strutting on the stage and comfortable people lolling on plush-covered seats, eating chocolates and smiling.

Mr. Gilhooley was quite drunk. His eyes stared fixedly. But in spite of his intoxication and the dullness in front of his eyes, he still felt bored and miserable. His increased intoxication had merely increased his misery instead of relieving it. No misery is as great as that of the lonely voluptuary who feels that his life is wrecked without any hope. Neither the misery of hunger, nor of homelessness, nor of disease. Because in all these miseries there is hope and a sense of righteousness. But in the misery of the bored voluptuary there is no hope nor sense of righteousness.

Mr. Gilhooley looked at the bright lights of the theatre. It occurred to him to go in for an hour. He strutted aimlessly across the street and glanced at the bill. The loafer came up.

'Good thing on, sir,' he said. 'Hot stuff, I believe,' he added, subtly measuring the character of the tippled gentleman.

Mr. Gilhooley stared contemptuously at the loafer with blurred eyes. He threw him a copper and walked away. He entered Grafton Street once more, and without troubling to think where he was going, he began to walk down towards College Green. The lights of the cinema struck his eyes, and he started slightly. Something pleasant occurred to him. He swallowed his breath and licked his lips slightly. He decided to enter the place.

This time he did not glance at the bill but entered rapidly, received an aluminium disc at the box office in exchange for his money, handed the disc to the door porter and passed through the hangings into the theatre.

The lights were turned low. Something was being exhibited on the screen. It was impossible to see whether the theatre was full or empty. Not a sound was heard from the audience if there was one. On the screen there were Americans dancing in a cabaret, while behind a curtain, on the screen, of course, a dark man was whispering to a half-naked woman.

A faint perfume reached Mr. Gilhooley, as he stood breathing heavily with his hat in his hand, waiting for the attendant to lead him to a seat. This perfume was a curious feminine scent, which was familiar to him, for he was an habitué of the cinema for certain reasons; and that curious feminine scent is peculiar to the cinema. So many well-dressed women sitting in silence in the half-darkness. There was an air of mystery about it. An air of romance and of remoteness from actual life. With the mind drugged by the spectacle on the screen, the body hidden from observation by the darkness, yet in contact with others, eavesdropping on the absurd display of emotion exhibited on the screen, passions were aroused which in the cold air outside would bring a flush to the cheek.

The attendant flashed his torch on Mr. Gilhooley, murmured, and led him along. Mr. Gilhooley became very excited. He breathed still more heavily. A feeling of extraordinary passion pervaded his body. His movements were no longer under control of his brain. He could not see, and had he tried to speak at that moment his lips could have uttered no sound. Moisture filled his eyes. He was intoxicated with passion. To the degree that he had been miserable a minute ago, suddenly he had now become deliriously happy, plunged suddenly into that intoxication of the voluptuary by the environment, which suggested strange things to his imagination, and by the prospect of a subtle amusement to which he was addicted.

The attendant pointed with his lighted torch to a row of seats. People rose in a row, one after the other, slowly, to let Mr. Gilhooley pass along. Blindly, without seeing anybody, guided by the forceful arm of the attendant, Mr. Gilhooley found the entrance to the row. Then he pushed along, brushing against the knees and bodies of one man and three women. At last he dropped into a vacant seat, closed his eyes and remained perfectly still. His head was swimming. His mind was empty and as light as a feather. His body was rising into the air, as it were. It kept rising and vanishing. Then another body rose and vanished, leaving another body that rose and vanished to give place to another body that rose and vanished. Body after body kept rising and vanishing. But Mr. Gilhooley kept on sitting there without moving, quite whole and substantial in spite of the numberless bodies that rose and vanished endlessly. And instead of being disturbed by these numberless bodies that rose out of himself and vanished, he kept laughing with great glee within himself, although his face was fixed and flabby. Gradually his breathing became more heavy. The bodies rose more slowly, vanished with difficulty and then ceased rising and vanishing. With a little snap stray ideas floated into his brain. A sort of mischievous idea began to ferment in his mind. His intoxication ceased to be formless and completely stupefied. His passions began to grow angry, as it were. His muscles wanted to take part in this peculiar form of debauchery. His intellect also began to make an effort to have a hand in it, giving it direction and suggesting methods and ideas. Mr. Gilhooley opened one eye and stared straight in front of him at an indistinct object which was the back of a lady's brown fur coat. Then he moved his right knee about a quarter of an inch. It came in contact with something soft. A shock went through his whole body.

He turned slightly and saw a woman sitting on his right. She was a stout woman and, from the line of her sturdy face, a woman of middle-age. But her form, her age, her personality, were not of interest to his mind, nor to his body. His self-centred passion merely toyed with the subtlest form of lust, which does not depend on the object desired, but on the suggestions brought to bear on the object. He touched her knee again and it seemed there was a slight response, that nervous twitching of a muscle that is caused involuntarily, as if the muscle hit back to find out what hit it.

Mr. Gilhooley became very calm suddenly. He slowly took off his coat, doubled it and drew it across his lap. He did this very slowly and it took him a considerable time to do it. While he was doing it, his mind was busy enjoying to the utmost the pleasure which he contemplated. Cunningly aware that the realisation would not be as pleasant as this preparation, it delayed as much as possible the completion of the act of taking off the coat and of doubling it across the knees. The woman remained perfectly still. Although now and for a whole minute past, there had been ripples of laughter eddying through the audience at some buffoonery represented on the screen, the line of her face remained absolutely stiff and motionless. Her chin was raised and her bosom heaved irregularly, her prominent bust jutting out.

With his hand concealed beneath the folded overcoat, Mr. Gilhooley swayed his knee over towards her knee again, until his hand touched her knee. It touched her with the fingers ever so gently. They remained motionless thus for over a minute. Mr. Gilhooley, during this pause, did not feel any emotion at all. Everything, his body, his mind, everything was quite dead. Feeling was completely suspended. Then suddenly the fingers that touched her knee began to tremble. Imperceptibly they began to move along towards her thigh. His legs, then his arms, began to tremble. Shortly this trembling spread all over his body and he no longer knew whether his fingers were moving over her thigh, or indeed where he was. A minute passed, while the woman remained perfectly still, except that her bosom moved still more violently. The most extraordinary visions flashed across Mr. Gilhooley's mind, became more and more exotic and unbelievable. He felt that. . . .

There was a violent shock which sent a shiver down his spine. The woman had moved abruptly, drawing in a deep breath through her nostrils, like a gasp.

'God Almighty!' muttered Mr. Gilhooley, clenching his teeth, drawing back his lower lip and becoming motionless.

The woman rose to her feet, making a considerable noise on purpose, as if making an effort to point out to the audience why she was going. He heard her say: 'Pardon,' in a gruff voice to whoever sat on the far side. And he heard the loud chorus of laughter that greeted some further buffoonery on the screen. Then her dress rustled against the seat in front as she passed out. Mr. Gilhooley became terror-stricken. His body, disturbed in the middle of its debauch, exhausted by the vicious excitement of the nerves, was shivering with fear.

One, two, three, four, five. . . . He kept counting, expecting at every moment to hear a disturbance caused by the lady coming along with an attendant and pointing him out. 'There he is. Seize him.' And the audience would cry: 'Pervert. Away with him. Lynch him.' He would be publicly ruined, disgraced.

The moments became minutes, while he sat there with his lower lip drawn back and his teeth clenched. Still nobody came. The audience, tired now of laughing, watched the buffoonery of their favourite screen buffoon with tears in their eyes, holding their exhausted stomachs. Mr. Gilhooley's fear of detection lessened. Then it vanished. But as soon as his fear vanished it gave place to shame. Nothing could be more horrible than that shame.

It was so powerful that it became physical and he had to press his hands against his lungs to prevent himself crying out. He made his body rigid, planted his right heel on the carpet of the floor, stiffened his calf and pressed his elbows into his sides, while he drew in a deep breath through his clenched teeth. His eyes were popping out of his head. He was in the throes of the mania of guilt which follows in the wake of a perversion.

Terrified by the intensity of his feelings, thinking that he was going mad, that he was going to die, or that he was being stricken by that unknown form of paralysis with which the priest threatened them at school if they persisted in a certain practice, he used various subterfuges to allay his fear and calm his body. He told himself that in an hour at most he would have forgotten it. He told himself that thousands of others were committing acts far more disgraceful at the very moment. But these excuses had no effect on him, until his body of its own accord began to recover from the nervous effects of the debauch. Then his mental attitude to it also underwent a change. Instead of loathing for himself he now felt pity.

The misery of his life, the hopelessness of his future, his solitude, the grossness of the set of imbeciles in which he moved, regrets for the life of activity and of social utility which he had prematurely abandoned, mingled into a sort of shame, which was no longer entirely unpleasant. It had now become a sentimental pity for himself.

His mouth slowly fell open. Tears came into his eyes. He became maudlin. He began to sob in his throat. Tears trickled down his cheeks. The feeling of purity and of being cleansed of something foul, which penitents feel leaving the confessional, took possession of him. He fixed his tearful eyes on a spot in front, a little to the left. His vision formed a little red spot there. In that little red spot he saw his whole life, as he had lived it, futile, unhappy, vicious and degrading. Now there was no good in it, not even the great amount of useful work he had done, the many years of healthy, fierce labour under the hot suns of South America. In his penitential savagery he denied that too to himself. While on the other hand, with a grovelling joy he formed a picture of the life he would like to lead in the future, of the life he *would* lead in the future. Something simple, an innocent country wife, children, a house in the country, pigs, cows, ploughed land, the music of a river, birds, new-mown hay, everything. He thought of the rabbit-farm which he had contemplated recently during similar fits of penitence. He thought of a bee-farm. 'Anything at all,' he mumbled, licking the salt tears that trickled into his mouth with his tongue, 'anything at all, provided it's simple and useful and . . . and healthy.'

Then he grew calmer. His mind underwent a further change. The grovelling penitence became repugnant to him, as gradually his body recovered its strength. His jaws set and his mind contemplated something at a distance: above his head, somewhere in the air, as is usual when a mind contemplates something abstract. There was pride and dignity in this contemplation and this attitude of his mind. There was also sincerity and truth in it, which there was not in the grovelling and despicable penitence of the former abject state.

He thought now of love. Love. Love. Love. He repeated the word several times. And as he repeated it, he was aware that he did not mean sensual love, but that ideal, pure love of which even the most degraded human beings are aware, which they treasure in their inmost hearts, perhaps unknown to themselves, their conception of that ultimate good which man calls God and which in moments of great pain comes to the surface of their consciousness, hurting them and making their souls cry out in anguish.

Soothed by this refreshing thought, his muscles became lax. His weary limbs stretched out limply. Trembling slightly and spasmodically, he closed his eyes and began to breathe gently through his half-open lips. His head swayed forward a little. He was beginning to fall asleep.

He thought of leaving the city, of settling in the country and changing his whole life. A picture formed in his mind. He could hear sounds. He could smell the summer, hawthorn bushes in bloom and the heavy perfume of clover fields, the drunkening perfume of summer with its sounds of sleepy insects, drugged with sap, murmuring in the hot fields. Cows lowed far away, and even though they were far away the sweet odour of their bodies, an odour of new milk, reached his nostrils. In an ivy-covered limestone hill over a river birds were twittering. He himself loafed on a stone fence at the cross-roads, smoking a clay pipe, yawning and conversing with the peasants about some idiotic subject. Soothed by the sounds and the torporous smells, he was falling asleep on the wall. Not on the wall, but in the cinema. He was very happy.

Just before he fell asleep he had a vision of God, a being with a white surplice around his body, girdled at the waist with a gold band, with enormous soft white limbs and a square head, smiling benignantly.

Moisture began to ooze from his forehead. He drew in a deep breath through his nostrils and then let it out in a deep, long snore. He was asleep.

CHAPTER III

It was half-past ten when Mr. Gilhooley awoke.

Somebody began to shake him by the shoulder. Opening his eyes, he jumped to his feet and murmured immediately: 'How much do I owe you? Eh?' There was a murmur of laughter around him. Mr. Gilhooley had been dreaming that he was being tried for the murder of an old woman under gruesome circumstances, and awaking, he thought the hand on his shoulder was the hand of an official of the court who was asking him to pay the fine. Rubbing his eyes, however, he saw a moving crowd around him and a laughing voice was saying close to his ear: 'Here's your hat.' Mr. Gilhooley, without making an effort to arouse himself from his sleep or from the effect of his dream, accepted the hat, gathered up his coat and began to move out with the people.

Yawning in silence, with that feeling of exhaustion which follows a session in a cinema, the audience shuffled out, blinked when they reached the open air, shuddered and darted away in various directions with that sudden access of energy peculiar to animals which have been loosed after a period of confinement in a stable.

While he was being herded out among the multitude, Mr. Gilhooley went along with drooping head and furrowed forehead, with sleep in his eyes, without thought. Suddenly he found himself outside in the street, on the pavement, quite alone, like a fish left on a shore after the retirement of a wave. With a start he came completely to his senses. He looked about him and said to himself: 'Where am I? What has happened?' Then immediately afterwards, he shook his coat which, until then, had been trailing after him drunkenly, and said to himself: 'Where am I going to go?'

He stood for some moments, perhaps three, with his shaken coat held out in front of him. Then a policeman, on patrol, passed slowly in front of him in the roadway. Noting that the gentleman was not sober, the policeman halted for a moment and, lifting his chin slightly, he said: 'Come on, now.' He passed on but a little lower down he halted sideways and looked back. Mr. Gilhooley was busily putting on his coat and scowling.

The mist had now lifted. One could see the sky quite near, still almost covered with dark clouds, but with spots of blue here and there. The blue spots were immeasurably farther away than the clouds, like a patch of blue sea seen from the top of a cliff through a hole in a sea fog. The streets were becoming deserted. Now the tap of a heel sounded loud, and the ear followed the tapping of a particular pair of heels until the tapping died away around a corner. The streets were becoming long empty tunnels instead of streets and a human being going along a street looked very queer and small. The electric lights in the big shops had been turned off and the hats perched on stands in the drapery shops looked very tawdry in this gloom. A strange silence was falling over the city, and every sound, no matter how loud, appeared to be very far off. The sounds also seemed to be making as little sound as possible, as if ashamed of themselves for making sounds when people were taking off their boots, yawning on to the backs of their hands and getting into bed. One could hear a train of some sort clanking on a railway, rumbling, halting for a moment, and then banging against something immovable, then clanking again with the noise of a chain falling in a heap. A ship's siren screamed in the docks at a great distance. Around corners there was an icy current of air without the noise of any wind to say where it came from. A very still night, very cold and forbidding.

Mr. Gilhooley walked away as hurriedly as he he could towards Stephen's Green. He found it difficult to walk straight and insisted on walking at the brink of the pavement. It seemed to him that he must walk on the brink of the pavement in order to prove to himself that he was quite sober, although he was continually swaying out over the brink and in danger of toppling over into the roadway. With the exertion of trying to walk in a perfectly straight line perspiration streamed down his face. The break in the pavement at Chatham Street relieved him of this sort of delusion by compelling him to walk on the roadway. He slackened his pace and began to think coherently. He felt desperately lonely. He thought of his boarding-house and he felt that it would be horrible to return to it in this condition. Sometimes, after experiences of this sort, he spent a night in agony, sitting in his bed, thinking. He remembered Macaward, Hanrahan and Culbertson. As soon as he remembered them, he felt a maudlin affection for them and decided that he must find them immediately and spend the night with them, probably at Culbertson's flat. The desire to find them sharpened his memory at one point, so that he remembered clearly that in the public-house while they were arguing, they had stated they were going to the rooms of the student Stevens, who belonged to the set.

'I'll head off for Stevens,' thought Mr. Gilhooley, suddenly quickening his pace.

Feeling very tired, however, and not at all sure of his ability to reach Stevens' rooms without falling in the roadway and getting arrested, he hailed a cab in Stephen's Green and gave the address to a little crooked cabman, who was wearing three overcoats, with an old sack across his shoulders.

In the dark interior of the cab, leaning back, with his hands clasped on his stomach, he felt a curious sensation of being pursued by somebody with a big club or a gun of some sort. The fellow was behind him, and although he was running up at a tremendous pace, with his head turned sideways, he kept at the same distance and did not succeed in striking or in firing. Mr. Gilhooley could not decide whether he had a stick or a gun, and this doubt kept him busy until the cab halted with a jolt in a street off Fitzwilliam Square, where Stevens had rooms. He stumbled out eagerly and immediately forgot the man who was pursuing him. He felt a great relief and spoke in a very cheerful voice to the cabman, as if he were unexpectedly relieved from a very perilous situation. He paid the cabman double his fare and dismissed him with a cheerful: 'Good-night.' Then he walked up the steps to the door, coughing in his throat and saying to himself: 'I'm all right now. We'll have a great night of it.' He rang and then waited. While he waited, an extraordinary feeling of exhilaration possessed him. With his eyes fixed on the door-knob, with his head reaching forward slightly, he kept thinking, or rather feeling, that this was a great life, and that presently he would be laughing, telling stories, drinking and having the time of his life. The thought of Macaward and the the others aroused in him a great enthusiasm, and he felt that these fellows were the most original, interesting and worthy fellows he had ever met, that he would be for ever happy in their company, and that a life of this sort was the only one worth living. Then suddenly the door opened and an old woman, with a sour, wrinkled face, wearing a black, indistinct frock, appeared at the slit, which she had made, about three inches in the doorway.

'Who is it?' she said cautiously.

It was the caretaker of the house. The house had recently been converted into apartments, of which the student Stevens possessed the one on the top floor. Formerly the house belonged to a retired army officer who bred horses somewhere down the country on his estate. But he had been either forced to convert it through poverty, or having become deeply engrossed in the breeding of horses had given up having a place in the city altogether.

'Is Mr. Stevens . . . eh . . . at home?' said Mr. Gilhooley, speaking in a gentle, rather timorous and hesitating voice.

'No, then, he isn't,' said the woman, gathering her clothes at her breast with a bony, shrivelled hand and glancing around the doorpost down the street with a scowl as if she were expecting something unpleasant from that quarter. 'He's gone out with . . . ' She shuddered from the cold, paused and glanced at Mr. Gilhooley with evident disapproval. She added curtly: 'Your friends came for him and indeed they kicked up an awful row, as if he had anything to do with it.'

'Heh, heh,' said Mr. Gilhooley timorously. 'What about? Where did they go?'

'There's no necessity for him to be mixed up in anything like that,' said the woman. 'His mother came to see him the other week in a motor car, wearin' a fur coat that cost pounds an' pounds. What would he want with forgin' cheques?'

Again she glanced sideways down the street around the doorpost, suspiciously, as if she were deeply interested in what she might see there, whereas she had no interest in Mr. Gilhooley or in what she was saying to him.

'Sure he had . . . he had . . . he had nothing to do with that cheque,' said Mr. Gilhooley. 'It was only a . . . only a joke. It was Macaward. . . . But where did they go? Did they say they'd be coming back shortly?'

The woman did not answer him for several moments, looking around the doorpost down the street suspiciously. Then grunting something, she retreated a pace, shuddered, glanced at him with aversion in her queer face, and closed the door. She opened it again an inch or two and said:

'He's not in. It's down the country they're gone . . . somewhere.'

She paused, looking out through the slit at him with one eye. Mr. Gilhooley pursed up his lips, drooped his head, shrugged his shoulders and walked down the steps. The woman stuck out her head again and glanced suspiciously around the corner of the doorpost down the street. Then mumbling to herself, she closed the door with a bang. Mr. Gilhooley shuddered when he heard the bang and he said to himself:

'That puts the tin hat on it. I'll have to go home.'

He had walked to the end of the street before he began to feel miserable again. Then the feeling of acute depression swooped down on him and he sharpened his pace, glancing around him from side to side, like an animal that has been struck suddenly on the haunches from behind. But presently he slackened his pace again. A fit of shuddering seized him, giving away gradually to a feeling of torpor. His jaws set. His teeth pressed together. He contemplated himself inwardly and he toyed with a romantic desire for death. He walked aimlessly, feeling that as long as he walked about aimlessly he was quite safe and these accusing spectres would not approach him, with clubs in their hands . . . or was it a gun?

He met nobody at all. In the distance now and again he saw the figure of a policeman, erect and substantial, symbol of security, good citizenship and smug propriety. Everything that he himself was not. He always made a little détour to avoid these figures. And at length he discovered that he was just walking to and fro among the streets that border on the National University Buildings. He halted and drew in a deep breath and shook himself.

'Come on,' he said to himself. 'There's nothing else for it. I must go home. I must face it.'

It really appeared terrible, going home to spend a night alone in his room, sitting up in bed, with his hands clasped around his bended knees, shuddering and thinking.

He looked at his watch. It was a quarter-past eleven.

He was standing at the juncture of three small streets, A lamp-post was near him on the right. At his back there was a brick wall, with little bare trees jutting over it. In the distance there was the gloomy whitish building of the University. Then, at other points, bulky shadows of rows of houses arose. There was a dark avenue ending in a group of trees that were quite naked. There was no sound in the neighbourhood, although in the distance there were sounds, light sounds and heavy sounds. There were merely shadows in the neighbourhood and dark lines, winding, sharply curving and stiff, angular lines. There were colours too, although everything had a superficial contour of gloom. Whitish colours and brown colours and pitch-black colours stood out distinctly. The roads were white, if contrasted with the mouths of lanes. And the hulks of streets, whole rows of houses, were brown, standing above the white roads. He contemplated these colours and sounds and shadows with great interest inwardly. And they seemed to press in on him, surrounding him, the colours, the sounds and the shadows.

There was silence quite near him. Then a little sound reached his ears. Although he did not see the human being, he knew that a human being approached. Not so much by the light sound he heard, of the sole of a shoe scraping lightly, as by the indistinct smell of a human being, an instinctive smell. He glanced over his shoulder, watched a corner closely, and presently the figure of a woman, walking very slowly, turned the corner, about five yards away. It was only then he heard the light tapping of her heels, she was walking so lightly and slowly. When she was beside him, she halted aimlessly and spoke.

'Good-night,' she said in a gentle voice, uttering the first syllable on a much higher note than the second, with a thrill in her accent like the voice of a bird.

'Good-night,' he said thickly, in his throat.

There was a pause. The woman looked into the distance. He looked at the woman, frowning.

She was quite a girl, young, slim, her features not yet hardened by age nor by the vice which might be expected (and which Mr. Gilhooley did expect) to be portrayed in them. Her face looked innocent, naïve, sad, like the face of a child that has lost its way and cannot find its mother. In the curious light formed by the lamp, the white roadway, the dark lane mouths, the sky that had now a dark belly overhead moving slightly, a dark belly of massing clouds, windlessly massing, the girl's face looked tiny and very white. Her slim body was shivering in a thin brown raincoat. Thin because her other clothes formed sharp lines showing beneath it like straight veins. The coat was held at the waist by a narrow yellow belt, obviously not the one bought with the coat but one that was bought in a sixpenny shop, with bright brass-edged holes in it. Her two gloveless hands were toying with the end of this belt, in front. Her hands were red with the cold. The overcoat was fastened at her throat with a safety-pin. She wore a little black skull-cap, with a stork embroidered in silver on the front. Even though she was not tall, the raincoat did not reach much below her knees. Her legs were beautiful, slim, elegantly shaped, encased in black stockings.

Mr. Gilhooley stood very still, gazing at her, moving his white eyebrows. His eyes at last met her eyes. He started slightly. An unpleasant frown passed over his slightly wrinkled face. Then his lips opened and he contracted his white eyebrows. He made a movement in his throat as if he were about to speak but he did not. Her eyes were staring into his, without movement. They stared so tensely, like the eyes of a dog that is begging for pity. He remembered the eyes of the cur in the public-house and he curled up his lips. But again his face relaxed. His lips fell open. These eyes were magnificent blue eyes, so beautiful compared to the tawdry clothes, the white face, the red hands. And they had a look of terror in them. This look of terror was making an appeal to Mr. Gilhooley. He found it unpleasant.

Suddenly the girl broke the silence by laughing nervously. She stood on one leg and then on the other. She shook her head and then shuddered all over.

'It's very cold,' she said timidly, looking into his eyes, then smiled, then suddenly cast a glance to one side, with the same look of terror in her eyes. She looked back into his eyes again suddenly. When her eyes moved, they moved jerkily, afraid of pursuers.

The same feeling of unpleasantness made Mr. Gilhooley contract his white eyebrows again. The girl looked repulsive to him, with her white face, her skimpy body, the safety-pin at her throat, and the look of terror in her eyes.

'What's that?' he said.

'It's very cold,' she repeated.

'What d'ye expect?' he said, shrugging his shoulder. 'It's winter. Eh?'

There was another pause. Somehow, Mr. Gilhooley had become very angry with her. All the time that he stood looking at her, a feeling of pity was growing in him, and he hated it. It made him feel very unhappy. He wanted another sort of feeling to grow in him, in order to rid him of his depression and give a promise of amusement for the night, as a last resort, although he had long since given up this form of amusement. But this charmless waif with her skimpy body and her shabby clothes did not arouse that feeling.

The girl, wrinkling her little forehead and biting her thin lips, one after the other, was looking into the distance at the sky.

'I've nowhere to go,' she said at length vehemently, striking the ground with the tip of her right shoe, a little to the rear of her left heel.

Mr. Gilhooley made a sound like a sarcastic laugh. 'There's a lot of people in the same boat,' he said sourly. 'Can't ye find anybody?'

'How do you mean?' she said seriously.

'Aw! For God sake,' said Mr. Gilhooley, 'don't be putting on airs. Yer too young.'

Her lips began to blubber. Mr. Gilhooley cursed under his breath. The feeling of pity was getting the mastery over him and he hated himself for speaking so harshly. He glanced at her breasts. They were very slight.

'How d'ye make out ye've nowhere to go?' he said, in a softer voice.

'Honest,' she said, biting her underlip to control her voice, 'I have been walking the streets for three nights. Nearly four, because I spent the best part of another night at the railway station. The night I came,' she added in a lower tone, as if the memory of her sleepless nights had made her too weary to finish properly.

'I better be going,' thought Mr. Gilhooley, feeling himself overcome by pity. Lately, since he became a voluptuary, he had been able to smother this feeling in himself and he did not want to awaken it again. 'She's pulling my leg. I had better be going.'

Still he did not move. When he thought of moving, he also thought of his empty room.

'Where did ye come from,' he said, 'if yer only four days here?'

'Belfast.'

'Ha, Belfast. Ye live in Belfast?'

'No. I just came from there.'

'Ha. Working there?'

'No.'

'Damn the little bitch,' thought Mr. Gilhooley. 'Only because I'm drunk I'm standing here jawing with her.'

'Well, good-night,' he said, moving away.

The girl jumped forward, seized him by the overcoat and whispered excitedly:

'For God sake, sir, whoever you are, don't leave me. I'm very hungry. I'm cold . . . cold . . . so cold. It's very cold and . . . and I'm afraid. I'm afraid. I don't know anybody. Not a soul. I don't know anybody. Don't leave me.'

She began to tremble violently as if she were going into hysterics. Mr. Gilhooley became very excited. Forgetting everything, except this feeling of pity which now assumed a complete mastery over him, he put his two arms around her and crushed her to him violently in an effort to stop her hysterics.

'Easy there. Easy there,' he almost shouted.

The girl stopped immediately. He loosed his hold.

'God, ye. . . . Ye gave me a fright,' he said. 'What are ye shiverin' for? Are ye hungry? Sure nobody is going to bite ye.'

The girl nodded her head, baring her short white teeth as she did so and furrowing her forehead. Her struggle had pushed back her cap a little and now a row of yellow curls were visible across her forehead. That made her face look prettier. What charm the curls gave her face! Standing over her, however, Mr. Gilhooley did not see the curls, nor the charm their appearance gave her face. It was still with the same feeling of repulsion and pity that he said:

'Come on, then, if yer hungry. Couldn't let a dog go hungry. Not to mind a . . . not to mind a . . . Eh?'

'Thanks,' said the girl almost inaudibly. Then she snivelled.

He walked off, a little in front, taking long steps. As soon as he moved he became aware of his drunkenness, the heaviness of his body and the immense weight of the still cold night pressing in on him. He seemed to be dragging a great load in the shape of his body. In this strange sensation of pity, he felt a great load, dragging at his heels, weighing him down, yet pleasant. His breath, when he drew it heavily into his lungs, felt salt, as after heavy weeping.

The girl walked a little behind him with little short steps. She was sobbing aloud. She held a handkerchief twined around the fingers of her left hand and she was biting into the handkerchief. After a while Mr. Gilhooley told her angrily to stop crying. Her crying seemed to increase the weight at his heels. She stopped crying. She suddenly raised her head, tossed it, like a schoolgirl, and her face became suffused with a brilliant light. She smiled, a strange smile. She looked into the distance at the sky and smiled again at something there, in the sky. In the smile there was now some precocious knowledge, a knowledge of bacchanalian joy and of feminine subtlety.

CHAPTER IV

He brought her to a supper house in King Street, across the road from the theatre. Being slightly ashamed of her shabby dress (for even though he was drunk he still retained his characteristic respect for the conventions) he seated her in the room within the door. Through the door that led to the inner room he saw a group of whom he recognized one man, a Government official with whom he had recently some business dealings. It was a matter relating to shares in South Russian Railways which he was trying to recover. They had been rendered worthless by the revolution in Russia. With a tenacity unexpected in an indolent man, he was still pestering the Government about them, even though it was long ago certain that he was wasting his stamps. This official and some others were entertaining chorus girls in the inner room.

'Don't want to let that fellow see me,' thought Mr. Gilhooley, getting right into the corner.

'Order what ye want,' he said gruffly to the girl.

The big, fat proprietress came. The girl ordered a mixed grill.

'Nothing for me,' said Mr. Gilhooley sourly.

The big, fat woman pressed him, however, so he ordered coffee. Then taking his face in his hands, he rested his elbows on the table and fell into a doze. The girl, who was sitting opposite him, very timidly touched him on the arm. He started up. The food had already been served. Strangely enough, although he had only ordered coffee, a mixed grill was given him also. He stared at it stupidly and felt too dull to offer any resistance to the cupidity of the proprietress.

'Go ahead,' he said to the girl. 'Eat. I'll just have some coffee. I feel a bit dry.'

The girl had neither moved her eyes nor spoken since she entered. She had sat with her hands clasped under the table, quivering slightly. The food had been placed on the table for nearly half a minute before she mustered courage to tip Mr. Gilhooley's arm, and even after he asked her to begin she did not do so. She kept glancing from her plate to his with a hunted look in her eyes. Mr. Gilhooley, taking pity on her timidity, sighed and made a show of seasoning his food with salt and pepper and handled his knife and fork and began to sip his coffee, making wry faces and watching the girl from the corners of his eyes.

She put the first morsel in her mouth timidly. She tasted it gently, nibbling small nibbles like a rabbit. She swallowed. Then she fell on the food like a hungry wolf, stuffing her mouth and rolling her large eyes around the table with a fierce expression in them. Now and again she cast a savage glance in the direction of Mr. Gilhooley. Then suddenly she would flush, drop her knife and fork, swallow something in her throat and smile faintly, as if making an apology.

'Go ahead, go ahead,' said Mr. Gilhooley tenderly.

'Poor little devil,' he said to himself. 'She's famished. Curse it.'

After each pause she began with greater avidity. The more she ate the more fierce she became, losing all traces of her timidity and of good manners. This made her still more repulsive to Mr. Gilhooley physically, and yet at the same time it increased his pity for her.

So that he groaned inwardly, cursing himself, the world, and his drunken state, which he felt sure was responsible for this weakness in him. For it seemed to him now that the girl had already attached herself to him, that he was responsible for her, that he would have to look after her, and yet . . . get nothing for it.

The girl finished her food, glanced at Mr. Gilhooley's downcast face and began to stir her coffee. After she glanced at Mr. Gilhooley her forehead wrinkled. She looked into the coffee with open lips, and then bit one lip after the other. Suddenly she raised her head, swallowed something in her throat, and smiled.

'Thanks very much,' she said. 'You're very kind. You're a kind man.'

'Eh?' said Mr. Gilhooley, wrinkling his white eyebrows and scowling with his thin, sallow lips, embarrassed and a trifle vexed. 'None of that now. Did you have enough?'

'Yes, yes,' she said, smiling again.

The smile illuminated her face. There was a knowledge of bacchanalian joy in her face when she smiled. It did not make her pale face prettier, but it illuminated the eyes, and it seemed that it disclosed a joyous personality, capable of strange transports of pleasure. It fascinated Mr. Gilhooley and he looked at her in wonder. She raised her upper lip slightly, showing her short white teeth. Like a merry little wild animal.

'Could you give me a cigarette?' she said.

'Pleasure,' mumbled Mr. Gilhooley.

While he was getting the cigarette, she took off her cap and looking at herself in the wall mirror, she tossed her head, so that the curls jumped about. When Mr. Gilhooley looked again, an astonishing sight met his eyes. The girl was transformed.

Instead of the miserable waif, with a skimpy body, a shabby raincoat, with a safety-pin at her throat, he saw a charming, impish, smiling face, crowned with a thick mass of golden curls. They shone in the light. Suddenly released from the close pressure of the black cap, they bubbled up in little hillocks, disentwining like writhing snakes, sparkling and trembling. Beneath them the white face had now taken a different light. The short white teeth and the brilliant, blue, laughing, big eyes mocked him, as if they suddenly disclosed a secret they had been hiding. They mocked with the same look of gaiety, as when she smiled before, but now it was different, for the sparkling yellow curls, like a golden treasure, stood above them explaining this gay madness.

Mr. Gilhooley was dazzled with this sight. He could not prevent himself from smiling and leaning forward to touch the curls. They crackled as his hand passed over them. Immediately he forgot the pity and that other feeling possessed him, which he had desired before as an amusement, but which now made him tremble and be afraid.

'That's a . . . that's a . . . that's a fine head of . . . head of hair,' he mumbled.

'Hm . . . hm,' said the girl, taking a cigarette from the packet he had dropped on the table.

When she spoke he recovered himself. Her voice had been dry and calm. They smoked in silence, until she had finished her cigarette.

He paid the bill and they went out.

A little to the right of the door outside, Mr. Gilhooley halted, with his hands in his overcoat pockets, staring at his outstretched right boot. He mused in silence for a time, scowling and moving his jaws. The girl did not speak, standing a little in front of him, arranging her cap and staring into the distance at the sky. The look of hopelessness and destitution had come into her face again. Her shoulders were shivering spasmodically with the cold. At last Mr. Gilhooley straightened himself and walked on with a jerk.

'Come on,' he muttered. 'There's nothing else for it. Ye might as well come to my place. We'll manage somehow. Though it is . . . never mind.'

They got a cab at the rank on Stephen's Green and Mr. Gilhooley told the driver to go to a square near the street in which he lived. He did not want to drive to the door for obvious reasons. They sat in the cab in silence until it reached its destination. During this time Mr. Gilhooley's mind was very disturbed, though not unpleasantly so. He had a curious idea that his meeting with this girl and his taking her home was an important thing in his life. He did not know why it was so. But, looking out through the cab window at the queer, deserted-looking buildings, at the stretches of whitish streets, utterly deserted and vast-looking, at the comic-looking monuments in O'Connel Street, he felt the same sensation as he had once experienced when a young lad, driving in a mourning coach at his father's funeral. Then, he had felt no sorrow for his father. He did not understand the solemnity of the occasion. But he was deeply impressed by the silence of the long line of mourning coaches, of traps, of jaunting cars and of men on horseback. He was near the front and he could hear the steady rhythm of feet, of the marchers behind the hearse. He could see the gently swaying countryside, bleak with winter and naked trees, swaying to the slow swaying of the mourning coach. He could see the naked blue sky, sour-looking with winter and cold. And he sat very still, impressed by this silence, this nakedness, this steady tramping of feet and by the memory of his mother, who had sat all the previous night in the room next to where the coffin was, with her lips screwed together in a stitch. Something impressive was being enacted which he did not understand. At that time . . . and now too . . . something impressive was being enacted . . . either because lately he had been turning in upon himself through loneliness or because there was something mysterious in the girl who sat in silence beside him, shivering slightly. He could feel her shoulders shivering, as she leaned over with the swaying of the cab.

They dismissed the cab in a square which was falling into decay. Then they walked until they reached a street of three-storeyed red brick houses. The street was built down an incline, giving the houses a curious shape. They were level at the tops. But their bottoms slanted. There were no lights in the houses. All was still. Mr. Gilhooley halted by a little dairy, the front of which was covered with black wooden shutters. He whispered to the girl:

'Not a word now. Not a word.'

The girl nodded. They came to the house on tiptoe. On tiptoe they ascended the four stone steps leading to the door. There Mr. Gilhooley put his fingers to his lips and stooped down. He found the key in his waistcoat pocket and gently opened the door, holding the knob firmly as he did so. The door made a tiny soft squeak as he pushed gently inward. It was quite dark within. He pawed about for the girl, caught her arm and squeezing it very hard, guided her into the hall. Then he entered and closed the door noiselessly. With a low grunt, he stooped and began to unlace his boots. While he was doing so, she made a little sound, drawing in her breath through her teeth. He clutched at her right leg above the ankle and squeezed it but said nothing. Presently he stood erect, tying the bootlaces together. Then he slung the boots around his neck, letting them hang in front over his chest. He pawed for the girl again and took her by both shoulders.

'On my back,' he muttered.

He got her on his back and set off slowly, moving his hands around in the darkness like a blind man. He began to ascend the stairs, planting his feet square and making his shoulders rigid, pausing now and again to listen for sounds. There seemed to be nothing on his powerful back.

The girl lay perfectly still on his back, clutching his coat lapels with her red, thin hands, hanging limply. He could feel her body shivering with fright or cold.

Mr. Gilhooley's room was on the third floor, sharing that floor with a smaller room, which was occupied by a medical student. Mr. Gilhooley's room faced the front and it had a white goatskin mat outside it. The third door on that landing did not lead to a room but to a little naked deal stairs that reached to the attic overhead, where the family slept, the landlady's family.

He dropped the girl lightly on the white goatskin mat, opened the door carefully, entered the room, drew her in after him and then, losing control of his muscles after the tension, closed the door with a bang. Startled by the noise he became rigid, said: 'Hist,' and then listened. Not a sound. The girl was somewhere near, breathing excitedly. It was pitch-black in the room. He turned the key in the lock and then abstracted it. He was about to feel along the wall for the electric switch, when he paused, licked his upper lip with his under lip, in the darkness, and frowned.

'Better hide the key,' he thought, 'before turning on the light. She looks innocent, but still. . . .'

Groping with his left hand in front of him, he stooped down by the wall, rummaged about a little and touched a heap of papers that lay on the floor with the groping hand. This heap of papers were Sunday papers which he read in bed each Sunday morning and kept, piling one on top of the other, out of the miserly instinct which had lately developed in him; miserly regarding things of no consequence. He placed the key in among them and rose erect, moving carefully so as not to let the girl know where he was, what he was doing; or if she did know what he was doing, where he had hidden it.

He moved towards the electric switch again. As he moved over the dark-stained bare boards of the floor, the boards creaked under the weight of his carefully-stepping, heavy, stockinged feet.

He turned on the light. The room lit up. The girl started and put her hands to her chin. Slowly she looked around from corner to corner, saw the bed, shuddered, then looked at Mr. Gilhooley from head to foot carefully, as if she had just seen him for the first time, or as if she had been with him somewhere in darkness for a long time and now saw him for the first time in clear light.

'Well,' said Mr. Gilhooley, smiling faintly and

waving his hand towards the room uncertainly. 'Sit down.'

She did not move. He unslung his boots and moved quickly over towards the gas fire. Stooping and grunting, he lit it. *Puff*, *paff*. The queer thing, like a bone with holes in it, became full of flame. Mr. Gilhooley, without looking at the girl, sat down in a chair by it and said again :

'Pull up a chair and warm yerself.'

She obeyed this time.

The big, square room, with long, high walls, was very silent. Everything was in a straight line, the walls, the windows, the enormous bed, with its head to the wall and its end to the space between the two windows, the tall wardrobe, with its door, holding a mirror, standing a little ajar, the big oblong steamer trunk, the straight-backed chairs, the wash-hand-stand. The room looked empty. The only two articles of furniture that impressed themselves on the eye after a short examination were the enormous bed and the shabby square carpet in the centre of the floor. The carpet was purple. The bed was a wooden one, on four stout posts, with a canopy over its head and an enormous feather mattress covering it.

They sat over the fire for nearly a minute without speaking. The silence became very embarrassing. Mr. Gilhooley, being in the habit of living alone, both since his return to Ireland and during the twenty years he spent in South America in sparsely populated places, was not clever at conversation.

Further, he was not quite at home with this girl If she were coarse, he could easily approach her in a casual, coarse manner. But she obviously was not coarse. Yet, it was absolutely necessary to get on some more intimate footing with her.

He got to his feet, took off his overcoat and put it away.

'Take off yer coat,' he said.

She jumped up and began to unloose her belt. Then she tossed her head, suddenly assumed a pert expression and said, as she opened out her coat :

'I had to sell my coat in Belfast to a Jew to get my fare to Dublin. He gave me this.'

She laughed a little laugh and looked very 'tough,' obviously on purpose, but her face was strained and almost immediately, without releasing her sleeves from the shabby thing, she put her hands to her eyes and burst into tears. Mr. Gilhooley, walking towards the gas fire, started and became very angry.

'Here now, here now,' he said, clutching and unclutching the fingers of his right hand. 'What's up now? What's up?'

'What's going to happen to me?' she wailed, shaking her shoulders.

'Ech?' said Mr. Gilhooley, 'there's nothing going to happen to ye.' He paused and scratched his poll, under the rim of the hat which he had not yet taken off. 'Are ye afraid or what?' he added. ''Fraid of me?'

'No, no,' she said quite calmly, taking away her

hands and licking her lower lip with the tip of her tongue. She examined him carefully from head to foot. Then she looked towards the door. 'No. Not you,' she said. 'It's him. I'm afraid of Matt. I'm afraid of him. I'm afraid.'

Her bosom heaved and her eyes seemed to enlarge with fear. Mr. Gilhooley felt a little shiver down his spine at first. Then he mused suspiciously.

'She's putting it on,' he thought. 'Hm. This is a nice how-d'ye-do.'

'Oh, sit down, for God's sake,' he said. 'Take off yer coat and sit down. Have a fa . . . a cigarette?'

'Thanks,' she said, rapidly taking off her coat and reaching out with a trembling hand for the cigarette. long before he had taken it from the packet. As soon as she received it, she put it between her lips and holding her thumb and forefinger to it, reached forward her mouth towards him for a light, trembling and blinking. He gave her a light. Then she put away her coat and sat down. Mr. Gilhooley took off his hat. While he was putting it on a peg at the back of the door, he felt the pint bottle of whisky on his hip and he uttered an exclamation.

'Saved,' he cried joyfully. 'Be the hokey, I had clean forgotten it. What d'ye think of that, now?' he cried, pulling it out and examining it joyfully against the light. 'A pint. Well, well. There's luck. Never say die. What?'

From under the bed, he drew his slippers, put his feet into them and then shuffled to the wash-hand-stand, pulling out his knife as he went. Opening the corkscrew in the knife with one hand, he picked up the glass off the neck of the carafe and approached the girl hurriedly.

'You have the glass,' he said. 'I'll drink out of the bottle.'

The girl refused at first, but at length she took the glass. He gave her a little. She drank. Gilhooley also drank. When the bottle went to his lips, he forgot the girl and everything. He had a long drink, pausing several times with the bottle to his lips. When he lowered the bottle it was half empty. His eyes were dim. And he felt very far away and careless. He kept blowing out his breath through his nose, heaving his chest and shaking his head slightly. The girl was still sipping her glass and staring at the fire.

'I say,' he said, ' eh . . . what name ? '

'Nelly,' she said. Then she added after a little pause: 'Fitzpatrick.'

'I see,' he said. 'Whereabouts is that now? Fitzpatrick. The west would it be?'

'Yes,' she said, ' I'm from Galway. Well, I was reared there, anyway. Though I don't know where I was born.'

'Don't know where ye were born?' said Mr. Gilhooley, beginning to hiccough and having no interest at all where she was born. Since his drink he had suddenly grown careless about everything, indifferent to the world, suddenly wafted into that delicious state of intoxication which had evaded him all the evening and which had now come upon him unawares after that last drink.

'I'm an orphan,' she said. 'I believe I was born in America and my mother came over here with me when I was little. She died. I was reared by a woman in Galway who took me from the nuns for charity. That's why, you see. . . .'

'I see. You were reared. I see.'

'They didn't tell me anything about . . . about it. I know very little about it.'

'How do you mean? Yes . . . of course. Oh! Of course. There's a convent in Galway.'

'Horrid woman.'

'What woman is this? The nun? Ye shouldn't speak about nuns that way.'

'No. Not the nuns. They were nice. But aunty. She wasn't my aunty but she made me call her. . . .'

'Hold on a mo'. How old would ye be now?'

'Twenty-two last month. She used to beat me.'

'What for?'

'Don't know. She was queer. Pure wickedness, I think. She wanted me to be a nun: I didn't want to be a nun.'

'Have another drop.'

Without thinking she held out her glass, but withdrew it again and shuddered, glancing at him almost with aversion. He pressed her, however, carelessly, still enjoying the exquisite pleasure of being happily drunk. She allowed a little into her glass and immediately tasted it. He had another sip.

'Go on,' he said. 'What next? Where does Matt come in? Eh?'

'Horrid,' she said, shuddering. She took a last puff at her cigarette and threw it into the fire.

'Have another,' he said.

'Thanks. That's a long story. Can you blame me? What did I know? There she was, with a black band around her throat, wearing the same black dress day after day. God! How I hated that black band and that black dress and the holy way she had with customers. She kept a little hat-shop. In our street there were no shops, only boarding-houses for students and a few solicitors and that sort of thing, you could see little hats in the window all of a sudden, modiste in French, it looked so funny in that street and hardly anybody came, but she had a little income of her own, from the death of her husband, he was an excise officer. She used to beat me, though, with her holy looks, and drink too . . . on the quiet.'

The girl spoke viciously of this woman. She paused and then she almost hissed through her teeth.

'I hate her, with her black band around her throat. The eyes she had, like an eel, and the funny, scabby-looking skin on the backs of her hands.'

'Eh?' said Mr. Gilhooley, blinking at her distantly and holding out the bottle from him. He was very happy. 'There are beautiful women in Galway right enough. There's a garrison there for God knows how long. Spanish trade and the wine they talk about . . . but like the coal mines in Pheonix Park it's only all nationalist propaganda. They are a lot of . . . well, there's a big mixture of blood there, anyway. Once there with my father when I was a young lad. Salthill, with all the old farmers warming their bellies in the sun. Once a year to the seaside and then never wash again. Ha, ha. Heh.'

Dangling the glass in her left hand, the girl leaned her right elbow on her crooked knee, rested her chin in her right palm and drew back the left corner of her upper lip. Her face had an ugly expression, as the faces of all people have when they are thinking of something with hatred.

'Well,' said Mr. Gilhooley stretching out his legs and drawing up his white eyebrows contentedly, 'so you went on the wallaby from the old hag. Proper order.'

'What's that?' said the girl, starting angrily, perhaps thinking that it was the old woman who spoke to her.

'On the wallaby, on the wallaby,' said Mr. Gilhooley, smiling. His face looked very simple, boyish and happy as he smiled. 'That's a saying we have in the Argentine. Fellows go off on a hike with only a toothpick in their pocket. Just head off God knows where, sleep out, rob, never work and just knock about, maybe going five hundred miles before they flop down.'

The girl made a little grimace. Her face became more remote, reserved, and as it were contemptuous.

She evidently did not approve of Mr. Gilhooley's light acceptance of her story. She also seemed a different person altogether from the skimpy waif of the street, with the shabby raincoat and the safety-pin at her throat. Although Mr. Gilhooley had not noticed it, the blue tailormade costume she wore was quite new and elegantly fashioned. It hung well from her square shoulders, and she carried herself like a woman who is used to interiors and feels quite at home in them, in any company. In fact, Mr. Gilhooley, with his rather drunken joy and the looseness of his conversation, looked rather bad form compared with her.

Still, the canker that seemed to be biting at her mind forced her to go on talking.

'I don't know about that,' she said. 'I've never robbed. I worked hard enough. I worked for her too. I didn't want to be educated, or reared either. I don't know why they rear orphans like me. She kept telling me all the money she spent on me, but I didn't want her to spend money on me. If she had let me sell her hats and blouses I'd sell them all right instead of going to the stuffy old convent. She could see I didn't want to be a nun.'

'Ye need a vocation,' said Mr. Gilhooley seriously, opening the lower buttons of his waistcoat. 'It's like everything else. People are born for it.'

The girl looked at him, as if to see was he making a joke.

' I just went off one day on an excursion to Dublin and never came back. Another girl was with me, but she turned back at Kingstown or Dunleary, as they call it now. I went on to London.'

'Ho! To London. Did ye, though? Like London? Too big, I think.'

'It's all right if you have money. I had to go to work in a teashop. Glad to get it too. Then I met a podgy little man. A horrid man. He just was sober one minute, then he'd take one glass after another and in five minutes he was staggering about on his little short thick legs, as drunk as a larry.'

'Ha, ha,' said Mr. Gilhooley. 'An Englishman? They're the devils for their beer.'

'No, he was Irish. A bockey. Fellow called Tutty. Lots of money and knew how to keep it. He gave me a job as his secretary when he found I was well educated, but I could soon see what he was after.'

'Same old game since Adam,' said Mr. Gilhooley. 'Was *he* Matt? Ye're not drinking, though. Drink up . . . or I'll have it all finished.'

''Deed he wasn't Matt,' said the girl contemptuously.

She uttered that word Matt with such force that Mr. Gilhooley started. The same little shiver went down his spine. He became uneasy.

'Don't worry about him,' he said. Then he added, looking at his watch : 'It's getting time for . . . time for bed.'

The girl did not take any notice.

'He was a Galway man, too. Can you blame me?' she cried.

'Hush,' said Mr. Gilhooley getting to his feet.

'Don't speak so loud.' He pointed at the ceiling. 'They're overhead.'

The girl leaned back in her chair and threw her head to one side with a weary gesture, wrinkling her forehead. Mr. Gilhooley went to the wash-hand-stand, took two pills out of a bottle, put them in his mouth and swallowed them with the assistance of a little water from the carafe. Then he took off his coat and opened the remaining buttons of his waistcoat. Suddenly the girl jumped to her feet. Her face was a little flushed with the whiskey she had drunk. It was obvious now that she was a woman of very violent temper.

'I'm not a street woman,' she said excitedly.

Her eyes were pointed. She pulled off her cap and put one hand palm downwards on her hip. Mr. Gilhooley looked at her in amazement, tried to say something, swallowed his breath and then began to button up the waistcoat which he had just unbuttoned.

'Do you believe me?' she said in a low tense voice.

'Well, well . . .' began Mr. Gilhooley, utterly at a loss.

'I lived with Matt for two years and . . . well. When I spoke to you . . . well there was. . . ' Her bosom heaved suddenly. She bared her teeth, swayed the upper part of her body rapidly like a boxer ducking a blow and added: 'I don't care now. But . . . you have to understand that . . . it's the first time. Else I'm . . . I'm going right out . . . see?'

'What put that idea into yer head?' said Mr. Gilhooley, staggering forward a little. 'Who said a word? Lord above! I never said . . . . What the devil do I care? Ye mean yer a . . . married woman?'

'Oh, rot,' she said, making a pass with her cap and taking a step to one side with her head thrown back. She sobbed. 'I'm not married. Not he. If he had . . . I was faithful to him, only his insane jealousy . . . I couldn't stick it. . . . All very well for a man. A woman has got to . . . God! I'm fed up. Look here,' she said, in the same tense voice as before, approaching him a little, 'there's going to be no love-making about this. It's just . . . Ach!'

Again she turned aside, fluttered her hands, threw away her cap and beat her chest with one hand.

'Give me a drink, for God's sake,' she said in a coarse voice.

Mr. Gilhooley gave her the bottle and was going for the glass she had placed on the mantelpiece, but she motioned him away with her head and put the bottle to her lips. She took a heavy drink. Then she smiled wildly, handing him back the bottle.

The bacchanalian look was in her eyes. Her rich golden curls sparkled. Her little chin was raised and the veins moved in her full white throat, dancing like fishes darting about in a stream. She stretched out her hands towards him. Her lips were open showing her short white teeth clenched tightly. One little ear was cocking out over the curls.

Amazed, he stood stupidly looking at her.

'Come, come,' she muttered angrily, panting. 'Kiss me."

Clumsily he took a pace forward and touched her shoulders.

With a bound, uttering a sound of some sort, she encircled his neck with fierce hands and fastened her thin lips to his thin sallow lips.

Something began to whirl around and around in his brain at an incredible speed.

Almost immediately she drew back and holding him by the waistcoat with her two hands, she whispered tensely :

'You've been kind to me. That's all.'

Then she walked rapidly to her chair and sat, sweeping out her skirt under her with a graceful gesture. Mr. Gilhooley took a pace after her but she said coldly, without looking at him.

'You go first. I'll take another of your cigarettes.'

She rose smartly and took a cigarette from the packet he had placed on the mantelpiece. He looked at her curiously as she lit it, with his mouth open, utterly amazed. Then he began to undress. She did not look around. Suddenly, while he was taking off his trousers in the middle of the floor as was his habit, he became ashamed. He went to the far side of the bed, sat down and took them off. He stood up in his underwear and looked around at her to say something, he didn't know what, but he remained, gently scratching his stomach, without saying anything. He looked funny in his underwear.

The bosom of the vest was unbottoned showing strong dark hairs and at the top-button of the pants, the slight protuberance of his stomach pressed out, gently straining the whitish button. He was pawing for his pyjamas from under the pillow. He was in the habit of stripping naked to put on his pyjamas. But in her presence he was ashamed of stripping naked. So he just tumbled into the big feather mattress hurriedly. It sank down under his weight. He concealed his body under the covering.

'Right you are,' he said with affected carelessness, though his heart was thumping.

She arose.

'Turn that off,' he said.

She turned off the fire. Then she began to undress. Struggling with his drunkenness he watched her, and all sorts of ideas wandered through his brain. But they were by no means connected with the relationship she was about to assume with him. He was a little terrified and at the same time exalted, by the unexpected development of his adventure, which began so drably and undesirably; by the strange power of this girl, who had so recently appealed to him like a stray dog. Then she had a safety-pin at her skimpy throat. Now she was pulling a frilly, dainty blouse over her little head with the delicate movements of a woman perfectly controlled and at ease, while she blew two thin columns of cigarette smoke from her nostrils. . . . All this amazed him. And the kiss . . . and the feeling that all his past, even the ride in the cab during which he had seen his father's funeral and the shrivelled face of the students' caretaker . . . all seemed far away and never to be remembered again.

His body was warm. His brain was agreeably unable to concentrate on any one thing. Yet everything seemed strange. And even though he told himself to sit up and say something and struggle to do something indefinite, to assert his mastery over this feeling that was gaining control over him, he lay still, breathing heavily.

And all the time she was undressing slowly, carefully, perfectly at ease. He could now see her slender, finely shaped arms bare to the shoulders and the little white straps over her bare shoulders, a different whiteness from the light whiteness of the straps. But this flesh did not arouse any desire. He merely wondered at it, wondering what was this feeling which prevented him from sitting up and saying something that would permit him to re-assert that control over her which he had outside in the cab and carrying her up the stairs on his back.

She put out the electric light and finished undressing. He could hear her move in the darkness, the rustle of her stockings even. Then he began to tremble.

And when her warm, soft body crept silently under the clothes by his side he did not move, but lay perfectly still, thinking rapidly without thinking anything.

Then he felt her hands, as it were mechanically, begin to fondle his person.

CHAPTER V

At six o'clock next morning, life began as usual in Mr. Gilhooley's boarding house.

Cissy, the dirty female servant with flabby red arms and flabby breasts, rolled off her narrow bed in the basement. She stopped the alarm clock. She pulled her rags over her head, muttering her morning prayers and muttering curses through her prayers. She shuffled along the narrow smelly stone passage into the large kitchen. She threw a little paraffin oil over the fire set in the range. She lit the fire. She put the big porridge pot and the kettle, full overnight with water, on the reddening circle of flame.

Gradually her prayers and her curses ceased, as her mind, stirred into a little activity by the night's feverish rest, relapsed again into the comatose state brought on by the ceaseless drudgery of the day. The pains in her back, in the upper parts of her thighs and in her calves lessened and then ceased to hurt. Her innumerable tasks, which had once terrified her and which she did excitedly, with a mind tremulously watching for errors, hoping for promotion, dreaming of having a house of her own one day, a husband, children who would succour her in her old age, now met her hands, one after the other, without thought, like the movements of a soldier digging a trench in ' no man's land' under fire. His mind, listening only to the frothing curses of the sergeant, heeds not the crash of the bursting shells. His eyes don't see the flare of the explosions, nor the distorted face of the dead man the stretcher-bearers are hauling around the corners of the traverse. His mind and hers are concentrated on the idiotic tasks that are performed by their enslaved limbs.

The same smells, the same sounds, the same articles of furniture, the same food reacted on her senses, offering no incentive to thought. Although she had human appearance and although there were potentialities for love hidden in her being, she moved and lived exactly like an old horse that has hauled a plough, up and down, up and down furrows for ten years. A soul stupefied by labour and misery.

Cissy had never the cunning to become a coutesan, nor indeed the wisdom. For there is some pleasure in a life of sin. There is danger and variety. But in Cissy's life there was the horror of sin without variety or pleasurable danger. She surrendered her virtue to the first comer long ago. She wept and was horrified afterwards. But again she sinned and again. She had two children that suckled at her flabby breasts. They were both dead. One died in the workhouse. The other died in the care of a harpy on the south side of the city. The harpy offered to rear him—it was a boy—for five pounds. And it promptly died. Cissy lost her job after each child was born, for no honest matron is willing to keep a fallen woman in her house, even though her son or husband may be the father of the child; or perhaps just because of that. Anyway, these falls and these misfortunes wrought a savage change in the mind and the body of Cissy.

We see a playful animal in the first joy of youth,

frolic at its mother's side, romp over fields and gambol fearlessly towards a stranger. And we see the same animal, reared brutally by a brutal master, become brutal, timorous and snarling. So, like a constantly beaten brute, Cissy's mind and soul had become brutal and pitiless.

Having arranged the table in the kitchen for breakfast she went to call the family, the medical student who went to mass every morning before breakfast and the two grocer's curates who ate in the kitchen because they were not considered fit to mix socially with the other boarders. The two grocer's curates shared a room on the first floor above the dining-room. She called them first, dropping a hot-water jug at their door. She went straight to the garret, called the family and dropped the other hot-water just at their door. Then she went to call the student on Mr. Gilhooley's floor. She had no jug for him, because he had no beard and he washed in cold water as a sort of religious penance. He belonged to the new sect of ardent nationalists who believe in mortification as a means of saving the national soul.

Just before she knocked at the student's door, she heard a sound of whispering from Mr. Gilhooley's room. She started. A malicious gleam came into her stupid eyes.

'It's Molly,' she whispered to herself. 'She's inside with him.'

She meant Molly Davin, the landlady's only daughter and Cissy's chief enemy in life. It was

Molly who was boss of the household, who bullied her father, her mother, the servant and the poor lodgers who ate in the kitchen, who flirted, or tried to flirt, with the religious medical student and who was angling for Mr. Gilhooley as a husband. Cissy hated her for all this. But she principally hated her for being able to preserve her virtue untarnished until she could make a good bargain with it at the altar steps. For although Molly flirted with all the well-to-do boarders who came to the house, she allowed them to go a certain distance and no further. Cissy respected the two girl boarders who were students at a commercial college. They were virtuous through refinement and religious idealism. Cissy envied those two. But Molly was virtuous through mercenary feelings and Cissy hated her. Cissy had no interest in women other than in their virtue or the lack of it.

'He's got hold of her at last,' she thought, moving to the door.

She put her ear to the keyhole and listened.

'Aw! God in heaven!' Mr. Gilhooley was saying, obviously from the bed. 'Hurry, for God sake. Open the door and beat it.'

Cissy heard a sob and she giggled.

'She's been sleepin' with him,' she thought.

Then she started. Her lips fell open. She rolled her eyes from side to side. She heard a strange female voice.

'It's locked,' said the strange female voice. 'The key is not here.'

'Holy God!' muttered Cissy in horror. 'It's a tart he brought in with 'im.'

Disappointed that it was not Molly and moved by another feeling of moral indignation which it would be difficult to explain, a violent feeling of hatred for this strange voice overwhelmed her.

She heard a muttered oath and then the heaving of Mr. Gilhooley's body as he got out of the bed. Then there was silence for a moment.

'What? What?' came Mr. Gilhooley's voice, almost inarticulate with anger and terror. 'The key. What? It's not in it. Where the . . . Where the . . . Where . . . Hey, where. . . Holy God! What are ye talkin' about? Lemme . . . Lemme look.'

Cissy drew back a little as he approached the door. Still, she could hear his violent breathing.

'Isn't he the shameless ruffian!' thought Cissy.

Her hatred was transferred from the strange female voice to Mr. Gilhooley. She remembered suddenly the day he was in bed with a 'bad head' and she was cleaning up his room. She said to him: 'Know anybody ud give us a fiver?' It was a saying she had. And he said, after examining her with aversion: 'Get away, ye slut.'

'Now where the hell did I put it?' said Mr. Gilhooley. 'Where did I put it? Where did I put it I say? Can't ye speak? Can't ye tell me where I put it?''

'I . . . I . . . I don't know,' sobbed the other voice.

'Divil mend him,' muttered Cissy, 'I hope she robs him, spending his money on them.'

'Aw! Now I'm ruined,' muttered Mr. Gilhooley in a weak voice. 'I'm done for. The shame of it. What are we going to do? Eh? What? I can't remember. Will I burst it? What? No use. They're up. They'd . . . . What time? Eh? It's all up. Why the blazes didn't ye . . . but wait . . . . What a head! Oh! The curse of . . . .'

A footstep pattered down the stairs and somebody was whistling. Cissy moved away from Mr. Gilhooley's door and called the student. She waited until she heard his sleepy answer and then she hurried downstairs to the kitchen.

Rubbing his hands together like a shopman, curling his whitish moustache and stamping about the kitchen, Pollard, one of the grocer's curates, was waiting for his breakfast when Cissy entered. He had merely doused his head in cold water and had not shaved. A grizzly fair stubble covered his fat white chin. His short stocky body bulged through his shabby blue suit that was shiny at the seat and along the thighs. His very fair hair, swept straight back to the poll and soaked with brilliantine, his sleek fat hands, the look of saucy servility in his blue eyes and the way he rubbed his hands, all gave him a peculiar character, the character of a shopman. 'Yes, ma'am. Best Limerick, ma'am. Yes, ma'am.' Always in good humour and never really disturbed by any emotional trouble, he went up to Cissy and gave her a hug and a slap on the back. The fact that he slept with her now and again did not embarrass him in her presence. He saw no harm in it. When drinking with his comrades on pay night, he was in the habit of saying : 'Hey, lads. We have a skivvy in our diggs. Mum's the word.'

'Hands off!' said Cissy, wiping her forehead. 'Lord! I got a fright.'

'What's up? What's up?' said Pollard, curling his moustache nervously.

When anything untoward happened in the boarding-house Pollard thought it had reference to his own relations with the servant.

'Mr. Gilhooley,' whispered Cissy. 'Now she can give herself airs, I'm telling ye, an' she only a police sergeant's daughter that had to clear out from the I.R.A. for fear he'd get murdered for giving information to the Black-an'-Tans.'

'Holy God! Can't ye tell us?' said Pollard excitedly.

'I'll have me own back, I'm telling ye. She with her rabbit-teeth and her goitre, thinkin' she'd land him. Faith, she might as well clear back to Meath or wherever she came from, the cow.'

'Is it Molly?' cried Pollard.

Cissy drew her scraggy black hair off her forehead and gaped at him.

'It's not,' she said grumpily. 'It's a tart he brought in. 'She pointed towards the ceiling. 'I heard them whispering.'

'A tart! A tart! Ja-aney! A tart!'

'Whist, will, ye, for God sake. Sit down to yer breakfast. He's got her within in the room.'

As he ate his porridge she told him every word she heard, adding generously, while she stood by the table with a bowl of porridge in her hand, gesticulating with the spoon, gulping noisily.

'Aw! Janey Mac!' Pollard kept saying, shifting his shiny seat about on the chair. 'That's too much of a good thing. There's a limit, so there is. God! He's going to be run out of this diggs or I'm not staying in it.'

Shaughnessy, the second grocer's curate, a big rustic, who still remained a rustic after ten years in Dublin, came in slowly, coughing and sniffing alternately. He was tall and lean and dour, with feet like a policeman and a lean, wrinkled neck that rose high over his stiff collar, like the neck of a doll that turns round and shoots up from its body when a child pulls a string. He had a gentle face.

'Hey, Tom,' said Pollard, rising a little from his chair and then waggling his haunches, 'did ye hear the latest?'

Shaughnessy frowned shyly when he heard the story. Making coarse noises, he began to eat his porridge.

'Mind yer own business,' was all he said. Then he added angrily: 'What's it got to do with you?'

'Hasn't it, though?' cried Pollard, rising to cut a slice off the loaf and waving the yellow-handled bread-knife, like a cavalry officer ordering a charge. 'If you have no respect for yer reputation, there's others that has.'

'Aw!' said Shaughnessy, banging a crust on the

table. 'Cissy, is this the only kind of bread ye have? This is a week old.' He frowned at Pollard. Then he said: 'I've no truck with women, but that's none of my business.'

'Who're ye referrin' to, Tom?' cried Pollard, dropping the knife and the slice he had cut. 'None o' that, now. I'm as good a Catholic as you are.'

'Well, shut your gob, then,' said Shaughnessy, taking the new loaf Cissy had brought. 'That's the way ye go suckin' to the boss about everything in the shop.'

An argument began about 'scabs' and trade unions and working overtime, which finally caused little Pollard to pull off his coat and hand it to Cissy, who did not move to take it, so that it fell on the floor. In his dirty shirt, Pollard offered to 'have it all out then and there.' But Shaughnessy crunched his black pudding without looking at him. Pollard put on his coat again and was going to sit down when Molly Davin came striding in.

'What's this noise all about?' she said angrily, surveying them, one after the other, coldly and with obvious contempt.

She was a stout woman of thirty, very ugly in features, although her powerfully-developed body had a certain animal charm, which attracts men in the country, but which repels men in towns. She was wearing a yellow golf jacket over a knitted white jumper, that jutted out at her breasts, with the stitches strained and exposing to view the white band of her camisole through the little holes. Her upper teeth showed, flat and broad, even when her mouth was shut. Her face was coarse and red. Her neck was swollen with goitre. Her eyes were small and cunning. Yet there was a curious expression lurking in her eyes and in her features, beneath the surface expression of cunning and coarseness. This half-hidden expression told of a gentle nature weak and conscious of its stupidity, intentionally being submerged under this brutal covering by circumstance, by fate. It seemed that some fear, perhaps the fear of not getting a husband, of not being able to satisfy that craving for a family which her powerful peasant body felt, caused this gentle expression to give way to that of brutality.

Her father had been a police-sergeant before he married her mother. He sold the little farm his wife had and came to live in Dublin, when he retired on pension after the disbandment of the R.I.C.

'What are you talking about?' she said to Pollard, as nobody answered her first question.

'It wasn't me, Miss Davin,' said Pollard, immediately becoming calm and deferential. 'I didn't start it. Better ask him. It's Mr. Shaughnessy, the socialist, who jumped down me throat when I said a few words about what —"

'You shut yer gob,' said Shaughnessy angrily, without moving.

'Who told you you were master in this house, Mr. Shaughnessy?' cried Molly in her loud voice, hoarse with goitre.

'No, I won't shut me gob,' said Pollard. 'I'm a

man and I've more respect for meself than to sit here and say nothing while these . . . .'

'Now I warn ye to go no further,' said Shaughnessy rising from his seat.

I suppose it's because he doesn't go to Mass yer so fond of him,' cried Pollard, edging towards the door.

Shaughnessy sat down again and coolly began to finish his cup of tea. Pollard, seeing him sit down, was coming up to him aggressively, but Molly caught him by the shoulder.

'What-are-you-rowing-about?' she said slowly.

'It's only what she told me I said to him,' said Pollard, 'an' be Janey, he let fly at me. About Mr. Gilhooley having a tart in his room.'

'What?' shrieked Molly. 'You liar, what are you saying?'

'You're a dirty scut of an informer,' shouted Shaughnessy, rising and rapidly leaving the room. 'God, he spoilt my breakfast again this morning,' he said plaintively, going out the door.

Molly turned to Cissy.

'Ye can go up an' see for yerself,' said Cissy sullenly. 'I heard her inside. She's locked in and he can't find the key.'

'God!' said Molly, clasping her bosom and rushing to the water-tap.

She swallowed a glass of water and dashed out of the room, muttering something. Pollard looked at Cissy.

'Now, be Janey,' he said foolishly, 'the fat's in the fire. It's all on account of Shaughnessy.'

He left the room, also muttering and threatening somebody with his fist.

'He, he, he,' tittered Cissy at the range, with a cup of tea in her hand.

Her face was creased from ear to ear in a motionless smile. Her flabby chest heaved with laughter. Then the laughter died within her. She sighed. The lines of dark laughter vanished from her face and the lines of dark melancholy took their place. A dead soul.

Molly passed the student on the stairs. He was rushing down, pulling on a brown raincoat as he ran. His ascetic, pale face glanced at her. Then his eyes dropped as he saluted. Without answering, she put her back to the wall to let him pass, and she thought as he passed:

'He doesn't know what I'm suffering.'

For she considered herself practically engaged to Mr. Gilhooley, although nothing had ever passed between them, except that one night, when he came home, weak from a bout of heavy drinking, with a sore throat, thinking he had diphtheria and so overpowered by loneliness that he longed for some human being to be near him, she had sat beside him on the bed, with her hand around his shoulder, comforting him. Under the influence of his drinking, his sore throat and his loneliness, he had been sentimental that night and said that she was a mother to him and that he wouldn't forget it. Ever since, she looked upon him as her own property, even going so far as to scold Mrs. Hourigan, the publican in the next street, for 'enticing him to drink.' She sat sewing white jumpers every morning in the dining-room while he was having breakfast and tried to conduct a business conversation with him about the rise and fall of the stock market, which he carefully studied every day.

With this feeling of maudlin pity for herself, she stepped cautiously up to his door, put her ear to the keyhole as Cissy had done and listened. She heard nothing.

'That wretch,' she said, 'she made it all up.'

Eager to disbelieve the servant's story, she was going away, when she started and put her ear to the keyhole again.

'It's no use,' Mr. Gilhooley was saying. 'Somebody is bound to find out. The people here have the eyes of hawks.'

'God! What am I to do?' said a strange female voice.

Molly nearly fainted. She was going to scream, but she put her hands to her mouth, snatched open the little door leading to the garret, pulled it after her, and bounded up the narrow stairs, weakly screaming: 'Mamma, mamma.'

On the little landing of the attic, Mrs. Davin was standing, fastening her capacious skirt at the back, looking over the banister excitedly, with three hairpins between her large white teeth, like daggers in a conjuror's mouth. She was an enormous woman and the only difference between her countenance and that of her daughter's was that the mother's countenance was twenty years older, and instead of the brutal expression being the dominant one it was the subsidiary one, while the weak, gentle expression was on the surface. She was a mountain of flesh.

'What's this?' she said, not excitedly, but calmly, as if she were used to these childish pranks from her overgrown baby of a daughter.

Uttering strange little cries, Molly advanced until she reached the landing. Then she hurled herself upon her mother's enormous chest and went limp. Mrs. Davin, from the force of the impact, retreated one, two, three paces until she fell plump on to the lid of a big laundry wicker basket. She also went limp and her head fell on the limp body of her daughter that lay on her bosom. Mr. Davin, with a pipe in his mouth and his braces trailing behind him, came out of the far bedroom. Holding up his trousers with one hand and in the other holding a necktie, he looked with amazement at his wife and daughter.

'Eh?' he said. He paused. Then he said again: 'Eh?'

'Pull her off me,' said Mrs. Davin.

Mr. Davin, suddenly becoming excited at hearing his wife's voice, dropped the necktie on the floor and rushed over. Between them, they brought Molly into her own little bedroom and laid her on her bed.

'It's that cursed goitre,' said Mr. Davin to his wife. 'She'll be all right in a moment.'

'Well, something musta terrified her,' said Mrs. Davin, in that funny plaintive voice that comes so unexpectedly from the seemingly enormous lungs of very fat people.

'Give her a nip o' brandy,' said Mr. Davin.

At that moment Molly started up, rubbed her eyes and grabbed her mother by the arms.

'Protect me, mummy,' she wailed. 'I'm ruined.'

'What? What?' cried both parents at once.

'Leave us a minute, dad,' said Molly.

Mrs. Davin motioned away her husband brusquely. Mr. Davin went out, pulling up the trousers which he had allowed to fall about his thighs in his excitement. Mrs. Davin banged the door. Mr. Davin went back to his own bedorom.

'What could it be?' he said to himself, standing just inside the door.

Then he shrugged his shoulders and said: 'Oh! Well!' He immediately forgot about it and allowed his mind to dwell again on the interrupted pleasure of wondering what there would be in the paper this morning.

Mr. Davin belonged to that class of men with whom it is a pleasure to converse, who are loved by all except their wives, who are always clean, smiling and gentlemanly-looking in public, who are always happy because their natures are unable to contemplate a difficulty of any kind for more than a moment. They can feel sympathy with the difficulties of their neighbours because it does not hurt them and the neighbours require only sympathy. But with the difficulties of their own family sympathy is the least estimable emotion. So that their wives curse them for their indolence of mind and of body. And Mr. Davin had chosen the very best profession for a man of his peculiar nature. Never, in all his thirty years of service among a community hostile to police of any kind, did he experience any trouble or arouse any enmity against his person. When arresting a wild mountaineer for the manufacture of potheen, he could smile in such a gentle manner that the wild man, who had the previous week, with his wife and seven sons routed the district inspector's posse, went meekly to the police barracks, manacled, while his captor lit his pipe for him and chatted about the best way to smoke out a badger.

He was not rendered unhappy even by the disbandment of the police force, athough he had spent so many luxurious years of idleness in its service. For in his new Dublin environment, he soon formed a circle of cronies who admired him. Without drinking more than a glass of mild stout, he could spend two hours in a public-house among choice citizens. And even citizens who were not choice became tame and good-mannered in his company.

But towards his own household, his own family, and his own affairs, he still showed the same good-natured indifference. Such, apparently, and unfortunately for the prosperity of our country, is the secret of Irish happiness.

Mr. Davin was approaching the age of sixty, but one would hardly believe it. His hair was of that grizzly colour, grey-black, which makes a florid countenance look so handsome. The pimple on his right cheek, the unchanging expression of his blue eyes, the broadness of his shoulders, the extreme length of his arms, body, legs and feet and the way he said: 'Heh,' in his throat before setting off anywhere were his chief characteristics.

Mr. Davin continued dressing. He heard his wife and daughter come out of the other bedroom and go down the stairs slowly, whispering. He paid no attention. He had forgotten their existence. He was buttoning his waistcoat when he heard their footsteps mount the stairs again. Now he paid attention to them, because he detected a peculiar whistling sound in his wife's breathing, which told him that she was about to attack him violently. Throwing on his coat hurriedly over his half-buttoned waistcoat, he went out on the landing to receive her.

His wife immediately grabbed him by the coat lapel.

'We're ruined,' she said. 'An' yer standing there like a fool without lifting a hand. Get down an' charge him. Charge him at once.'

'No, don't, mummy. Don't, daddy. Don't,' said Molly, standing behind her mother, wringing her hands and shivering.

'Who in the name of God will I charge?' murmured Mr. Davin.

'Mr. Gilhooley,' ejaculated Mrs. Davin with difficulty. Short of breath, she pronounced the name-'Shiloole.'

'What for?' said Mr. Davin.

Mrs. Davin glanced at her daughter and said coldly:

'This is not fit for your ears, Molly. Go into yer bedroom, child.'

Then she pushed Mr. Davin before her into his bedroom and followed him, holding up her skirt in front, thinking she was still mounting the stairs.

In whispers, she told him all about it.

'Oh! Well!' said Mr. Davin. 'Oh! Well! I suppose. . . .'

'What d'ye suppose?' said Mrs. Davin furiously, recovering her breath.

'I suppose,' said Mr. Davin, 'that . . . well, ye can do what ye please. It all depends on . . . on . . . well, ye see. . . .'

'You lazy, idle ruffian. You. . . .'

Mrs. Davin burst forth and Mr. Davin, as usual, shrugged his shoulders, curled his moustaches and wagged his head from side to side.

'D'ye know that he might have married Molly only for this?'

'I know nothing, Mrs. Davin,' said Mr. Davin.

'No, ye don't know nothing,' wailed Mrs. Davin. 'Oh, Blessed Virgin Mary, don't ye look down in pity on me, a Child of Mary, married to this ruffian? Go down and charge him.'

'What' l I charge him with? Sure ye know I'm not in the Force now.'

'Charge him,' said Mrs. Davin, beside herself with rage.

Suddenly Molly burst into the room, completely recovered from her weakness.

'Come on,' she said in her hoarse voice. 'Out he goes. He mustn't stay another minute in the house. Get the key of his room, mother, and open the door. Call a cab, father, and pack him off.'

Both parents were taken unawares by this development and gaped at her. Mr. Davin, who seemed not to have paid any attention to the affair, was the first to interfere.

'Now, Molly,' he said calmly. 'Heh. Don't rush at things. Heh. The two young women down there' – he raised his eyebrows –'are they up yet? It's best not to . . . . '

'Yes, yes,' said Mrs. Davin.

'All right,' said Mr. Davin, 'let me handle this. He must go, no doubt. But still. . . . There's ways an' ways for everything. Gimme the key. And . . . now that we're here . . . draw up the bill . . . how much does he owe? . . . . Is there laundry? . . . These things . . . . Well! There's no end to this world. So it seems.'

With amazing tact and subtlety, Mr. Davin went about the objectionable business of getting rid of Mr. Gilhooley. And it was extraordinary too, that in his own mind he considered himself to be acting not on behalf of his own family (he never took himself into consideration at all) but on behalf of Mr. Gilhooley. Which indeed accounts for his success in life.

He first of all transported his family downstairs,

past the objectionable door. Then he rapped at the door.

'Yes,' said Mr. Gilhooley.

'Heh!' said Mr. Davin, wiping his feet for some unknown reason on the white goatskin mat. 'I'm very sorry, Mr. Gilhooley, but . . . the wife, ye understand . . . and . . . well . . . ye know how it is. . . . I'll be sorry to lose yer very pleasant company and . . . indeed I wish ye the best of luck . . . and . . . well . . . ye know me well enough be now, Mr. Gilhooley.'

'Hold on there, Mr. Davin,' said Mr. Gilhooley.

'Not a word of apology, Mr. Gilhooley,' said Mr. Davin. 'Human nature is human nature, as the saying is.'

'For God sake, open this bloody door and let me out,' Mr. Gilhooley almost roared.

'Now, now,' said Mr. Davin soothingly, 'don't take me up like that. Listen. Pack yer things. Then I'll get yer breakfast sent into the room. As soon as yer ready to move, I'll call a cab or a taxi, whichever ye like. D'ye see? The two young ladies, ye understand . . . . Now don't put yerself about. . . . Heh! Sure we're up against it, all of us from the day we're born. . . . Heh! . . . I'm slipping the bill under the door. Ye can leave the cheque on the dressing-table and . . . I'll settle about the laundry if ye . . . . "

'Oh! For God sake, shut yer gob and let me out. I've locked meself in.'

'No offence. No offence, Mr. Gilhooley,' said Mr. Davin. 'I'll get yer breakfast sent up to yer room.'

'Mick Davin,' bawled Mr. Gilhooley at the top of his voice.

But Mr. Davin moved away, downstairs into the kitchen to order Mr. Gilhooley's breakfast. Then he moved all over the house and somehow, by his presence, the unchanging expression of his eyes and his merry pimple, he restored order everywhere.

It was nine o'clock before Mr. Davin thought it advisable to allow Mr. Gilhooley out of the house. By that time the house was clear of boarders, and Mr. Davin felt that Mr. Gilhooley would not be embarrassed by setting forth to look for another lodging at that hour, accompanied as he was by 'an undesirable person.'

Nobody in the house saw Mr. Gilhooley come down. Not even Mr. Davin. Because that gentleman, with his innate delicacy, pointed out the room to the cabman and then retired, thinking perhaps that sight of him would be embarrassing to Mr. Gilhooley.

However, as soon as the door banged after the retiring Mr. Gilhooley, four pairs of eyes peered out of windows in various parts of the house. Mr. Davin could not prevent himself from peering out of the attic front window. Cissy was gaping up through the basement window, although she could only catch a glimpse of Mr. Gilhooley's legs and of the 'tart's' stockings. At the dining-room window, Mrs. Davin and Molly were peering out, clutching one another and almost hysterical.

The four pair of eyes watched excitedly while Mr.

Gilhooley ushered the girl into the cab and then went in himself after whispering to the cabman. Four pair of ears unconsciously strained to catch that whisper, but they heard nothing. The cab door closed with a click. The jarvey cracked his whip. The cab rumbled off.

'Oh!' said each person that had been watching.

Then by common instinct the four of them rushed to Mr. Gilhooley's room, and such was the common excitement to see where 'she' had spent the night that nobody turned Cissy away.

In this manner, Mr. Gilhooley was evicted from his boarding-house.

CHAPTER VI

When Mr. Gilhooley got into the cab, he was in a state of abject terror. He lay back, pressing his head against the rear of the cab. His hands fell limply by his sides. His legs were twitching. His body was limp. But his head was rigid up from the neck and so hot that his tongue kept rubbing against the roof of his mouth for moisture. His eyes were bloodshot. His face, darkened by a day's growth of beard, was heavily lined and drawn. The wrinkles that usually creased it, after the manner of one who has lived a long time in hot countries, were now straightened out into deep furrows along his cheeks, ending at the corners of his lips. A cold sweat oozed from his pores.

With the immovable and unreasoning fatalism of the voluptuary, he firmly believed that he was in the hands of an evil spirit, that there was no escape, and that he was moving towards some inevitable catastrophe, slowly, but with unchangeable certainty. He cast a nervous, furtive glance at her who sat mute and motionless at his right. He twitched his white eyebrows. He distended his nostrils after the manner of an animal staring at something it does not understand. The pockmarks on his nose seemed to have become an unseemly blemish in his fear.

And yet . . . what, what, he asked himself, was this fear? It had come upon him last night when he lay in bed awaiting her approach. The subtle power of her personality had suddenly made itself aware to his mind. And the futile attempt he had made to rise up that time and say something, to free himself, had made his helplessness so manifest to him. The events of the night, during which he had abandoned himself to her devilish charms, now evoked horror in his mind. For how could such vitality be possessed by a slim frail creature, unless it were some charm of an evil spirit?

When he awoke in the morning, a frenzy of hatred made him lean over her, with his hand clawed, desiring to choke her. Every nerve in his body was vibrating, exhausted by the savage excitement, to which he had been a stranger for the past three years. The stored energy of his powerful body had suddenly found an outlet, and like a dam that bursts its banks it was carrying him along in a mad rush, tearing everything down in its passage. How strong he felt then! And yet . . . fate, this unescapable destiny, had stood in his way. The key couldn't be found after he had flung a present at her and told her to be gone. But would he not have followed her 'like a dog'! He knew now he would. For even now, in his abject terror, as he sat beside her, he could hardly keep his hands off her. For it was this insane passion for her, for the memory of that drunken excitement of the night. her eel-like body, that filled his mind with terror. He was slipping over the brink of the precipice, over the edge of which he had been hanging for three years. He had now lost the last hold, his respectability. He was unmoored, in her possession. Where was he going?

Again he saw the fellow, a long way off now, standing still, grinning, with a club in his hand. It was a club for sure, and not a gun. And the fellow was unmistakably Matt, the man whom she feared.

'The key, the key,' he kept muttering to himself, without understanding what he was saying, with his mind fixed on the man standing afar off and at the same time thinking in a jumble of all that happened since the moment he had met her, down to the terrible moment when he had walked down the stairs and out into the street . . . for ever.

The past too tumbled into his mind, but very far off, farther than the menacing fellow with the club. For the past was now dead and never would he get an opportunity of fleeing from this approaching catastrophe by leaving the city and starting his bee-farm. He had lost the opportunity of escaping from the grinning brute who stood at a distance.

He hunched up his shoulders, drew in a deep breath, gripped his lower lip with the tips of his upper teeth and looked at her. She was staring fixedly in front of her. Her eyes were closed. There was an angelic, childlike expression in her pale countenance. A rim of yellow curls strayed from the brim of the hat. Her little nostrils were quivering. He swallowed his breath and, in spite of himself, his right hand moved over and caught her bare red hand. It was not so red now. And as soon as his hand touched hers, he trembled. All his fear vanished. A cloak of some sort, a mist, swooped down over his head. His head whirled. There was a fever in his body. In a strange voice which he did not recognize, he said to her:

'It's all over now. It's my fault. D'ye see?'

She opened her eyes and looked at him coldly, as from a great distance. There seemed to be contempt, for a moment, in her far-seeing eyes. Then the expression changed. She slightly shrugged her shoulders, making a little noise in her nostrils as she did so. Then she smiled, stopped smiling suddenly, clenched her short white teeth and then burst into a laugh.

He started. His mouth fell open. She stopped laughing and seized his right arm below the shoulder with both hands and hugged it. She looked up into his eyes.

'Cheer up, you damn fool,' she said in a low voice. 'D'you hear? Cheer up. I didn't hide the key. You hid it. But . . . what about it? What will be, will be.' She stared in front of her gloomily and shuddered. 'I know it,' she added in a whisper. 'It always does.' She turned to him again, surveyed him slowly and said: 'But I'll go through with it. I'll play the game. Whatever you like. It's done now. God! I didn't think I'd come to this.'

She suddenly began to beat her breast with her clenched fists and moan hysterically through her teeth:

'Matt, Matt, don't kill me. Don't kill me. Let me out. Let me out.'

She was trying to rise up in the cab, but he

clutched her around the body, pressed her violently with his powerful hands and muttered in her ear:

'Quiet, will you, damn it? Quiet. See? I . . . I . . . I'll kill you. . . . See? None o' that.'

Immediately all was still. In the cab, there were only sounds of violent breathing, and over the roof rain began to patter heavily, making a loud noise. Each listened to the other's violent breathing and to the loud pattering of the rain. Then she looked up into his face. There was a stern look in his bloodshot eyes. She sighed and leaned her head weakly against his chest. For a moment he stared at her recumbent head, twitching his white eyebrows. Then his eyes grew dim. His mouth quivered. He began to stroke her cheek slowly with the tips of his fingers.

The cab stopped.

'Here we are, sir,' came the voice of the cabman at the window.

It was a house he knew by reputation, but where he was unknown. Friel, the fellow who had married the house agent's daughter, had told him about it. A shudder passed through him when he heard the cabman's voice. The girl sat up and began to arrange her hat. He tried to rise, but a curious disgust at taking the final step overcame him and he sat motionless until the cabman, shielding his face from the gusts of rain, opened the door. Then he rose abruptly and stepped on to the wet pavement.

He told the cabman to wait, and lowering his head, as if he shunned recognition by any chance passer-by, he rushed up the steps to the door. He knocked, and waited with downcast head, staring at the bottom of the door.

This street was long and straight, intersected a little to the left by a main thoroughfare through which traffic rattled and to the right mounting a hill to a square. The houses were very tall and gloomy. To the right they were proper, and even elegant. But to the left, quite near, the beautiful uniform structures had decayed into tenements, at the doors of which there were women conversing idly, overcoats thrown over their shoulders with the sleeves hanging empty and their hands on their bosoms. There were balconies to each window and over the doors were the fanlights typical of the eighteenth century. In the unkempt roadway, the sudden heavy rain had already formed tiny rivulets, along which light débris was tentatively floating. Overhead the dark, shapeless sky formed a sagging roof, from which ice-cold rain pattered smartly, straight down, without wind to slant its fall.

A woman raised the dusty window to the left of the door and put out her head for a moment. She ducked it inwards immediately, feeling the rain. Then she said:

'Yes, mister?'

'Room,' said Mr. Gilhooley. 'Room for two.'

'Room for two,' said the woman in a thin voice, which pronounced the words in a rippling murmur, very pleasant to hear.

After a few moments she opened the door and

bid him enter. In the hallway, he found her to be a frail, middle-aged woman, with her hair in curls, clutching a shabby dressing-gown about her. He began a long story about crossing on the night mail from Holyhead and having had breakfast at the Grosvenor and not wanting to knock about hotels, but she cut him short.

'Let me see,' she said, pursing up her lips and eyeing him very cutely. 'For how long?'

She glanced suspiciously at his unpolished shoes and his muddy trouser legs.

'Oh, well,' he said, 'at least a fortnight.'

'H'm,' she said. 'There's one on the second floor front. Thirty shillings a week bed and breakfast . . . each. Suitable? Pay in advance, of course, by the week. Unless ye want extras, like two rashers, or porridge of a morning. Porridge'll be extra and . . . and baths. There's a bath-room but ye have to pass through it to get at the . . . so we have to arrange for baths and . . . . '

'Eh . . . eh . . . eh . . . that'll be all right,' said Mr. Gilhooley hastily. 'That'll be O.K.'

The whole business was arranged in a few minutes. The woman in the shabby dressing-gown stood all the time behind the door, peering around its corner. She watched the luggage coming in. She examined the girl who raced headlong in from the rain. The girl had taken off her raincoat, from a feeling of delicacy. She received the money from Mr. Gilhooley and said she would give him change later. Did he mind? No. Then she went to the head of the stairway and hailed a servant to convey them to their room.

There was a curious air of poverty and disrespectability about the gaunt house. The majestic stairway with its shabby carpet, the carved roof of the hallway overhanging a dirty hall-stand, and two chairs, out of which hairs were protruding, the musty smell coming from the open door of the dining-room, all suggested a mansion seized by marauders during a revolution and allowed by them to go to ruin. Although it was after nine o'clock the blinds were yet drawn in the dining-room. The hall was unswept and the landlady was in her dressing-gown. There was nobody downstairs, but overhead there was a loud and varied babble of voices and the *clink-clink* of tea-cups and the patter of feet running to and fro, peals of laughter and merriment.

This noise, the landlady explained to Mr. Gilhooley, was caused by a theatrical troupe that was having their breakfast in bed. 'Four boys and three girls,' she said, as if she were enumerating her family.

Mr. Gilhooley and the girl were shown to their room. Their luggage was carried up. The cabman was paid and dismissed. The servant retired after bringing a towel and a jug full of water. They were alone.

Mr. Gilhooley sat on a chair near the bed, staring at the ground. He had the feeling of being in a foreign country, where one suspects that the inhabitants, although civilized like one's own people, are yet not quite clean or of doubtful morals or in the habit of eating with their knives. The atmosphere about him had an alien breath. The sounds were strange, unrestrained and unbalanced. The quilt on the bed was shabby. There was no gas-fire and the grate was stuffed with papers. There was a crack in one of the windows. The room was very large. The roof was high. There was quite an echo when one spoke. And over all that, there was the consciousness of the girl being near. He looked. She was sitting by the left window, with her chin in her hands, looking out. She was in his charge now. Or, rather, he was in her charge. What was to be done? Even his passion for her had subsided now. And the effect of the previous night's drinking overwhelmed him.

'Come, come,' he said at length, getting to his feet, anxious to escape from his thoughts. 'There's a lot to be done. Ye . . . ye must get a coat.'

She jumped to her feet gracefully and approached him.

'My things are at the station,' she said. 'Would you mind getting them down here? I don't like going out alone.'

'Your things?' he said with surprise.

It seemed strange that she could have any property or any connection with the world at all before he knew her. He was delighted. If she had *some* property, there was at least one ordinary circumstance of respectable life connected with her.

'Why, hang it,' he said. 'I never thought of asking

ye. Well. We'll go. There's a lot to be done. We'll take a cab and do it all. There's a lot.'

In a cab, Mr. Gilhooley and the girl rolled around town all day, procuring the girl's luggage, buying her a coat, going to the bank to arrange about a draught on Mr. Gilhooley's current account and notify them of his change of address, and ending up at a theatre, with Mr. Gilhooley thoroughly soused once more.

In this manner Mr. Gilhooley took a mistress.

CHAPTER VII

WERE there really such a place as hell, it would have now become a heaven to its tenants of long standing. For subtle nature, possibly foreseeing such a devilish contrivance, has so constituted the human soul that usage makes it inured to discomfort.

At the end of the first day, Mr. Gilhooley had completely forgotten his horror at leaving his boarding-house in the morning. Saturated afresh with drink, his mind was soothed, dreamy, and eager for pleasure. He had spent a good amount of money. He had paid seven guineas for her coat and given her a present 'as a little pocket-money.' And during the day, at odd moments, when a passing shadow crossed his mind, of the man standing at a distance, grinning and of the imminent catastrophe, he sneered and shrugged his shoulder with a braggart gesture. At the bank, when the cashier seemed to raise his eyebrows at the unusual size of the cheque, Mr. Gilhooley grew very indignant and said to himself: 'God! What's this country coming to at all? Ye'd think it wasn't yer own money they're giving ye.' And in spite of his habitual miserly inclinations, where personal luxuries were concerned other than drink and a certain kind of dissipation, miserly habits peculiar to voluptuaries, he was awfully extravagant that day, tipping everybody half-a-crown and ordering the best of everything.

The girl stolid and indifferent at first, gradually became animated. She ate with the same surprising appetite as on the previous night. She drank quite her share too, and after she put on her new coat and they had re-entered the cab, she put her arms suddenly around Mr. Gilhooley's neck and kissed him.

At midnight they dismissed the cab outside the door, paid the cabman a good deal over his heavy fare and mounted to their room, arm in arm, exactly like a honeymoon couple deeply in love. They were admitted by the landlady, but they merely nodded to her, without pausing a moment to think of her existence. And although the theatrical troupe were having supper in the dining-room and quarrelling loudly over the distribution of their common victuals, using vulgar language, very surprising from ladies and gentlemen who had just been dukes and duchesses on the stage in some theatre, Mr. Gilhooley and his mistress did not hear one word they were saying. The gaunt staircase that had presented such a tawdry appearance in the morning was now a majestic avenue leading to delights of the most delicious kind. The hollow room, still smelling faintly of mustiness in spite of the fire that had been lit by Mr. Gilhooley's orders, had somehow changed its character since morning. For it had now the cloak of night to give it a character with peculiar significance for their present relations.

Both as tipsy as could be, they sat on the side of the bed, with their arms round one another, for a long while before they went to bed, babbling idiocies.

And in bed, after embracing with the same fervency as on the previous night, they lay a long time awake, while Mr. Gilhooley, holding an unlighted cigarette in one hand and gesticulating with the other hand, told her the history of his life, dwelling proudly on the fact that his father was the engineer-in-charge at the building of a certain section of railway up north and that he himself had galloped two hundred miles into Antofagasta to get a cure for snakebite for a pal. And the girl lay high up on her pillow, puffing rapidly at a cigarette, listening with dazed, happy eyes, without understanding one word he was saying.

Everything was forgotten by both of them. They had even forgotten one another, the one his passion, the other her aversion caused by the indelicacy of their meeting. They were united in a perfect intimacy by the common delight of humanity at escaping from the consciousness of existence and the fear of death, through lust and drunkenness. And after further embraces, deliciously exhausted, they fell asleep in one another's arms as gently as children. They slept soundly, without moving, until morning.

Quite early the girl jumped out of bed. Mr. Gilhooley still lay sound asleep. While putting on her knickers, she gazed at him in a curious way, coldly and, as it were, contemptuously. Then, moved by some extraordinary feeling, her lips trembled, she let the folds of her nightdress drop over her undergarments and approaching the bed on tiptoe, she gently kissed the big, sun-tanned hand that lay over the quilt. Why? Was it because Mr. Gilhooley's face in sleep had that childlike expression which was natural to it, but which the manner of his life and the innumerable circumstances of social intercourse kept hidden while he was awake? Truly, he looked like a big baby asleep, with his lower lip sagging comically. Or perhaps it was through a feeling of gratitude, or pity? Or even love?

Inexplicable mind of woman!

She rapidly dressed herself, having rummaged in her trunk and procured another dress, a pretty one of a mauve colour. But although she paid the strictest attention to the powdering of her face, arms and shoulders, to the cleansing of her teeth and to the arrangement of her clothes in the daintiest manner possible, she used very little water on her person.

Dressed, she immediately busied herself with the room, changing articles of furniture and using a piece of cloth from her trunk as a duster. In quite a short time, without making the least noise, she had completely changed the aspect of the place. Some way or other, although the changes she made were trifling, there was now an air of sprightliness. The dressing-table's varnish shone. The basin on the washhand-stand had lost its stains. The beautiful eighteenth-century mantelpiece was dusted and all the trash that had rested on top of it was hidden away in a corner. When she had finished, she sat down and surveyed it for a moment. She nodded her head and got to her feet again. Taking Mr. Gilhooley's boots, she left the room.

At half-past nine, when Mr. Gilhooley was gently awakened, an astonishing change in his life was made manifest to him. Before he had time to feel angry and disgusted with himself, as usually happened after a night's debauch, a glass of whiskey and soda was handed to him by the girl, with a smile. He took it in his trembling hand, stared at her a moment, and then swallowed it without a word. The effect was instantaneous. Like these American hoboes in Southern California, who, getting drunk overnight on a certain wine, awake in the morning in a sad condition and then turning around three times rapidly are quite drunk and happy once more – I say, Mr. Gilhooley, before he had time to awaken, was just as pleasurably intoxicated as he had been the previous night. So much so, that he had a splendid appetite for the breakfast which was served to him in bed, on a tray with legs. The morning paper was also there, and beside the bed, he saw his boots, brightly polished. And there was the girl, having her breakfast separately at a little table, talking seriously, as she ate with relish her bacon and egg, with little wrinkles in her forehead, after the manner of a young zealous housewife.

Mr. Gilhooley never said a word. He was trying to reconcile this experience with all his preconceptions of a disreputable life. He could not. He felt himself happy and he was trying to persuade himself that he should not be happy. He had never awakened in the morning, for the past three years, in a happy mood like this, with pleasant surroundings, in comfort, waited upon by a charming woman. He was not in the habit of being happy at this hour of the day, and he was worried. But gradually his indolent mind gave up trying to explain things. Just as, when a strong young man, reared in careful ignorance of sin, meets his first temptation of the flesh, is warned by his conscience to resist, makes gestures with his arms and moves his lips, as if talking to his conscience, shooing it away, so Mr. Gilhooley, listening to the girl's chatter, combated his cynical pessimism and his superstitious fears until they were vanquished. Then he hunched up his shoulders. His eyes twinkled merrily and he scratched his stomach under the bedclothes.

'Well, well,' he said. 'Who invented work? Well . . . There's something to be said for it. If there was no such thing as work, it would be no fun lying in bed while other people were working.'

She looked at him over the edge of her teacup, so that he could just see her eyelashes and the upper parts of her eyes over the edge.

'Lazy wretch,' she said, grinning, as she put down the cup.

'Oho,' thought Mr. Gilhooley, as he smiled at her, 'we're getting on. Yes, begob, we are.'

'Well,' he said, raising his shoulders and his white eyebrows, 'I've done me share of work.' He reached for the packet of cigarettes she had put on the tray. 'Twenty years of it in South America alone. What ye might *call* work. Nothing on above the waist sometimes. An' ye never knew when one of those peons 'ud land a knife in yer kidneys.' He lit his cigarette. 'Well, it's all done now.'

Scratching his chest idly, he lay back, smoking and thinking comfortably, replete and content, for the first time in three years.

'This is a funny house,' said the girl, lighting a cigarette. 'Do you know the people?'

'Only from a friend,' said Mr. Gilhooley.

'I'm sure the landlady takes dope or something. She has queer eyes.'

'Nonsense,' said Mr. Gilhooley. 'Nobody takes dope in this country. What's the matter with her?'

'Don't like the look of her,' said the girl, shrugging her shoulder. 'The way she looked at me when I was coming up from the kitchen. And you should see the kitchen. O! My God! I lived for a year in Germany. I'm afraid it has spoiled me for this country again. Such filth!'

'Well,' said Mr. Gilhooley with a sigh. 'It's there. Ye can't escape it. So why worry?'

'Don't be silly,' she said. 'Of course you can escape it. Why not get a flat? I'll look after it for you. I'm a good housekeeper.'

Mr. Gilhooley looked at her with his mouth open and a gleam of suspicion in his eyes. The thought flashed through his head: 'I see what ye're driving at.' But she immediately broke into a merry laugh and jumped to her feet. Cutting a figure round the room, with her hands on her hips and throwing up her shapely legs like a dancer, she cried:

'Do you like this dress?'

'It's dandy, sure enough,' said Mr. Gilhooley, swallowing his breath.

Her seductiveness made him flush.

'Matt bought it for me in Paris,' she said carelessly.

Mr. Gilhooley felt a curious sensation of embarrassment, which rapidly changed into discomfort, and then into hatred of something unknown. He felt the presence of an unpleasant idea somewhere in his mind and sulkily pretended to be unaware of it. Dropping his head and picking up the paper, he refused to look at the girl, and listened to her humming as she tidied her hair at the mirror with a feeling of repulsion and a determination to injure her feelings in some manner, with some biting remark.

But when she addressed a gentle remark to him a little later, he answered her politely, very politely, determined not to let her know that that idea was skulking in his mind.

That day he bought her a new hat and a new pair of gloves.

Ten days passed, almost identical with the first, but with the difference that their drinking and dissipation grew less and less, gradually. They became gradually more intimate. Little by little, the girl took under her care all his life, his wants and his habits. Seeing him use a soiled handkerchief, if in the room, she immediately offered him a clean one from among his linen, which she had completely overhauled; if in the street, she never failed to remember that he needed a clean one on arriving home. He no longer wore a frayed tie, for she had borrowed a smoothing iron from the landlady's servant, an old and very ugly peasant woman, with whom she had almost immediately contracted an extraordinary friendship. She pressed his ties, his soft collars and his shirts. She carefully brushed all his clothes and got them creased and pressed. A great deal of rubbishy things which had accumulated in his boxes owing to his miserly habits, she persuaded him to throw away. And at her suggestion, on the third day he bought a gorgeous dressing-gown in Clery's, an article of clothing he had never used before, but of which he became passionately fond as soon as he wore it.

Mr. Gilhooley was aware that Nelly (he now called her Nelly and she called him uncle, a name which suited him remarkably well), was gradually becoming a necessity. The moments he thought of it, it gave him an unpleasant feeling. But such was the rush of life under these new circumstances that he seldom had a moment to spare for those morbid meditations which occupied so much of his time previously. Almost every hour of the day, for they hardly ever separated, she was making him conscious of her body by a subtle movement or exposure of some limb, of her voice humming a strange tune, of her personality by some act in the interest of his comfort. And the resources of her nature were so numerous and varied that his naturally indolent mind was not able to foresee her actions or immediately to detect her motives . . . if, indeed, she had any beyond a craze for activity and a desire to please mankind.

He manifested his displeasure at her taking control over him at times by giving her a gruff order, as if to show he was the master. But instead of feeling hurt, she obeyed still more meekly. And then perhaps, half an hour later, he would notice her sad and silent.

'What's the matter, Nelly?'

She would burst into tears.

'What's up? Damn it, can't you tell me what's up?'

'Do you want me to go away? Are you tired of me already?'

'Who the hell said anything. . . .'

'You were so cross when you told me to . . . . '

'Oh, hell, that's all right. That's all right.'

'I know, but I . . . . '

'Yes, yes. I didn't mean anything. It's only . . . . '

He felt very miserable and ashamed of himself after these outbursts. But on one point he was adamant. When she led the conversation, as she often did, towards the desirability of moving to a flat, he would close up like an oyster and drop the conversation. For the reason that even though he was getting passionately fond of her, even though she pleased him in every sense as no woman ever had, he still was not aware of being in love with her, or of not being able to go away and leave her when it occurred to him that he had stayed long enough. Particularly when she made him jealous of Matt, or of somebody who passed in the street, admiring her, or of a waiter in a restaurant, or of the actors who lived in the house, he lay back, smiling within himself and chuckling: 'That's all right, me lady. Don't think ye can work that game on me. I'm off if ye try it and ye should know that.'

But a trifling event happened which sealed his fate as surely as the hiding of the key or the fact that the student Stevens was not at home that night. . . . But. . . . Faugh! It's ridiculous to say that trifling events change the course of a man's life or that either of these events determined the manner of Mr. Gilhooley's. . . . However, there is something in chance which scientists have not yet explained.

A jockey named Patrick Shirley occupied a room on the third floor. As Mr. Gilhooley himself said, this jockey was 'a hard case.' He was a dour man and nobody ever saw him smile. He came and went away again frequently, crossing to France, to England, and even to Germany on occasion. But whenever he stayed in the house, everybody in the house knew it, because he brought a curious odour with him. Not an odour of the stable, as might be supposed, but a curious odour, like a perfume. He and the landlady were on very intimate terms, and Nelly said to Mr. Gilhooley that the 'old hag' had some hold over him. In fact, when the jockey tried to break into the other room on the third floor one night, in order to get at the two confectioners who occupied it, the landlady took his part and fiercely attacked the two girls for being offended. He was so ugly, in fact, that he fascinated women by his ugliness. And yet his appetites seemed to be insatiable.

Mr. Gilhooley tried several times to get into conversation with him, but the man merely scowled and never replied. A perfect boor. Towards Nelly, however, he was very courteous in a crude way. On the sixth day – the theatrical troupe had disappeared that morning – he offered her a large pot of French preserves which 'he had smuggled across.' She accepted it with a charming smile and made Mr. Gilhooley very jealous when she told him about it.

'Better steer clear of that fellah,' said Mr. Gilhooley. 'He's rotten. I know by the look of him.'

The girl said nothing. On the tenth night, Mr. Gilhooley went out alone at about ten o'clock to get some fruit at the corner shop before it closed. They were staying indoors that night. He returned quite soon, and was amazed to find the jockey coming out of his room on his return. The two men stood looking at one another outside the door. The jockey calmly closed the door behind him and tossed his head.

'Well,' he said, 'd'ye think ye own the universe?'

Mr. Gilhooley started, so utterly amazed that he didn't know what to do until the jockey walked up the stairs past him, whistling, with his hands in his pockets. Mr. Gilhooley stared after the little midget of a fellow with his mouth open. Then he strode into the room. Nelly was sewing something at the table by the window. She hardly looked up.

'What was that fellah doing in here?' said Mr. Gilhooley.

Nelly flushed and didn't reply for a moment.

'He wanted to know would I come to the theatre with him?' she said.

'What?' cried Mr. Gilhooley. 'I'll soon answer his question for him.'

He was rushing towards the door when she jumped up and cried:

'Where are you going?'

'I'm going to him,' he roared like a bull. 'I'll show him.'

She darted to the door and put her back to it. Her face was like the face of an angry cat.

'Who gave you any right over me?' she cried. 'Eh?'

'Eh?' said Mr. Gilhooley. 'Eh?' he shouted, rushing at her.

With one large hand he caught her by the shoulder and swung her out of the way. She staggered back three paces and tumbled head over heels on to the bed. He opened the door, dashed out and up the stairs.

'Come out,' he yelled, standing between the two doors on the third floor, not knowing which was occupied by the jockey. 'Come out, you hound. Come out here, you son of a . . . . '

The jockey opened his door suddenly and rushed out with a poker. His coat was off. His waistcoat was unbuttoned and the sleeves of his little check shirt were rolled up. His short stubby nose was twitching and his oily hair was shining like black velvet. He rushed at Mr. Gilhooley and made a swipe with the poker. Mr. Gilhooley caught the poker just as it grazed his shoulder. With the other hand he seized the jockey by the face. His large hand covered the jockey's face and gripped it by the forehead and one ear. They closed. In an effort to put his other arm around the jockey's body, Mr. Gilhooley staggered and fell over him with a groan. They rolled around on the floor, yelling and cursing. The two confectioners ran out of their room, the big one wearing her dressing-gown, the thin, hollow-cheeked one in her stockinged feet.

'Help, help,' they cried. 'Mother of Mercy! They're fighting. Mrs. Brennan!'

People came, both from the attic overhead and from the floors underneath. Frowsy old Mrs. Brennan, with a long dyed curl in her mouth and her bare, wrinkled old arms dirty, came tumbling up, calling loudly and followed by a tall, puffy man, who was trying to peer over her head at the scene above. Two other men came running up together, one with his braces trailing behind him, the other wearing his hat and overcoat, fresh from the street. There was a hubbub around the two struggling men.

By now Mr. Gilhooley's rage had suddenly evaporated. A good-natured man, he rapidly became ashamed of himself for fighting in such a disreputable quarter, and also for fighting with such a puny man, who did not fight like a man, but availed himself of all the cunning artifices of a child struggling with a grown-up person, biting, kicking and screaming. Mr. Gilhooley held him under the armpits and he was trying to put his knee on his back. The jockey was twisting around his head. His jaws were open and he was trying to bury his yellowish teeth in Mr. Gilhooley's knee.

'Quiet, now, ye little devil,' Mr. Gilhooley kept saying.

'God! He has a fighting jag on him,' said the puffy man, who arrived with Mrs. Brennan. 'Throw water on him.'

'Stand back,' said somebody else. 'Make room.'

'Mrs. Brennan, Mrs. Brennan,' the big confectioner in the dressing-gown kept saying, with her knuckles between her teeth, staring at the fighters in a fascinated way.

The man in the hat and overcoat did not approach but stood half-way down the flight of stairs, laughing in an idiotic way. He was slightly intoxicated. The little crowd of people, rallied by the puffy fellow, closed in on the fighters and began to shout.

Then Nelly came running up. Opening a passage with her hands, she seized Mr. Gilhooley by the coat and pulled him, whispering excitedly:

'Larry, what are you doing? What are you doing?'

'Eh?' cried Mr. Gilhooley, dropping the jockey and standing bolt upright.

He was amazed, hearing himself called Larry, amazed that any of his friends should be present in such a place. In the excitement of the struggle he had forgotten about the girl. She led him away like a lamb. The others seized the frantic jockey and bundled him into his room, hauling him along by the arms and head, while his dainty little feet scraped along the floor, kicking wildly. They closed the door on him. Mrs. Brennan went inside to pacify him. People kept going to and fro, murmuring, laughing and shouting. For a long time this lasted. Mr. Gilhooley kept coming out of his room to talk to the landlady or to remonstrate with the slightly tipsy man who was making wild statements and had to be restrained by the man with his braces trailing. The jockey broke loose from his room and began to brandish his arms on the landing. The two confectioners screamed in their room. Two men seized the jockey once more and pushed him back into his room. Finally Mrs. Brennan went into hysterics and had to be given rum and water.

It was almost midnight before the whole thing had been explained away and before everybody was pacified. It was really very scandalous and the two confectioners said within Nelly's hearing that they were not going to stay in the same house with that rowdy, meaning Mr. Gilhooley. Yet in the end everything was settled in a very satisfactory manner. And it seemed that everybody was pleased with the excitement except the principals.

At midnight Mr. Gilhooley was still walking

around the room, with his hands in the sleeves of his new dressing-gown, staring at the ground, in a violent temper, and yet thoroughly ashamed of himself. Nelly was sitting on the bed, reading a novel, so silent, that he knew very well she was not reading at all, but waiting for him to say something.

'Why the devil don't you go to bed?' he said at last.

She turned her head towards him slowly, noiselessly laid down the novel and yawned.

'So sorry,' she said.

That maddened him. He bounded over to her. He stood over her with his hands clenched. The veins stood out in his neck. His eyes were bloodshot.

'I'll . . . I'll . . . I'll . . . ' he cried.

He glared at her, panting. She became paralyzed with fear and crouching low, with her hands up limply, like a dog crouching before its master, she stared into his eyes, shivering. It seemed there was pleasure in her eyes, and hatred and fear, all together. Mr. Gilhooley seemed to be making an effort to lower his hands to her throat and to stoop forward to fall on her, judging by the convulsing of his features and the movements of his shoulders and fingers. But he stood there, stooping forward, glaring impotently.

'Don't murder me,' she said at last, in a faint voice.

Immediately he fell forward over her and caught her knees in both hands. He violently pushed his head against her lap. Strange smothered sounds came from his lips. They were like sobs, ferocious sobs. His body was trembling. She slowly raised her head and looked down at his head. Then she touched the bald spot on top of it lightly with her hand, stroking it gently. There was a wild light in her eyes, her lips quivered and her little forehead kept wrinkling tremulously like a person making a great effort to lift something too heavy.

But as soon as she touched his head he started up and stared at her. His eyes roamed over her face, rested on her lips, and he said in a hoarse whisper:

'Don't do it again. For Christ's sake, don't madden me. You don't know me. I won't stand for it. See?'

'I don't know what's the matter with you,' she said slowly, shaking her head from side to side.

'Ach!' he cried, standing up and swinging his arms over his head. He held out his two hands and looked at them. 'Hell! Why can't I? . . . Do you hear?' He whirled around. 'Are you glad?'

'What? What?' she said, with her eyebrows raised.

'Ach!' he said again, striding over to the window.

He stood there, clenching his hands behind his back, muttering curses. She watched him for a while, motionless, her eyelids lowered. Then she cracked her thumb against the second finger and said:

'Come here.'

He didn't move. She jumped off the bed lightly and came towards him, swinging her hips. He turned around suddenly. His face had a look of agony in it. She halted and stretched out her hands. She threw back her head.

'Here, here,' she cried. 'Kill me if you like. I deserve it. What am I? What have I come to? A . . . .'

He had seized her in his arms before she finished. Covering her face with kisses, he kept muttering. Perfectly calm, she tried to catch his words, but they were indistinct. Then she too gave way . . . abandoning herself to a transport of passion, which seemed to be a mixture of amorousness and hatred. For she bit his cheeks and kissed them alternately.

That night, when their passion subsided and they were smoking cigarettes side by side in bed, Mr. Gilhooley capitulated. It was arranged that he was to go in the morning to procure a flat, a furnished one, for a term of a few months.

They were to live as man and wife publicly.

CHAPTER VIII

NEXT morning, shortly after eleven o'clock, Mr. Gilhooley set out alone to engage a flat. His mind was in a ferment. The fight of the previous night, the quarrel with Nelly, the humiliating apologies that morning to the landlady and the ridiculous promise he had made under the influence of the sudden realization of his insane passion, all caused him agonies. For all these things seemed to him to be the result of some disease that was growing on him, the local pains caused by a deadly disease, like the dizziness, the prickly heat and the stabbing muscular pains that presage a physical malady.

And as the mind of the sickening man is driven by these trivial signs to concentrate not on the coming malady itself, but on its result, death, so Mr. Gilhooley's mind was concentrated on an indefinable horror of something remote.

This thing remote and indefinable was connected in his mind with vague superstitious fears, with ideas of God and eternity, with rotting of the limbs and a slow paralysis of the mind. It was an irresistible force slowly surrounding him and about to overwhelm him. Human society and the normal circumstances of existence gradually slipped away one by one; just as the limbs are shorn by the wind from a dying tree, until the rotting trunk totters and then falls among the vermin.

The joyous days of lust and dissipation he had spent with her in the lodging-house had ended suddenly in a misery even worse than his former misery. For this love which he felt burning within him was not the form of ideal love of which he dreamt but its opposite. And instead of going along the avenue to escape he felt himself dragged the opposite way.

These thoughts were remote and unformed, but unformed thoughts are always more menacing and convincing. Like a vague feeling of unrest that spreads among an inarticulate peasantry and causes them to rise without leadership and commit extraordinary acts of heroism and barbarity in pursuit of some objective, which no single individual of their mass is able to understand.

There seemed to be several individuals waging war in his being. One savage fellow, half naked and incapable of argument, was standing apart, pursuing the girl, drunk with passion and indifferent to the past, the present and the future. Another, a mild man, eager to take offence, was moving about, muttering apologies and conversing energetically with extraordinary spiritual fetishes that remained silent and offered the man no assistance. Another, an indolent, tired man, who seemed to be the central and controlling figure of this trio, was walking along moodily, with compressed, sallow lips, incapable of action, nodding his head with a fatalist gesture.

He walked along O'Connel Street towards the bridge, going into the south side of the city.

It was a beautiful Irish spring day. As it were, summer had sent a day in advance to encourage the people. There was a fresh wind, but it had no bite.

The sky was clear and blue. The sun was a brilliant silver disc, with innumerable spears sticking from its edges, like the vessel which the priest raises aloft at benediction. Walking in the open air was like running along the bank of a river quite naked after a plunge into the water, in early morning. This freshness and eagerness of nature was reflected in the rapid, happy movements of the people who walked along and even in the faces of the motionless carters, who rumbled along in their carts, with their legs hanging through holes at the back.

A procession of unemployed workers was marching along the street, also going into the south side of the city, either to show their destitute condition to the wealthy citizens of the south side, to interview the city authority, or perhaps to take some exercise. There was a small fife and drum band in front. The front ranks kept step to the music. The rear ranks did not hear the music at all. There were women with babies marching. Along the sides men ran among the pedestrians with boxes, shaking their boxes and mutely asking for alms. Great crowds of other unemployed workers followed the procession, too timid to join and yet eyeing it eagerly. People of the wealthier class paused to look at the marchers. They saw the banner carried in the front ranks on two shabby sticks, bearing a skull and crossbones painted in white on a black ground. Some faces filled with pity watching the marchers. Others scowled in anger, angry perhaps that in a city like Dublin, where there are so many fat priests, there should be so many thin workers. Here and there a face, watching, bore a faint smile, a sour old wise man, who had long since become convinced that humanity is stupid, barbarous and destitute of philosophy and therefore refrained from feeling pity for the skinny, uncouth marchers. Only one young man, standing near O'Connel Bridge, waved his hand in the air and cried: 'Long Live . . . . ' He probably was a poet and saw in this marching throng a sign for some obscure human movement. But nobody paid any attention to him.

Mr. Gilhooley walked along beside the procession utterly unaware of its existence. He noticed that there were crowds of people in the streets, but he was too melancholy to endeavour to find out whether they were the Third Order of Saint Christopher, with sashes and Holy Water, or a temperance guild or unemployed workers. It was a matter of indifference to him. The ambitions, prejudices, woes and joys of his fellow-citizens had already ceased to have any interest for him. In fact, feeling a great movement of people about him, hearing music and the tramping of feet, he felt envious. He felt there was a mass of people near him, leaning on one another for support, co-operating for some purpose and therefore eluding the thought of death by fixing their minds on some concrete human enterprise. And in that they were happy, lucky and filled with hope . . . whereas he was alone, without hope, with his mind fixed on death.

Seeing him walk along among them, the unemployed workers on the pavements murmured angrily among themselves. They saw his handsome, tall, plump body, well-clothed, well-groomed, with a distinguished carriage and the slow, measured tread of the idler. They saw his melancholy, drawn face, with creases in the cheeks and a tired look in the blue eyes, the sallow, thin lips pressed together, the pockmarked nose twitching slightly, the thick red nape of his neck and the dark lines on the backs of his gloves.

'That b—d,' one said. 'He's all right. Never did a day's work in his life.'

'Jay,' said another. 'There's nothin' for them buggers but the bayonet.'

'No use shakin' a box at that fellah,' said a man with a box. 'He was never hungry in his life. He doesn't know what sufferin' is.'

'No. He ain't got a wife an' kiddies. . . .'

Mr. Gilhooley did not hear.

Soon the procession passed him, with its crowds of followers. He reached Grafton Street. He inquired for Friel at the house agent's office. Friel had not yet arrived. He went away again without stating his business, because he was shy of speaking to anybody about this affair, unless he knew the person. And Friel was the very man for this sort of thing. He decided to wait in a public-house for a little and then return for Friel.

Going up Grafton Street, on his way to the public-house, he saw a group of his friends. His first thought was to turn back to avoid them. Since his meeting with the girl, he had managed to avoid all his acquaintances except the son of a Welsh parson, who had nodded to him casually and winked. The Welshman was in the habit of borrowing money from Mr. Gilhooley whenever they met, but on this occasion, seeing Nelly with Mr. Gilhooley, he walked past with a wink, as much as to say: 'That gay dog Gilhooley has hooked a pretty one. I won't butt in. Oh! No. I'm a sport.' Mr. Gilhooley did not like that wink, however. And now, seeing a group of his friends, even though the girl was not with him and they could not possibly know of her existence, he wanted to avoid them.

'There it is,' he thought with shame. 'I'm ruined. I'm afraid to face the people. What's the use, though?'

Then it occurred to him that since he was going to live publicly with her as man and wife, he might as well face them now and tell them all about it. He advanced towards them. 'But why should I tell them about it?' he thought. He became very nervous, realizing that there were various social ties attached to a relation of this sort, objectionable ties. They recognized him. Macaward, standing against the wall of a shop, raised his stick in salute. Mr. Gilhooley flushed. 'That fellow is disreputable,' he thought. 'But now he too 'll be able to crow over me.' Why? He did not know why.

He approached, raising his white eyebrows, his favourite form of salutation, and assuming a bored look. With Macaward there were Culbertson, Hanrahan and the student Stevens. Another man, whom Mr. Gilhooley did not know, stood in the background, obviously imparting some sort of secret to Hanrahan, who seemed to be eager to get rid of him.

'Ha,' said Culbertson, in his harsh, loud voice. 'He has returned. Where have you been?'

Mr. Gilhooley, with a dry smile, made some sort of remark about making a change in his affairs. Nobody paid any attention to his remarks. They all seemed to be sober and not in a very good temper. The reason for this was explained very soon. Culbertson seized Mr. Gilhooley by the arm and, gazing very intently into his eyes, murmured:

'Do you want to save three lives?'

'How?' said Mr. Gilhooley.

'You have only to say the word,' said Culbertson.

'Silence in the court,' said Macaward to Stevens, who had begun to laugh dreamily.

'Not a word,' said Culbertson, turning around to his companions. 'The prophet is going to prophesy. Say the word, Gilhooley. *Introibo ad altare dei.*'

'Oho,' said Mr. Gilhooley, beginning to laugh, although he felt very miserable. 'I see the joke. Nothing in the bank.'

'A seer. A seer,' said Culbertson. 'Come on, Hanrahan. You take part in the ceremony. I don't know your friend, but perhaps he also might be prevailed on to make a poisonous offering.'

'Well, so long, Klem,' said Hanrahan, at last

managing to shake hands with his friend, whoever he was. 'Next time, we'll talk it over. By-bye.'

The stranger disappeared, very rapidly, down the side street, at the corner of which he had been standing. Hanrahan approached the others, looking even more bloated than on the previous occasion, with his thick purple lips open, as if about to kiss.

They all turned towards him eagerly.

'Why didn't you bring him along?' said Culbertson.

'No go,' said Hanrahan. 'Nothing stirring in that quarter.'

'Who is that chap?' said the tall student Stevens, curling a little faint black moustache that was growing on his upper lip.

'Ex-Colonel——" said Hanrahan casually, but with pride, mentioning the name of a famous revolutionary gunman, who had been one of the leaders in the intrigue which got Hanrahan dismissed from the army.

'Oho!' said Mr. Gilhooley, looking around suspiciously in the direction in which the stranger had disappeared.

It suddenly occurred to him that this fellow, ex-Colonel—— had killed a number of men, had tried to organise some sort of a revolution and was still abroad with a gun on his person, revered by a few, feared by many and looked upon by all as an interesting individual. Whereas he himself had never killed anybody in his life, had never organized a revolution and hardly ever fired a gun, even to kill a rabbit . . . and yet nobody revered him, nobody had any interest in him, and if he died nobody would say: 'That was an interesting chap, Larry Gilhooley.' It was very strange.

'Gunmen,' said Macaward contemptuously. 'They put them in jail in America. Here they make them colonels.'

'No time for recriminations,' said Culbertson, rubbing his large hands on his puffed-out chest. 'We have to offer sacrifice very soon or I'll have ulcers on my throat. Come on, Gilhooley. Name the cathedral.'

'Eh . . . Eh,' Mr. Gilhooley began, but Hanrahan interrupted him.

'None o' that,' said Hanrahan to Macaward, sadly and arrogantly. 'It's easy talking now. But there was a day. . . .'

'Yes, yes,' said Culbertson impatiently. 'Never mind. Let's go.'

'And don't you forget it,' cried Hanrahan, with a wild look in his eyes. 'That day'll come again, when the fighting man'll come into his own.'

'*Der tag*, gentlemen,' said Culbertson. 'Fill your glasses. Come on, Gilhooley.'

'I say,' said Mr. Gilhooley nervously. 'I can't go. I'm sorry.'

'What?' cried Culbertson.

'Good God!' said Macaward, dropping his pipe to the street. 'The blow is as sudden as it was unexpected.'

'That's all right,' said Mr. Gilhooley, putting his hand in his pocket. 'I'll stand all the same.'

'But why not come along? Damn it, man, be sociable,' said Culbertson. 'We haven't seen you for . . . . '

'Private business,' said Mr. Gilhooley, nervously handing Culbertson a pound-note. 'Pay me any time. I'm making . . . eh . . . a change in my life.'

They all looked at him curiously, with serious faces. Even Culbertson, while he carefully pushed the crumpled note into his trousers pocket, opened his eyes wide. The student Stevens, lighting a tiny pipe, which he had just bought for a penny in Woolworth's 'for a cod,' let the match burn his fingers.

'What?' somebody said.

It was so extraordinary that Mr. Gilhooley should make a change in his life. And he looked so sad and serious.

'Well,' said Mr. Gilhooley sheepishly, 'everybody does it . . . sometimes. We are all mor . . . I mean human.'

'Hell to my soul,' said Macaward, coming up and looking at Mr. Gilhooley's clothes. 'Has it happened already?'

'What?' said Mr. Gilhooley nervously and angrily.

'He, he,' said Macaward. 'I never saw his clothes brushed before. Is it the result or the preparation?'

'Let's drop the parables,' said Culbertson. 'My brain is watertight. What's it all about?'

'The connubial couch,' said Macaward. 'What else?'

'What are you talking about?' said Mr. Gilhooley angrily to Macaward. 'Has it happened already? How do you mean? Do you mean to say . . . . '

'This is getting very obscure,' said Culbertson. 'Do you mean to say you are married, Gilhooley?'

'Not yet,' said Mr. Gilhooley. 'But I expect to be married . . . eh . . . . '

Suddenly it occurred to him that he didn't know for certain whether the arrangement would be carried out, but flushing still more, he continued:

'Next week, I think.'

'Bravo!' said Culbertson. 'I knew you had it in you. Well. Sorry to lose you, old chap. Still. . . You know me. Culbertson.'

'Hope she is pretty,' said the student Stevens, spitting into the roadway.

'Larry,' said Hanrahan, coming up to Mr. Gilhooley and taking him by the right hand. 'Good luck.'

Hanrahan's blotched face assumed a melancholy, tender look. It seemed that his whole soul was stretching out towards Mr. Gilhooley, with love for Mr. Gilhooley and for some idea with which it had suddenly associated Mr. Gilhooley.

Mr. Gilhooley became terribly ashamed for some reason, seeing this look of tenderness and love, so strange in Hanrahan's face.

'Make a home,' said Hanrahan, gripping Mr. Gilhooley's hand so firmly that it hurt. 'Make a home. To hell with this life.'

'Public-house ballad entitled: "The Sinner's

Lament," ' said Culbertson. 'Come along, boys. First o' the month, Gilhooley. Name the cathedral.'

Hanrahan gave Mr. Gilhooley's hand another shake.

'A home,' he muttered, turning away.

'Good-day, gentlemen,' said Mr. Gilhooley.

They were moving off, when Macaward called out:

'I'll follow on, boys. Larry, just a word.'

The others disappeared around the corner. Mr. Gilhooley had turned down the street, going back to the house agent's. He halted and turned angrily towards Macaward.

'Vexed at what I said?' said Macaward solemnly. 'Don't deny it. I see it in your face. Know why I said that?'

'Why should I mind?' said Mr. Gilhooley. 'You just talk to be thought clever. Why should I mind what you say?'

'Listen,' said Macaward, becoming very melancholy and gazing down the street with tired eyes. 'We have something in common, you and I. That's why I spoke.'

'Eh?' said Mr. Gilhooley.

'I understand you,' continued Macaward solemnly gazing down the street, 'but you don't understand me.'

'Is it money ye want?' said Mr. Gilhooley offensively.

'No, then,' said Macaward, arrogantly drawing himself erect. 'It's not. I don't want money. But I want to say this. I understand you, though you don't understand me. I live in a lie. So do you. Do you think I like this life? No. My proper place is out there,' he waved his stick towards the country. 'There is life growing out there. New life.' He waved his stick again. 'Here there is only death. Corruption. You'll rot here. Living in a lie. You can't deceive me. You aren't fit for it, no more than me. Only where there are green fields and birds and life, growing and dying and growing and dying, all the year round. Not corruption like this. We're Irish. We were made for the hillsides and the fields . . . and the sea. That's our life.'

'Yes, yes,' said Mr. Gilhooley. 'How do you mean? You're driving at something.'

Macaward tapped him on the breast with the crook of his stick.

'Listen,' he said. 'Don't do it. Do you understand?'

'Ha,' said Mr. Gilhooley.

'Don't do it,' said Macaward. 'I don't want money. So you think I wanted money. Heh.'

His face assumed a ferocious expression.

'Money. To hell with your money.'

He suddenly moved back a pace and the ferocious expression left his face. The look of demonaic glee came into his eyes.

'The voluptuary is going to get married,' he cried, laughing without making any sound. 'A voluptuary's marriage. There is more joy in heaven for the salvation of one voluptuary. . . . Nice married man you'll make. Heh. Heh.'

He disappeared round the corner.

'Don't do it,' said Mr. Gilhooley to himself. 'Eh?'

He was very angry and yet . . . his anger turned in on himself instead of turning on Macaward.

'Will I go or not?' he said to himself.

'I'll not go,' he said, moving on down the street. 'I'll leave here. Just go without a word. To hell with my clothes. They can stay there. Settle by letter with the landlady. No. Begob. Paid in advance. There's no need to settle. I'll just step over to London for a few . . . . '

He began to shiver. The very thought of leaving her roused every part of his being, until a great shout seemed to be made by the multitude of nerves and tissues and veins that clamoured for her. His brain was overwhelmed.

For a few seconds this was unpleasant to his mind. Then it changed suddenly into a great joy, an eagerness like that of a lover awaiting his mistress. The people who passed, the sounds of the city, the shops, everything swam before him. Everything lost its meaning. Fear, caution and the desire for life itself melted away before the heat of his passion.

Smiling like a child, he muttered to himself.

'God! Wild horses couldn't tear her out of my arms. God help me.'

Smiling and trembling he walked along contemplating the pressure of his arms about her slim body, the eel-like wriggling of her body and the throbbing of his heart.

CHAPTER IX

MICHAEL FRIEL was just stepping out of his little motor car in front of the house agent's office as Mr. Gilhooley came up.

'Hey! Friel,' Mr. Gilhooley called out, 'hold on a moment.'

Friel turned around languidly, saw Mr. Gilhooley and smiled, by turning up one side of his little brown moustache. Then he sniffed, waved his little moustache up and down like a see-saw and shrugged his shoulders.

He was a stout fellow of low size, with powerful shoulders and a sunburnt face that seemed to be composed of large bones, coated with a heavy thick skin. His blue eyes looked extremely intelligent, although he was utterly devoid of intelligence. For the reason that his eyes always seemed to be laughing at something, sarcastically, like a goat's eyes. This make-believe intelligence expressed in his eyes did not go into his brain, but exhausted itself in an excessive physical vitality. He could not read the simplest book or understand the simplest problem relating to any abstract idea. But the most intricate sort of machinery provided an irresistible attraction for him and somehow or other, he understood it and mastered its complexity in half the time that a highly intellectual individual would take to master it. As long as he had something physical to occupy his body, either the pursuit of some bodily pleasure or the performance of some task requiring manual skill and a certain kind of animal cunning, he was restless, energetic and violently determined to finish the thing, whatever it was. But as soon as he was prevented from pursuing that sort of activity, he immediately fell asleep. If he went to church to hear Mass or listen to a sermon he fell asleep. If he were in a drawing-room where politics, religion, art or philosophy were discussed he fell asleep. Walking with somebody who was of an academic or scientific disposition, he became at first restless, then insulting and finally picked a quarrel for some foolish reason.

He was the third son of a prosperous middle-class family that had lately become rather high officials in the new Government. Michael was educated for the Bar, not because he had any inclination for the pursuit of that profession, but because the family thought it was a respectable one. For ten years he studied law without understanding a word of the rubbish. He drank, amused himself with women, got into trouble with the police, with women and with his friends among the middle classes, and at the same time he became the darling of the common people about town. Every policeman knew him and loved him. Every flower woman, tramp and beggar knew him and said: 'God bless yer honour' when they saw him. And yet with these people he was often impudent, rough, and even brutal. But he was generous and eager to assist everybody in a difficulty. Finally his family kicked him out, washed their hands of him and said he was a disgrace. This was after their accession to the Government circles.

Being compelled to earn a living and free to do what he liked, Friel married a house agent's only daughter and was taken into the business by his father-in-law as a partner. Then he turned out to be an invaluable citizen. In two years he had doubled the business. Nobody could resist his ingratiating manner, his frank blue eyes, and the way he moved his little moustache up and down like a see-saw. People who thought themselves wise thought him a fool and allowed him to overreach them, just because they thought it was impossible for a fool to over-reach a wise man. Fools saw in him only a silly fellow like themselves and allowed him to overreach them, out of pity for him. He was still the most popular figure in town among the poor people but the middle classes and respectable people still raised their hands in horror when his name was mentioned. He was an excellent husband to his plain wife, although he was still promiscuous in his relations with women. He had two children already and he was a devoted father to them. And such was the control that he had exerted over the affairs of his father-in-law, that the latter was thinking of retiring, as the business was getting too difficult for him; even though he was only fifty and quite a sturdy fellow two years before.

Mr. Gilhooley's face brightened when he came up to Friel. Friel had that effect on everybody of a simple nature. There was something innocent and joyous in his soul which attracted simple natures, while it terrified those who, though they may be very respectable, solid citizens, useful in their way and quite necessary for the progress of mankind and the salvation of black babies, are . . . rather dull and mean.

'Well,' said Friel. 'Frosty weather. How's it keeping? Frisky? Wha'?'

'Little bit of business,' said Mr. Gilhooley.

'Always welcome,' said Friel, tightening the belt of his raincoat and smiling broadly. 'Anything from a harem to a cycle lock-up. I'm your man for the usual commission.'

'Eh?' said Mr. Gilhooley. 'How do you mean? A harem?'

'Hush baby,' said Friel. Then the smile left his face. He assumed a melancholy expression. He spat into the street and wiped his lips with the back of his glove. Looking a little to one side first and then upwards at Mr. Gilhooley's eyes, he said confidentially, as if he and Mr. Gilhooley were united by the closest ties of friendship and love and they were going to embark on an expedition of great danger: 'What is it?'

'I want a . . . a . . . a . . . ' began Mr. Gilhooley flushing slightly.

'Ha, ha,' said Friel, drawing his chin into his throat and assuming an expression of boredom and of utter indifference.

'A furnished flat,' said Mr. Gilhooley.

'Heh, hm,' said Friel, dispassionately. 'I see. Let me see. A flat. Yes.'

'Ye see,' said Mr. Gilhooley, putting the crook

of his stick on his arm and searching for his cigarette case. 'I'm thinking of making a change . . . a big change I may say . . . in a way . . . I'm . . . I might as well say. . . .'

'Heh, hm,' said Friel. 'Just a moment.'

He went over to the little motor car and did something to the engine. He nodded to a policeman that passed. The policeman, with a smile, shook the folded cloak he carried on his shoulder. Friel returned to Mr. Gilhooley.

'Have a cigarette,' said Mr. Gilhooley. 'Point of fact . . . I'm . . . thinking of getting married.'

Taking the cigarette, Friel paused, looked at Mr. Gilhooley suspiciously for a moment, assumed a look of stupidity, smiled slightly, wagged his moustache and then raised his right shoulder.

'Holy Christ!' he said. 'Honest?'

'Why?'

'Well, you know,' said Friel, trying to curl his little moustache, 'you're a man . . . let me say . . . pretty good income . . . and . . . well, I'm a married man myself . . . best little wife in the country and two little peaches that I'd give my life for.' A brilliant light came into his eyes. 'Still. It's a tough proposition. Let me tell you . . . I know many a man. . . . It's all very well, let us say . . . have a bit of fun . . . flat and that sort of thing . . . the best in the country does it . . . and it's less bother but. . . .'

'Blast it,' thought Mr. Gilhooley, biting his sallow thin lip. 'If I told him the truth he'd make a laughing-stock of me around town and maybe call me a scoundrel, and yet he. . . .'

'Aw!' he said aloud. 'You fellows are all the same.'

'How is that?' said Friel.

'Preach one thing and practise another,' said Mr. Gilhooley.

Friel, without understanding what Mr. Gilhooley had said, clapped his hands together, laughed loudly and then suddenly became serious.

'Well, anyhow,' he said, 'let's think. Wait. I'll just rush in and see. . . .'

He dashed into the office. Mr. Gilhooley waited, afraid to think and yet pursued savagely by one persistent thought: 'It's all very well for them. No matter what they do they're all right. It washes off their backs like water off a duck. But I'm different. Why the devil it is, I don't know. I got to pay. I know it.'

Friel came out, putting some little pieces of paper into the inside of his cap and then jamming his cap tight on his head. He winked to Mr. Gilhooley, started his motor car, vaulted into the driver's seat and motioned Mr. Gilhooley to take a seat beside him.

'Fortunes of war,' he said. 'I have the very thing ye want.'

Mr. Gilhooley got into the car.

'What is it?' he said. 'Have ye got a . . . .'

Suddenly the little motor car dashed off, almost at full speed, stopped short for half a second and then darted off again with a loud noise, swerved around a corner, jerked aside and finally went ahead at a smart pace, while several enraged pedestrians, who had almost been knocked down by its savage movements, stared after it, gesticulating.

'Ye see,' said Friel, with one hand on the wheel, spitting into the roadway, 'ye want one in a good quarter so. . . . There's a fellow called Crimmins, a journalist. . . . There's something on in France . . . so he . . . they have to run off everywhere, maybe to South America supposing there's an earthquake or a fall in the franc . . . ye know . . . write something about damn all . . . so he has to go for a bit, tour around, he said to me . . . he's a decent fellow all the same.' He paused to spit again, settled his cap, shouted at a man on the opposite side of the street and then seeing a girl whom he knew, he winked at her. 'She's a great bit of skirt. Give ye an intro only we're in a hurry. Name's Molly Carroll. Stevens is on that trail but he hasn't a ghost. . . . Ye'd want it for six months I suppose, anyway, and then ye could look around. Seeing yer a friend I wouldn't put yer neck in a halter.'

'But—' said Mr. Gilhooley.

'Four rooms and a bath, on the second floor,' interrupted Friel. 'There's a fellow out of the —— Ministry on the floor below, but he's all right, I think. And on the top there's . . . what's his name? . . . a fellow with a beard, not in our crowd. Must be a civil servant, though. Lot's o' them around. The other lad out of the —— Ministry is called Fleming. He has a good-looking wife but ye better keep yer eye off her, 'cause she's. . . .'

'But look here,' said Mr. Gilhooley.

'Now, not a word,' interrupted Friel. 'I'll manage it all right. Crimmins is a good fellow. He's not exactly in our line but I know lots of his crowd. Ye see. . . . No use talking about Anatole France or what's that other fellah? . . . fellah wrote the hot stuff . . . it's in a big book . . . it doesn't do in a pub. . . . I can't stand them fellahs but only for that . . . otherwise, ye see, he's all right. You leave it to me. Ye might as well call it settled. I'll cut him down to two-pound-ten though he's asking three. There are lots of China lanterns or something, not China lanterns, what am I talking about? but pictures, artist stuff, that he's particular about, but you tell him to cart the damn things off. I'd rather have a French post-card.'

They arrived at the house where the flat was to let. It was in a street near Merrion Square. At one end there were little shops on the ground floor of houses. At the other end, there were rather pretentious houses and what looked like Government offices of some sort. Opposite the house where Friel halted there was an archway leading to a mews. The ground floor of the house had been converted into a tobacconist's shop. There was no separate door for the dwelling part of the house. One entered by the shop door but within that, the hallway had been divided in two by a wooden partition, that was now painted dark green. A little glass door led into the tobacco-shop on the left.

'Just a moment,' said Friel, with his hand on the door handle of the shop. 'You wait here. Ye see the advantage of the shop? Door open all day, so saves answering bells . . . up till ten o'clock at night. And knocks down the price ye see . . . remember that . . . say something about the shop to Crimmins if he . . . . Just wait . . . . Careful what ye say here, though. I'm known but they don't know me . . . know what I mean . . . just a little. . . .'

He winked to Mr. Gilhooley and passed into the shop. Within, Mr. Gilhooley could see two women, standing behind the counter, one large, buxom and approaching middle age, the other young, frail and handsome in a delicate way. Friel went up to the counter, leaned his elbows on it familiarly, took the buxom lady's hand, drew her towards him and tried to kiss her. The buxom lady giggled and struck at him. The young lady cocked up her head and frowned. Mr. Gilhooley saw Friel move around to the rear of the counter, put his arms around the buxom lady, embrace her while she almost screamed and then move over to the frail young lady, who kept on polishing cigarette cases without paying any attention to him.

'Damn the man,' said Mr. Gilhooley to himself. 'He's just fooling around for nothing.'

Suddenly he became conscious of Friel's youth and his own approaching old age. He became ashamed. He became angry and hated Friel. He looked with sudden jealousy at the black luxuriant curls of Friel's hair. Friel had taken off his cap and he was passing a little slip of paper, which had been concealed in the cap, furtively, to the frail young lady.

'The scoundrel,' thought Mr. Gilhooley. 'He's after her blood.'

With a pang of remorse he thought of a girl in Derbyshire, England, when he was working on his first job. For six months the affair lasted and then . . . he was afraid of the poverty it would mean to him, at the outset of his career. Then he thought of his father, angrily, with hatred. He was the cause of it all, dying in his prime, leaving a wife and three children penniless. Then he became suddenly melancholy, imagining a malignant fate pursuing him . . . the man with the club. He started. A host of visions crowded into his mind, Nelly dancing around the room in her red knickers, holding them out at the thighs on either side with the thumb and forefinger, his brother's farm he had visited after coming back, with turkeys screaming around the yard, turkeys, turkeys, turkeys and the marked hostility of his brother when he didn't offer to pay for young Harry's education, the shame of hiding the key and the problem of what was to be done with Matt supposing he turned up as she seemed to expect.

'If I only believed in God itself,' he muttered, looking at Friel pass into the room beyond the shop, with his arm around the now smiling buxom lady's waist, 'it would be some comfort. She doesn't love me. I'm not a fool. Anything to fill a gap . . . provided there's money. He has black curls and he's young . . . same as I was once. . . . None of them believe me, only that down and out Hanrahan. Larry Gilhooley getting married! That baldy codger! Good for a loan and for a drink, that's all.'

Then he became suddenly furious. He clenched his hands within his overcoat pockets. He glared through the glass window at the frail young woman, who was reading the little note, whatever it was, surreptitiously, under the ledge of the counter. He became furious with shame at his own incompetence, at his weakness of character in allowing himself to stand here in the hallway, waiting for the pleasure of a 'libertine' like Friel. He became furious with the whole process of society around him, which he envisaged going its way, smugly content within its web of religion, law and morality. He puffed out his chest. He made his muscles rigid. His thick, red neck became purple and he wanted to cry out.

What? He wanted to kill. What would he kill? He listened, not for physical noises or words but for an inner command. He heard nothing.

Terrified of the silence within his soul, the ignorance and the helplessness of his personality, his body relaxed. He emitted the breath from his dilated chest tremulously. His eyes grew dazed and his lips fell open. His helplessness became manifest to him. He knew that he could no longer escape. From what? Unconsciously he waved his right arm and rapidly struck his tongue against the roof of his mouth several times.

Then his eyes blazed again. His lips compressed. He said, almost aloud:

'But, by Christ, I'll keep her. If I have to murder her and him.'

Friel came out, smiling languidly and eating a bun. He blew a kiss to the frail young woman and left the shop.

'Just fixing a primus stove for Mrs. Burgess," he said in a low affectionate voice. 'Decent sort. Better be careful what ye say in there, though . . . she's very religious. Mass every morning. Good job somebody is praying,' he added, bounding up the stairs and throwing away the rind of the sweet bun. 'Come on, Larry.'

Irritated and anxious to show his dignity, Mr. Gilhooley walked up the stairs slowly.

Crimmins and his wife were in the flat, packing their things. Mr. Gilhooley was introduced to them. He murmured something and shook hands with Mrs. Crimmins. But when he moved to take Crimmins's hand, Crimmins bowed slightly and didn't offer to shake hands. Mr. Gilhooley drew back also and bowed. Crimmins scowled nervously. He treated both Mr. Gilhooley and Friel with very casual courtesy indeed. Friel, however, was indifferent to this reception and addressed all his remarks to Mrs. Crimmins, a pretty little woman with delicate hands, who kept running around and smiling.

Mr. Gilhooley stood apart, without looking at the rooms or understanding what was being said. He said, 'Yes, yes,' to every proposal, much to the disgust of Friel who wanted to drag the business out as far as possible, so as to have more time with Mrs. Crimmins. In fact he prevented himself from looking at the rooms and from receiving a close impression of them.

'Here,' he thought. 'Will it be here? How do I know? I'll know the worst, anyway, and it can't go on. But . . . Christ! Even one week. . . . They can do it . . . some people . . . like the Roman that opened his veins. What is time?'

The arrangement was concluded. Crimmins, who had been standing by the fireplace with his hands in his pockets, scowling, said:

'Yes, you get the contract, Friel. I simply detest these . . . these. . . .'

'But, my dear,' said Mrs. Crimmins, 'you must remember . . . dear, oh, dear, it's just the same . . . even with his letters, Mr. Friel. . . .'

'Ha, ha,' said Friel, 'it must be very hard on the brain all the same . . . writing ye know . . . wha'?'

'Yes . . . of course,' said Mr. Gilhooley dreamily. 'That arrangement will be perfectly satisfactory . . . er . . . I hope to both parties . . . very pleasant, I'm sure. . . .'

Then they said good day.

Going down the stairs behind the bounding, bulky figure of Friel, Mr. Gilhooley paused and touched the wall. Then he went on down.

'It feels just the same as any other wall and yet. . . . Superstition, that's what it is . . . it's in our blood. God! I hate that fellow, Friel.'

Outside at the car, Mr. Gilhooley refused a seat and an offer to have a drink at Mooney's. The sight of Friel's muscular young thighs vaulting into the driver's seat of the motor car so enraged him that he felt ashamed.

Friel drove away and Mr. Gilhooley walked on furiously, thinking of his careless insolence. The insolence of youth. His own youthful insolence of twenty years ago.

Then he straightened himself. Passion, tender, intoxicating and blinding passion, surged up into his head. He suddenly thought of her and of the flat, where he would soon have her alone. . . . .

All the way back to the lodging-house he walked slowly, drunkenly thinking of various forms of lust.

CHAPTER X

It was long after one o'clock when Mr. Gilhooley returned to the lodging-house. The old proprietress met him in the hallway and said excitedly.

'Oh, dear! I thought you'd never come back. Your wife had a bad turn.'

'What's that?' cried Mr. Gilhooley.

His mouth became very dry. He shivered and his heart stopped beating.

'Oh, dear!' said the old woman. There was a curious air of mystery and of secrecy in her expression. 'Poor thing! Last night brought it on, I suppose. You know, anything like that' – she lowered her voice – 'it gives them a fright . . . you should be very careful. . . .'

'She thinks,' thought Mr. Gilhooley, reddening, ' that she. . . . Good God! Suppose it had happened before she. . . .'

'How do you mean?' he said angrily.

The old woman looked at him cunningly. She saw in his face that he understood what she meant. She touched him gently on the arm.

'Don't take offence with an old woman,' she said. 'I thought I'd just. . . . I haven't got a grudge against ye . . . only sometimes men don't understand . . . they *don't* understand these things. . . .'

'But, damn it all,' said Mr. Gilhooley. 'I never. . . .'

'Hush,' said the old woman. 'You shouldn't leave her alone. You on up to her now. She was hysterical. I gave her a drop of brandy.'

'God!' thought Mr. Gilhooley, making an effort to run up the stairs and floundering cumbersomely. 'Supposing that . . . but it can't be . . . that devil, whoever he is. . . . .'

He halted outside the door of the room and listened. Not a sound. For some reason he took off his hat and was about to knock. But he changed his mind and opened the door.

'Hello, hello,' he said cheerfully, closing the door behind him and entering the room. 'I got it all right.'

Then, seeing her, he rushed forward.

She had been kneeling by her trunk when he entered, with letters in her hands and strewn about in the trunk. She made an effort to hide the letters and then jumped to her feet. She stood erect, with a tearful, terrified face, with her hands drawn down by her sides. Her lips twitched and her great blue eyes were brilliant with emotion.

'Nelly,' he said, 'what . . . what . . . what is it?'

She staggered forward and threw herself into his arms. She burst into tears, shivering.

'Now, now,' he muttered. 'Good God! What's it all about? I say. I say . . . don't cry now . . . for God sake, Nelly . . . ye know I'd do anything for you. . . . D'ye hear?'

'Don't leave me,' she sobbed. 'Don't . . . don't leave me. I became terrified.'

'Sit down, now, and be quiet. Here, now. Sit down.'

Her led her to the bed and put her sitting on it. She put her face into her hands. Standing over her, a frown came into his face and his eyes wandered over her figure suspiciously. Reassured, he drew in a deep breath and began to stroke her hair. He sat down beside her. They were silent for nearly a minute. Then she raised her head.

'You weren't going to leave me?' she said sharply, scrutinizing his face.

'Going to leave you!' he cried indignantly. With a pang he remembered that he had thought of running away. But he said: 'What could put that idea into your head? You know damn well that I couldn't tear myself away behind a . . . a . . . traction engine.'

'I got afraid,' she said, 'as soon as you had gone. Then I thought . . . every noise I heard, he was coming up the stairs. He said he'd kill me.'

'Who?' said Mr. Gilhooley, although he knew very well who it was.

'Matt,' she said.

Mr. Gilhooley got very angry.

'Now, look here,' he said fiercely. 'We're going to settle this once and for all. I didn't want to be inquisitive. I hate poking my nose into other people's business. Live and let live. But, as we're going to . . . live together, this blackguard — '

'Don't ,' she cried. 'Don't say that. I love him.'

He stiffened.

'No, no,' she cried, sobbing and clutching him feverishly by the shoulders, 'I don't. I hate him, only it was he; it's a long time now. You don't understand.'

'Come on,' said Mr. Gilhooley, resolutely pushing her away. 'We're going to settle this now. Who *is* this fellow? Who is he, I say? What hold has he over you? I'm not a woman-snatcher.'

He got to his feet and took a few paces towards the dressing-table. He thought: 'Here's a good chance of getting away.' In his jealousy, he thought himself quite capable of going away, returning her to Matt, whoever he was, and making peace with himself. These thoughts were vague, but very cunning.

'Well?' he said, halting by the dressing-table and taking up a long nail-file that belonged to her.

'I don't want to talk about it.' she said in a low voice.

'Come, come,' he said sharply, 'out with it. Otherwise, I finish here and now. There may be other things in this . . . which might . . . the landlady was under the impression that your sudden illness was caused by. . . .'

'By what?' she said, flaring up.

'There's no need to. . . .'

'I see,' she said harshly. 'No. You needn't be terrified. There's nothing of the kind. He's a gentleman. At least, he's that.' She got to her feet. 'And although he has brought me to this. . . . Oh! Why are men so cruel?'

She put her face in her hands and sat down on the bed again.

'Now, now,' said Mr. Gilhooley, endeavouring to speak in a cold voice, although his passion for her was again rising. 'Those tricks are no use. It's either yes or no. Here and now. Out with it.'

'What do you want to know?' she said, without uncovering her face.

'All,' he said. 'We'll leave nothing behind the bush.'

There was silence for a few moments. Somebody outside in the street began to play the 'Adeste Fideles' on a concertina.

'Damn that noise,' muttered Mr. Gilhooley.

'Come on,' he said, approaching the bed. 'What hold has he got over you? Speak up. Speak up, or I'm going out that door.'

'No, don't . . . don't be angry,' she cried, reaching out her hand and touching his coat. 'Don't be angry with me. I'll . . . I'll . . . He has no hold over me.'

'But then . . . in the name of God. . . .'

He sat down on the bed and scratched his left cheek.

'Eh?' he said.

'You needn't be afraid,' she said softly and sadly. 'We had a child, but it died. Three months old.'

'O . . . Hoh,' he said in a whisper. 'I wasn't referring to that.'

'Will you forgive me if I tell you?'

'Sure. I'm not a hypocrite.'

'You won't be angry?'

'Oh, go ahead. I merely . . . You see it's absolutely necessary to. . . . .'

'His name is Considine.'

'Matt Considine.'

'No. Matt is only a nickname. His real name is Francis.'

'That doesn't matter, anyway. Go ahead.'

'I met him in Galway. He was living there with his mother after coming out of the army. They were all crazy about him then, but I was only a school-girl . . . fifteen at the time. You see. . . ."

She paused and touched her lips with a little scented handkerchief.

Unconsciously her accent had changed. The natural richness of the soft western speech had left her voice and it was pitched on the high, dry note, affected by Englishwomen of fashion.

'We didn't see much of one another at that time. I was very shy at that time. Only fifteen. And he. . . . He was a genius and he had done all sorts of things in the war. His father, you see, was an officer in the Indian army. He married out in India and then, when his father died, he inherited an estate. . . . '

'Who is this?'

'Mr. Considine, Matt's father.'

'I see.'

'They came back from India. Then they had some quarrel. There was some talk of Mrs. Considine. Anyway, the father died, they said it was poison or suicide or something, it's just scandal I'm sure, but he left the property in his will to the eldest son, Louis, the mother to . . . what is it? . . . administer it during her lifetime. So I heard, anyway. That's how, you see, although she dotes on Matt, she can't give him very much but. . . . At school they said he was a genius, but he got expelled from several places in England and then they sent him to Trinity but the war broke out and he joined the Flying Corps.'

'That doesn't matter,' said Mr. Gilhooley. 'The point is. . . .'

'Just a moment,' she said. 'He fell out of an aeroplane in France, shot down or something, he got a decoration for that, the day Tommy Fitzgibbon, Mrs. Fitzgibbon's son, was killed. He was discharged with a wound in the head, you can see the scar yet, at the back, and then he joined up as a private under an assumed name and went to the East. He was at the taking of Jaffa or some place he told me and they gave him a commission, but he lost it again, I don't know what it was. Anyhow, when he came back, there were all sorts of rumours and they all tried their level best to . . . you could see it very well . . . dances and balls of all sorts, running around shamelessly after him, but he didn't give a pin for them. "As dull as ditchwater," he used to say.'

'Then you . . . when was this?'

'That was in 1918.'

'But you . . . you mean to say that you went off. . . .'

'No, just a moment. I used to go for drives in his car and that horrid beast used to beat me at night for it. How I hate her, with the black band around her throat. But . . . the Republicans were going about that time, terrorizing the country and putting an end, as they said, to all this immorality and drinking. So. . . . That was in 1919, though.'

'What?'

'They caught us one night out near C—, stopped the car and threatened to shoot him unless he cleared out of the country in twenty-four hours.'

'And did he go?'

'He did.'

'Bloody coward,' said Mr. Gilhooley. 'That's always the way with these desperadoes. They didn't turn him out for nothing. I suppose he had all the women in the place ruined. Eh?'

'No, he wasn't a coward,' she retorted angrily. 'It was his mother sent him away. She was living in Galway then. You should see her, so beautiful, with black hair and wonderful eyes, walks like a cat, only so tall. Like a queen. His eyes are like hers, but he's not tall.'

Mr. Gilhooley ground his teeth and muttered to himself: 'She's telling lies. She said nothing about that the first night.'

'Then I . . . I thought I'd die. I loved him and I thought he didn't love me. He couldn't have . . . he couldn't and never did. God! How I hate that man. Do you know? I detest him, with his sneering smile.'

Mr. Gilhooley got to his feet and then stood still, looking at the ground.

'Tell me,' he said, 'what's this fellow like?'

'Just a moment,' she said impatiently. 'Sit down.'

He sat down again. She seemed just as impatient now to tell the whole story as she had been reluctant to do so previously. Whereas Mr. Gilhooley felt anxious not to hear any more. Every word, every mention of the fellow caused him a pang. And yet . . . a part of him listened avidly, as if the recital were an interesting piece of scandal relating to somebody else.

'Shows you he wasn't a coward,' she said excitedly. 'He joined the Auxiliary Cadets against the Republicans.'

'What else?' muttered Mr. Gilhooley. 'Christ!'

'He wasn't around Galway, but I heard from Sidney Conners that he met him in Dublin . . . in them. At that time . . . of course later we all knew . . . but I told nobody. Then just before the Civil War he came back. . . . Oh! He was in an awful state, drinking, and nearly mad. Mr. Louis had sold out and they burned the house, the Republicans did, so that . . . somehow they made an arrangement, the mother and Louis, so much each, but the trustees had some hold over it, either in his favour or because of the will, well anyway, I never understood why it was. . . . He would never do it otherwise, I swear he wouldn't, it nearly broke my heart, because after he came back he was just the same as before, only a bit wild and queer and the mother of course. . . . I love her all the same, although she never spoke to me, I love her, she is like a queen, like a big lovely cat, with black hair. . . .'

'Oh! Damn it,' said Mr. Gilhooley. 'It's two o'clock. Well?' he cried angrily.

Now she seemed to be utterly indifferent to his presence. That enraged him still more. He got up and lit a cigarette.

'He became engaged to a widow, Mrs. Ryder, just for her money, I know it was his mother made him do it, because they had only what she had and he was too proud . . . he told me himself that was why it was. . . . It nearly broke my heart. I swore . . . I said to myself: "Never again. Not another word. If he went down on his knees." Then I ran away. And like a fool, I wrote to him from London. He came and I . . . how could I . . . can you understand . . . how he must despise me . . . and you too. . . .'

'Did he marry her?' said Mr. Gilhooley sarcastically.

'Yes, sneer,' she said. 'I knew it. But you never loved anyone and then had to hate him. Hate him. Yes. I'd drive a knife into him.'

She buried her face in her hands. She began to sob violently. Mr. Gilhooley, with his hands in his pockets, rolled the burning cigarette on his lower lip, looked at her and . . . his heart filled with pity. He could see, in spite of his jealousy, that her sorrow was sincere, that she was suffering now and that she had suffered, that she had a simple nature and that it was the extraordinary circumstances of her life that had wrought that veneer of callousness and hardness over her character. He saw a child, helpless in the power of this unique passion, half love, half hatred, and his heart was overcome with pity.

He realized at that moment that he had hated her until now, for awakening his passion, for being young and a burden to him. Looking at her sobbing body, the delicate contours of her loins, the slender, shapely arms and the curve of her graceful neck, all the memories of her amorous charms mingled with this new pity. He no longer hated her. He became sad, and his soul became tranquil.

'Where is he now?' he said calmly.

'What's the use?' she said, shaking her head. 'What's the use?'

'Listen,' he said, moving over and sitting on the bed beside her. 'We all have . . . we all, ye see . . . damn it, as you said, what's the use. In a few years we are all dead and forgotten; it's the end of it, so why . . . let's enjoy it and forget.'

'Don't say that,' she said, raising her head and looking at him in horror.

'Why, child?' he said calmly.

'I hate to think of death.'

'We all die,' he said calmly. 'It's a release.'

'No, no. I'm afraid of . . . of God.'

'Well,' he said, sighing. 'That may be, but. . . .'

Suddenly he paused, surprised. He remembered

his thoughts of that morning. He shuddered. Then he smiled.

'Tell me, though,' he said. 'Why are you afraid of him? He's gone, isn't he . . . for good? Didn't he marry this woman?'

'Yes,' she said weakly, 'but he left her again. 'Now he's gone back to her . . . no, no . . . I don't believe it, but . . . his mother was trying to make an arrangement. She wanted to pension me off. Still . . . I love her. He'll never live with that woman. And he got so terrible in the end, in Germany. There were Russian women there. Awful things. Used to be awful goings-on in Berlin. Then he said I was carrying on with a Jew, a banker, and wanted to shoot me and him. He rushed me off to London, his mother came and I ran away. I couldn't stand him. He could have every woman he liked, only no man must look at me, or he was out with his gun.'

'That's the way with every blackguard,' said Mr. Gilhooley quietly. 'Come, we better go out and have lunch. It's after two.'

Neither moved.

'Do you . . . still love him?' he asked gently, after a pause.

'No,' she said fervently, 'I hate him.'

'I wish I could kill him,' she added, 'but I couldn't. I tried.'

'Well,' he said, getting to his feet. 'Forget him. We'll have a good time, you and I. Top hole. You leave it to me. I know how to play the game.

I don't expect that you . . . but just . . . you know . . . we have both had a tough time and the high lights are not for everybody in this world. There's many a man, and a woman too, that would be glad to have a meal and a shirt and. . . . .'

'I can't forget him,' she said resolutely, staring stupidly in front of her. 'I can't. Honest. He said I ruined his life and that he'd kill me if he found me with another man. He said: "You're mine and. . . ."

'Oh! That be damned,' said Mr. Gilhooley, getting to his feet. 'You're just nervous. Forget it. Forget it. Let's go.'

He felt exhilarated and happy. His soul felt tranquil, and at the same time, he passionately remembered the eel-like movements of her naked body.

'Put on your things,' he said.

She got to her feet. She sighed. Suddenly she braced herself up. Wiping her eyes with her little scented handkerchief, she said quickly :

'Tell me about the flat?'

'Eh . . . eh,' he began, 'you see, it's a . . .'

He told her all he could. A cautious, hard expression came into her face, and she questioned him eagerly on every detail. She scolded him for not having tried the taps in the bathroom, seen to the meter and for not remembering the colour of the walls in the sitting-room.

CHAPTER XI

On the first of March they entered into possession of the flat.

Mr. Gilhooley was very excited all day. There were innumerable things to be done. He pottered about, perspiring, putting things in the wrong place, forgetting things, getting in the way and sighing with weariness.

'What am I to do with this?'

'Where is this to go?'

'Will I order some coal?'

'Where is the key for this?'

Her sleeves were rolled up. She wore a suit of overalls. She went about with rapid movements, hardly saying a word, working with that feverish energy which was peculiar to her. At last everything was set in order by tea-time. It was really a beautiful flat.

They both sighed and, before sitting down to the tea she had prepared, they went around to inspect everything.

The sitting-room was large. The walls were distempered a light brown. The floor was covered with a blue-and-black carpet. The furniture all corresponded with these colours. On the big divan in the corner there was a bright-coloured Turkish rug. In the corner opposite there was a little circular table, surmounted by a beautiful little statue of Venus, with one arm raised and the head lowered, as if she were trying to admire the fall of her arched loins. On the walls there were pictures by Italian painters, sombre and refined. The low chairs, the armchairs and settees strewn with cushions, the bright Turkish carpet on the divan, the luxurious floor covering, all mingled into an atmosphere of calm and expectation admirably suited to thoughts of love. There was an air of remoteness from primitive life, from the sordidness of poverty, even from the consciousness of life itself, which is always present, even in the fields under a bright sunlight, where the growth and decay of nature, moving conjointly, temper human joy with a grim realization of death. But in this room the ingenuity of man had successfully combated these vague premonitions. The hand of nature had been stayed and an effect was procured, of stability, of refinement, of civilization, of that soft charm which is so necessary to the proper encouragement of passionate desires. It seemed that the dyspeptic journalist, with the soul of an artistic lover and a body suited for a contemplative life in a monastery, had generously prepared this room for his tenant, having in view the special purpose for which he required it.

There was a slight perfume in the air, which Mr. Gilhooley had not noticed on entering, but which was now manifest to his senses. It was intoxicating.

There was a bedroom overlooking a small square, tree-covered and shady. The bedroom was decorated and furnished with the same taste as the sitting-room But here, the feminine influence was more manifest. There was an air of secrecy.

Another smaller room had been used as a study and workroom by the journalist. There was a narrow bed there, which he used himself. His nerves demanded this seclusion at night. This room was austere because the journalist had an idea that a proper enjoyment of life necessitated a respect for luxury and at the same time an appreciation of the teachings of Count Tolstoy. The kitchen caused Nelly to utter little cries of delight. It was the most beautiful room of all. As we say in the West: 'Ye could eat yer dinner on the floor.'

A little way down the flight of stairs was the bathroom.

'I say,' said Mr. Gilhooley with a beaming face while they were having tea. 'We must celebrate. What do you say? Eh?'

'Great,' she cried, with flashing eyes. 'What'll we do?'

'Champagne supper,' said Mr. Gilhooley with a sly wink.

She jumped up, threw her arms about his neck and kissed his forehead.

After tea they set forth to get the food and the wine. While she cooked supper, Mr. Gilhooley assisted by setting the table in the sitting-room, according to her orders. And while he did so very pleasant thoughts passed through his mind. He kept saying to himself: 'I'll keep her. By God, I will!' He thought that, at last, a life of happiness had arrived for him, that his melancholy, his fear of the future and his disillusionment had vanished and that nothing was now required but generosity to unite this girl with him forever in love. Before supper, he went into the bedroom and perfumed his hair, his nostrils, the backs of his ears and his forehead with her perfumes. He put on his best suit and a pair of shoes he had not worn since he used to dance in them at the cabarets in Argentine. Nelly also dressed for supper. She wore a dark silk dress, cut very low at the neck, with a curve at the waist, which gave her an appearance of great height and slimness.

Thus the feast began.

They toasted one another's health, happiness and prosperity with wine, as they ate, in the usual manner. Then, their hunger appeased, they cleared the table together, laughing, unmoored and restless, intoxicated by food, drink and by the merry thoughts aroused in their minds by the naughtiness of their intentions. Mr. Gilhooley followed every movement of her body with eager eyes and there was nothing but joy in his soul. Nelly's brilliant eyes shone. She allowed herself to be admired and took pleasure in the admiration. But the glances she cast at Mr. Gilhooley were not glances of personal love. There was a touch of sadness in them. For now and again, a ruminating look came in her face. She would pause and think of something: only, next moment, to utter a merry laugh and toss her golden curls.

Mr. Gilhooley, however, did not trouble himself, even if he had the power to do so, with watching the thoughts that flitted across her countenance. She was his and he would keep her. This would go on forever. That was all he thought.

They sat side by side on the divan, with a little table in front of them, on which there was wine, glasses, cigarettes, a box of chocolates, cigars and coffee.

They talked in whispers, foolishly. They became more and more intoxicated. Mr. Gilhooley made promises, he waved his arms, he swore, he sang snatches of song, he boasted of his past, he got to his feet and divested himself of his coat, his necktie and finally his waistcoat. Then going on his two knees at her feet he begged her to marry him and make him an honest man.

'Don't be a fool, don't be a fool,' she cried, laughing and getting to her feet unsteadily. She raised her hands above her head, then she whirled around on her toes and added: 'You never saw me dance, did you, uncle? Did you, my big poodle? Will I dance for my tame bear? Will I?'

With her head thrown back, her slim naked arms raised above her head and her voluptuous body trembling beneath the slight covering of her silk dress, she looked so seductive that Mr. Gilhooley's eyes grew dull and he could say nothing. Instead he uttered some sort of joyous sound and plunged towards her. With a little cry she sprang back. His hand, clumsily trying to grip her loins, snatched at her dress and ripped it.

'Oh!' she cried in terror. 'My dress. My dress.'

'Never mind,' he cried. 'I'll buy another, two, three, all ye want, my beauty . . . my . . . hey, come here to me, come here to me. . . .'

Laughing, she rushed out of the room. At the door she paused and blew him a kiss.

'A moment,' she said.

Then Mr. Gilhooley began to stumble around the room, gesticulating and conversing with himself in a low voice.

'I don't deserve this happiness,' he kept saying, with tears in his eyes.

Then he threw himself on the divan and lit a cigar, waiting for her to come.

At last she appeared noiselessly at the door, clad like a nun, all in white. But as she advanced across the floor, it appeared that her feet were bare. And then through his mist-covered eyes, he saw that she wore nothing but a veil, that her body, as she moved, showed through its folds, like something passing behind a curtain. She came towards him dancing, moving the folds of the veil, so that they unfolded slowly, as she danced. He did not see her dance and did not know whether it was beautiful or not. He only watched the gradual disclosure of her beautiful body, appearing from beneath the veil. Then with a cry, she dropped the veil and stood quite naked before him, shielding her eyes with her hands.

He got to his feet, with a glass of wine in his hand. He staggered towards her offering the wine. She uttered another cry, caught up the veil and fled. He followed her, staggering and muttering to himself. In the bedroom he found her wrapped in her dressing-gown, lying on the bed face downwards, sobbing loudly.

He was too drunk to understand. He sat on the bed and swaying the wineglass to and fro in his hand, he swayed his body and began to sing.

Then he fell asleep on the side of the bed.

After a short while, she sat up abruptly, looked around her wildly and said, raising her hands to the ceiling:

'Holy Saint Joseph, intercede for me.'

Then she listened. There was no sound but the sound of Mr. Gilhooley's irregular snoring. Then in the distance the bells began to ring the midnight chimes. The tears dried on her face and it became very cruel.

With her chin in her hands she watched him, her drawn-up knees knocking together angrily. She saw the bald spot on the top of his head, his thick red neck, the pockmark on his nose, his wrinkled cheeks and the limpness of his fleshy limbs. He looked like an old man in his sleep. And a great hatred of him was born within her.

Naked. He had seen her naked. He had abused her body. She had given herself to him for food.

Tears flowed from her eyes once more, with rage. And she called upon God to curse her and all who had ever possessed her. Rushing on to the floor she threw up her arms and screamed out to God to curse all mankind.

Mr. Gilhooley grunted, moved, raised his head, muttered something and fell prone again, babbling in his sleep: 'I don't deserve . . . deserve this . . . this . . . . '

CHAPTER XII

MR. GILHOOLEY awoke at dawn. Without becoming fully conscious, he stripped off his clothes and got into bed beside her. She was asleep, and his entering the bed did not awake her. He fell asleep again and slept until midday.

He awoke terribly frightened. Sitting up in bed, with his right hand under his hip, he stared about him, listening intently. There was no sound in the bedroom or in the other rooms. Outside, there was a distinct noise of traffic. Although his head pained him violently, he instantly thought of her.

'Has she gone?' he said aloud.

It was only then that he turned inwards and examined the bed, lifting the pillow on which her head rested and dropping it again. Then he touched the hollowed bed where she had lain. Then he held aloft his right forefinger and said:

'Christ! She wouldn't be gone. Eh?'

He jumped out of bed and rushed towards the door. But he halted when near it and listened again. He was afraid to go into the other rooms and find her gone. He wanted to hear some sound first to show that she was still here. While waiting for that sound he looked around the bedroom and saw her trunk and her toilet articles on the dressing-table. He sighed joyfully.

'God! I must be mad,' he said. 'She's not gone. Hey, Nelly.'

He rushed out of the room, barefooted, looked into the kitchen on his way, and then entered the sitting-room. There was nobody there. Everything was in order. But there was no sign of her. He became afraid again.

'Christ!' he said. 'She's gone and left me.'

'No, wait a minute,' he said again. 'She might be in the other room.'

Trembling, he walked to the other room and opened the door. There was nobody there. He was going to close the door again, when he noticed several sheets of paper lying on the writing-table by the window. All that had been tidied up, he thought. He walked over suspiciously, certain now that she was gone and that she had left some note. Craning his neck, he glanced at the papers from a distance. He could see nothing like a note. Then slowly he approached and picked them up one by one. They were sheets torn off a writing-pad. On each of them, there was the address of the flat and the date, while underneath, where one begins a letter, there were several things scratched out. It was difficult to make it out, but on close scrutiny, he could read something like 'Dear One,' and then 'Darling,' and then, as if she were beginning the letter without any introduction, there was an extraordinary line, written so hurriedly that the words were all joined: 'Just one word to tell you how I hate y . . . .'

He was at least twenty minutes examining these sheets of paper and the written words. He did not think at all. Then, dropping them all, he walked away with downcast head, out of the room, into the bedroom, to the bed, upon which he fell prone. He lay perfectly still, with his eyes closed, his forehead pressing against the bedsheet, without thought. He didn't want to think any more. But at last he was forced to get up and move his legs and hands. When he did so, he began to think. As soon as he began to think tears came into his eyes. His throat hurt him and his limbs trembled. A feeling of immeasurable sadness and tenderness took possession of him. He thought rapidly that this tenderness was the love which he sought and that it was infinitely beautiful, like the tears his mother shed over him in his childhood. He wanted to pray, to raise up his hands to the sky and cry out to God. What God? Any God. God, the spirit of love.

Very soon, however, his joy changed into agony, when he thought of the scribbling on the papers and the line: 'Just one word to tell you how I hate y . . . '

He beat his forehead with both hands and strode about the floor, hoisting his shoulders, one after the other, making his muscles rigid, groaning:

'She's gone,' he muttered repeatedly.

Then he started. He stood erect, quite stiff. His jaws set. He tore off his pyjamas, ripping the buttons off the jacket. Rapidly, he pulled on his underwear, inside out.

'I'll get after her, I'll get after her,' he muttered, almost in tears.

Without putting on his collar and tie, he reached for his overcoat and was putting it on, when he heard a footstep on the stairs. He dropped the overcoat to the ground and darted back to the bed. He sat down, listening. The outer door of the flat opened and he heard her humming a tune he knew very well. He wiped his forehead with his sleeve and sighed. Then he became very angry.

'Hey, where the devil have you been?' he cried.

'What's that?' she called lightly, outside in the hall.

He could hear her shake something, the overcoat she was taking off. It was raining outside.

'Huh!' he said, getting to his feet. 'Nice thing. . . . Where have you been?'

'Hello, hello, what's the matter?' she said, approaching rapidly. 'What's up?'

He sat down again on the bed. She entered the room, smiling, but with an expression in her eyes that he didn't like. They were hard, smiling eyes. They concealed something. Instantly he realised that they had been always so, but that he hadn't noticed them before. They looked at him as at a stranger.

They looked at one another in silence. Her eyes met his boldly, and even though he was thinking of that scribbled line, he could see nothing in her face to accuse. His eyes dropped from hers and he thought it strange that a moment ago he wanted to throw himself at her feet and kiss her knees, while now he seemed to hate her.

'Where have you been?' he said sulkily, without looking at her.

'Just out to get something,' she said quietly. 'Why?'

He tried to say that he had seen the scribbling on the sheets of paper, but he could not say it. Instead he said:

'Well, I just woke up and . . . . '

'Thought I had run away,' she said, laughing dryly.

'Why the devil would you run away?' he said angrily, looking her in the face.

'Why, what's the matter with you?' she said slowly. 'You're so cross. I thought it better not to wake you, so . . . I'll get your breakfast for you now in a tick. I'm awfully sorry, uncle.'

'Uncle be damned,' he said, scratching his left knee. 'Uncle!'

'There you are,' she said, shrugging her shoulders. 'Have a wash and a drink. Then you'll feel better.'

She went out of the room. He stared after her suspiciously.

'I know where she was,' he said to himself. 'Posting a letter. That's where she was. What's she up to?'

He threw off his coat and waistcoat and rolled up his shirt sleeves to shave himself. Then he paused again, thinking.

'Better say nothing,' he said. 'She was writing to him all right. But. . . . There are ways and ways. I'll see to that.'

When he entered the sitting-room after a bath and a shave, she had breakfast ready for him. He looked at the food and it made him feel ill.

'I don't want any breakfast,' he said.

'Have a cup of tea,' she said. 'It will do you good.'

'A lot you care,' he said. 'Lot you care about it.'

Then he sat down to the table and began to sip tea. She looked at him curiously. Then she walked past him towards the window. He glanced at her sideways as she passed quite close to him. She was wearing a two-piece frock, tight at the waist and bouncing at the hips. The skirt was pleated and it flapped as she walked. It made her very attractive. It accentuated her youth and suggested that extraordinary amorousness which had awakened his desire. She was so supple in her movements! No muscle or limb was static. The whole of her was resilient. It was impossible to ravish her. His passion exhausted itself against her body as a sea-wave exhausts itself buffeting a wind-filled, bouncing ball, that rebounds merrily when struck and offers itself wantonly to one wave's stroke and then to another's. Watching her move, he became enraged at the impossibility of crushing her body, making it limp with satiety.

She passed behind him and he heard her hum something in a low voice at the window. What was she thinking of? Of Matt? She wanted him to embrace her with the ferocity of youth. That other young blackguard, that had been 'gunned' out of Galway for raping all the women in the county, the low ruffian, the libertine, the murderer that joined the Black-an'-Tan cut-throats against his own countrymen. So he thought, while he listened to her humming behind him.

She passed again, going towards the door. He saw the slight hollow of her straight back and the yellow curls caressing her white, slender neck, the kitten-like bosses of her smooth jaws and the way she leaned slightly on the right hip walking, like a lazy filly.

'I say,' he said thickly, 'one moment.'

'Yes,' she said calmly, turning around.

He stared at her, with fixed eyes, in silence. Mastered by his love for her, he forgot for a few moments what he wanted to say. He got to his feet and took a step towards her. Then he laid his palm on the edge of the table and coughed.

'Who were you writing to?' he said.

She started slightly. But she looked him straight in the eyes without fear.

'I was writing to Matt,' she said calmly.

He had not expected this. He opened his lips to speak, but said nothing. His lips remained open, however, and he blinked his eyes.

'Why?' she said.

Her face became sad. He thought he saw a tear shining at the right corner of the left eye. Her lips twitched. Certainly it was a sincere sadness that came into her face. The very mention of his name overcame her. She turned away her head for a moment. Then she turned to Mr. Gilhooley again, looking almost fierce.

'Do you want to know what I wrote to him?' she said bitterly.

'No, no,' said Mr. Gilhooley, waving his hands slightly. 'I'm not a busybody. It's no business of mine. Only I like people to play the game.'

'Well, then,' she said, 'I'll tell you.'

'Ye needn't bother,' he said with a lordly raising of his eyebrows. 'What right have I to know?'

He walked over to the table and took up the copy of the *Daily Mail*, which the charwoman had brought up by his orders. He sat down.

'I'm only a baldy-headed old codger,' he said sarcastically. 'Why should I know anything? The . . . the . . . they are all the same. Around town . . . the lads . . . I know very well, by the look they give me, a smile at the corner of their lips, it's my money they want, not my company. But, mind my words, there's more ways than one for playing a tune on an old fiddle. It's the fashion nowadays to laugh at the old. "He's out of date, that fellah. His day is done." That's what every little whipper-snapper says. But I played the game. God knows, I'm no saint. But, by the Lord God, I never did a man down in my life.' He struck the table violently. 'I never double-crossed a man or woman in my life. Before Christ, I swear it. There's no man. . . .'

He got to his feet and waved his right hand over his head. He was speaking in a loud voice. She was staring at him and trembling slightly. He looked so majestic in his anger, which was not violence, but a cry from the sadness of his heart.

'There's no man,' he repeated in an exultant voice, 'can say that Larry Gilhooley did him down, or woman either. I may have been a kip hound and a boozer, but, before God, I paid my way. I paid my score. I declare to the Lord.'

'Don't swear so loudly,' she interrupted suddenly, moving towards him.

They both listened. There was no sound near them, only the slogging of the heavy rain, falling heavily now outside in the already sodden street-ways and the distant hum of human life, guiding many strident instruments, vehicles and factory machines.

'So you think I'm not playing the game,' she said angrily, but in a low voice.

He did not answer her. He muttered something and sat down.

'What do you want of me?' she said.

He opened the paper and began to read something.

'Very well,' she said quietly. 'It's all over.'

'What's all over?' he cried excitedly, dropping the paper.

'Do you think I'm going to stay here if you suspect everything I do is a plot against you?'

'Who said a word?' he cried.

'Then what's all this sermon about?'

'Eh . . . eh . . . I'm no good at this,' he said. 'I'm not clever. Only I see that there's . . . there's something on your mind. Is it something I said last night?'

She shuddered and knocked her clenched hands together.

'Don't talk about last night, for God sake,' she said.

'Why, why, what did I do?' he said, coming towards her.

'No, no,' she said, 'don't touch me.'

He put his arms around her. She leaned back her head and her body went limp. Moved by passion, he was going to embrace her with force, when he noticed that she had gone limp. The life, the resiliency, the buoyancy had left her body. It was now like a corpse, out of which the soul had vanished. He ceased to be angry. His throat filled with hardness and he dropped his head on her bosom. Again the tenderness overcame him. It was now a despairing tenderness. Hiding his head on her unresisting, smooth, warm bosom, he thought of his youth, of the brutality of youth, the joyous selfishness of youth, the cunning of mate-hunting youth. He thought how a youth would overwhelm her with passionate words, with wild promises, with the pressure of throbbing limbs, with feverishly warm lips.

'Let me go,' she said.

He loosed her. She stepped back a little and took him by the coat lapels.

'What did I say the first night I met you?' she said.

'Why?' he said stupidly. 'I don't know.'

'I said . . . I said there was to be no love-making

about this,' she replied coldly. 'You want something and . . . well, that's your business. I said I'd play the game and when you find that I'm not playing the game come and tell me. I'm as straight as you are. I never took something for nothing, no more than you did. See?'

'You mean?'

'Just what I say.'

'You mean to say you don't care for me?'

'Do you mean to say you care for me?'

'I . . . I . . . It's not a laughing matter.'

'I'm not laughing. God! Is there anything in this life to laugh at? Is there? I'm a workhouse brat, raised on charity. I have no parents and no relatives, and if I'm found in the gutter with my throat slit, they'll say it was the price of me. What have I to laugh at? You have had a good life. You were independent. You were beholding to nobody for your clothes and your food. And you're crying like a sick baby. You think women are all prostitutes.'

'That's a lie. I'm not a —'

'It comes to the same thing. You are all the same. You can buy a part of me but you can't buy . . . I tell you that it's only women are capable of love.'

'Listen,' he said. 'I —'

'Oh! I know what you are going to say,' she said, walking rapidly to a chair, off which she flicked a speck of dust. Then she sat down on the chair.

'You are soured,' he said. 'You have a kink in you.

I don't blame you. Mind, I don't blame you. I'm not a man for throwing stones. Says He: "Let him who is without sin . . . . "

'Oh! Leave that out,' she said.

'Can't we make a start?' he said excitedly.

She looked at him with wondering eyes.

'What do you mean?'

'I'm in earnest,' he said. 'Come. Leave here and clear out, the two of us. Marry me. Honest to God. . . .'

She laughed in a thrilling voice and got to her feet. He opened his eyes very wide.

She stretched her arms above her head and yawned.

'Listen, uncle,' she said, 'I wrote to tell him that I was living with you and that I never want to hear of him again. That was all I wrote to him. I was doing a lot of thinking last night in bed. I've been very silly. I'm not going to be silly any more. Don't you worry yourself. I'll give you a good time, provided you give me a good time. See the idea?'

Mr. Gilhooley put his hands in his trousers pockets and stared at the floor with drooping underlip. He jerked his head upwards three times and then let it sag again. He shrugged his shoulders and sighed. She watched him closely, with upward-looking, mysterious, cold eyes, in which there was either hatred or contempt. The vulgar old man, who had seen her naked, who had bought her hungry body, who wanted to be kind to her. Her vain soul watched him contemptuously. And all the corrupted tenderness of her being smiled scornfully at him.

'I'll admit it's beyond me,' he muttered, turning away. 'There's an old Irish proverb, "The day of the big wind is not the day for thatching the cabin." It's only when we feel death creeping towards us that we begin to make our nest. And it's a poor nest to rear young fledglings in. Well, well. They were wise people that made that proverb, but I have strayed a long way from the root; 'twould be a twisted, twisted path that leads back to it. How could I expect that you'd even have the memory of it? Ach! The foolishness, the bloody foolishness of these big towns. Sure, we are as ignorant as new-born calves that can't find their mother's teats. There's no going back. And I'll . . . well, I'll . . . pay the bloody piper. I've paid my score, so I have. I've paid the piper.'

He seemed to have fallen asleep, musing. She watched him very curiously.

'He's doting,' she thought. 'Too much drink and the warm climate.'

Then he raised his head until his eyes met hers. He looked into her eyes with infinite tenderness. in silence. He seemed to be very far away, among the wise old men, who brooded over proverbs on the Irish hills. A distant, slender root, withering in barren soil, yearning for the mother sap.

CHAPTER XIII

UNDER the influence of this tenderly melancholy mood, he came to a new arrangement with Nelly. He named a certain sum which she was to receive weekly for housekeeping purposes and a further weekly sum, which was to be her personal allowance. Her time was 'to be her own' during the day. He would make no conditions for her living with him, other than what she wanted to do herself.

Fully dressed for the street, with his hat and gloves in his hand, drawing the tip of his walking-stick back and forth along the carpet, he told her of this arrangement in a little speech, which he uttered slowly, pausing between each couple of words. She listened to him without making any movement whatsoever, and it was impossible to discover in her cold eyes whether she was grateful or just contemptuous of anything he might offer her. When he had finished she merely said:

'Very well. Whatever you please.'

He raised his eyes and looked at her sadly.

'Yes,' he said. 'That'll be all right. But . . . I'd like to say that I . . . if at any time you thought different . . . you could . . . . '

'Yes?' she said.

'Well! No,' he said. 'We won't talk of that now. I'm going out to make a little change in my . . . affairs. That'll be all right. Yes. If there is anything else, you can just tell me. So long.'

He went out. Going down the stairs he began to shake his head violently and he said to himself:

'I'm a damn fool. I'm putting my head in a halter. I know it. But I can't stop. It's very funny.'

The rain had stopped when he got into the street. There was brilliant sunlight, but there was no heat. It was quite cold. On the housetops, lit by the merry sunlight, the raindrops sparkled, freshly fallen. Children had rushed out into alleyways to play and they were shouting to one another. A policeman, with outstretched hands, stood at a triple-cornered crossing, guiding traffic. His helmet shone brightly. There were many people in the street, walking slowly.

Mr. Gilhooley, walking along the street, felt exalted. A weight passed from his body and he felt that he was moving with people of his kind, somewhere. Around him the houses were clean, secure, stately. The people were clean, stable, well-mannered. Here there was no danger from unseen forces, no public appearance of vice, only comfort and stability. And he thought more intently of the wise old men who saw in life only the making of warm nests where fledglings grow and are fed by loving parents.

He waved his stick.

'That's just it,' he said to himself. 'I want to settle down. And I want her. And the two things don't come together. Somehow, it doesn't work. But. . . . If I begin to worry myself this way I won't last long. How did I fall in love with her? Eh? She doesn't care a button for me and yet I'm in love with her. Isn't it awful?'

He caught a glimpse of himself passing a shop mirror, and he saw a face that looked gaunt, with a haunted look in the eyes. He didn't recognize it.

But he halted and hailed a cab that sauntered along on the far side of the street. He named his bank and entered the cab. At the bank he went into his affairs with the manager. While he was doing so he felt that the manager was watching him suspiciously, and that irritated him.

'That man thinks I'm going to the dogs,' he thought.

After that he went to his solicitor. The solicitor rose to meet him eagerly, then paused with outstretched hand and said:

'Why? What's up, Mr. Gilhooley?'

'What's the matter?' said Mr. Gilhooley indignantly.

'Nothing, only . . . . You look ill.'

'Ill? I'm not ill. Never felt as well in my life.'

'Glad to hear it, but you certainly have got thin since I saw you last.'

'Oh, that's nothing. I was up late last night. It always . . . . '

'Oh, yes,' said the solicitor, rubbing his hands; 'ha, ha, none of us are as young as we used to be.'

When he left the solicitor's office, Mr. Gilhooley entered a public-house and drank a stiff tumbler of hot brandy and water. Then, although he did not feel at all hungry, he went to a grill room and had a steak, fried potatoes and some strong cheese. Having eaten this meal he felt better. But the melancholy still remained. Now, however, it was pleasant, very pleasant.

He returned to the flat. Going up the stairs he heard loud laughter. He halted and touched the wall. Then he went on upwards. On the landing he heard Friel's voice within. He entered hurriedly.

Friel was sitting on the table in the centre of the room, while Nelly was curled upon the divan, smoking a cigarette and smiling. Friel jumped off the table and bowed his thighs after the habit he had.

'Hello, Larry,' he said, moving his little moustache and smiling in a friendly way. 'Thought I'd prowl up to see how ye were doing. So I met the missus here and we were having a talk. How's the body?'

'Very well, very well,' said Mr. Gilhooley.

'So he has smelt her out already,' he thought. 'He can be up to no good.'

He glanced at Nelly and saw her smiling at Friel in a friendly way. He felt hurt. But he instantly turned to Friel and said:

'Seen any of the boys lately?'

'Oh! Wait 'll I tell ye,' said Friel. 'This is the nuttiest story you ever heard in your life. Macaward got a goat somewhere up in Phoenix Park and brought her down on the end of a rope, yesterday it was, about four o'clock in the afternoon, I was telling the missus. What the hell d'ye think he did with the old nanny? Ye'll split yer sides laughing. He ties her up to a lamp-post in Grafton Street, goes into a shop and brings out a few heads of lettuces and he begins to feed her with them. Ye never saw such a commotion since the year one. Polismen and everybody trying to arrest the bloomin' goat and Sean waving his stick and making a speech about the rights of man an' . . . no end to it. Well! Anyway, they hauls off the goat from the lamp-post and . . . they didn't arrest him, d'ye see, only . . . I know him very well, the sergeant is a decent fellow . . . but the funny part was. . . .'

Then he suddenly laughed, broke off the story and lit a cigarette, which he had been taking from a big box.

Mr. Gilhooley tried to smile at the story, but he could not. He found it very dull. Nelly, on the other hand, was giggling rapturously and Friel, while he told the story, glanced at Mr. Gilhooley now and again, but concentrated all his attention on Nelly. When he looked at Mr. Gilhooley his face bore a respectful frown. But when he looked at Nelly his face was illuminated with an eager, passionate look. Mr. Gilhooley noticed this.

Friel, not a bit embarrassed by Mr. Gilhooley's silence, began to tell all the gossip of the town.

'But I say, Larry,' he said at length, laughing boisterously, 'this is not playing the game, ye know.'

'How d'ye mean?' said Mr. Gilhooley.

'Oh! Well, now, walking in here without a word, after getting married an' all.' He rubbed his palms together. 'What about a bit of a spree? Wha'? A few o' the boys and girls, we could have the liveliest time you ever saw up here. See? I'll square

Fleming below. He's in the —— Ministry. Not a word. Wha'? What do you say, Mrs. Gilhooley?

Smiling in a way Mr. Gilhooley never saw her smile before, Nelly shrugged her shoulders slightly, bared her teeth, and then nodded her head several times.

'I think it would be jolly,' she said.

'There ye are, Larry,' said Friel. 'Ye see. Leave it to me. I'll settle everything and . . . . '

'Hold on a moment,' said Mr. Gilhooley. 'Who said —'

'Now look here, Larry,' said Friel, 'ye can't go against yer wife the week after yer marriage. Can ye?'

'Well,' said Mr. Gilhooley, with a sigh. 'I don't give a damn. You settle it between you.'

'I knew what it would come to', he said to himself. 'That fellow is up to no good. But what can I do?'

Friel and Mrs. Gilhooley began to discuss the details for a party excitedly.

'Leave that to me,' Friel would say, wagging his moustache up and down, smiling at her in the curious way he had. 'It doesn't matter, ye see. Larry knows me, so anybody that comes'll be all right. Aw! Ye needn't be worried about Dublin people, Mrs. Gilhooley. Take it from me. Dublin people can take some beating. Ye see. This is how it is. . . .'

Then he would tap the palm of his right hand with his left forefinger, wink one eye, glance at Mr. Gilhooley, and say something totally irrevelant.

At last he went away, promising to call again that evening at eight o'clock and bring around his cousin, Maggie Dawson, to meet Mrs. Gilhooley.

'She's nutts,' he said. 'Be careful what ye say to her about Jews. She's nutts on Jews, but otherwise she's all right. I'll be around at eight. Honest to God. Well, so long, Larry. Keep up the old pecker.'

When he had gone Mr. Gilhooley sat down by the fire, lit a cigarette and thought in silence a long time. Nelly was outside in one of the other rooms.

'Hell,' he said. 'I'm feeling all upset. What's the matter with me? I wonder would it be the heart again? I'll go and see Bill Hanrahan. I can't stand this.'

He told Nelly that he might not be back until late, and he went out. She said nothing. He did not notice. He took it for granted now that their relations should be almost those of casual acquaintances. He was not even angry that Friel should be pursuing her, as he felt sure he was. He foresaw how all the idle fellows about town and the women who move in that circle would make the flat their common meeting-place, and yet he felt no interest in that now. He was not angry at that prospect. But . . . .

'It's hard to make it out,' he said, scratching his poll. 'There's something going to happen to me, though. That's certain. Something bloody awful. And I don't deserve it. No Honest to God, I don't. What did I ever do to deserve a thing like this? What thing? Hey now! What thing?'

In the hallway he brushed against a fashionably-dressed young woman and without expressing his sorrow for the fault, he dashed out into the street, flurried by his thoughts. He hurried away, thinking fearfully.

'How am I to know?' he asked himself. 'What did she write? God only knows. But I love her. That's certain. Well then, let's work it out this way. There's no question of being a criminal. I'm not a criminal. It's a question of either keeping her or letting her go. If I let her go, it's the end of me. I know that very well. I'm not going back to the old life. And yet, how am I to keep her! He's sure to turn up. I'm certain of that. And the other fellahs. . . . Don't I know them? D'ye think any of them'll believe it? That I'm married to her? God! What persuaded me to stay on here? Why didn't I go off? But where could I go? I don't want to leave Ireland?'

So immersed in his thinking, that he didn't notice where he was going, he was almost run down crossing the end of Kildare Street. A man going past in a motor car yelled something at him, but he took no notice. An old man, who was scratching his back against the wall of a shop, whispered to his mate:

'That fellah is canned.'

'Farmer,' said the other man.

'Naw,' said the first. 'He's an Englishman. I know be the cut of him.'

'Touch him,' said the other man.

The old man shuffled hurriedly after Mr. Gilhooley and whispered when close beside him:

'God bless yer honour an' give us the price of a cup o' tay. I didn't put a bite inside me mouth, yer honour. Blessin' o' God on ye, yer honour.'

Without looking at the old man, Mr. Gilhooley put his hand in his trousers pocket and pulled out three coins, one half-crown piece and two pennies. These he gave to the old man without looking. The old man looked at him with a curious look of contempt and suspicion in his face. Then he shuffled back to his mate.

'He's up the pole, sure enough,' he said, laughing raucously. 'He's a bloody Englishman an' no doubt about it. Farmer!'

'Christ!' said the other man enviously. 'Half a bloody dollar.'

'I wonder what it's like,' thought Mr. Gilhooley. 'Just stop breathing. But it's a different thing to make another stop breathing. The cool way they do it in Chile. God! They're strong men. It's a sin. But why do they call it a sin? What is sin? I never did it. It always made my blood curdle when I saw a man, remember the man at Bahia Blanca, sprawling across the café table, with the black-handled knife sticking out of his left shoulder blade. His tongue was out. They just came and hauled him out. The women, half naked, screaming and looking at the blood. Jabbering. Hush, hush. I mustn't think of that. Not of *that*. God forgive me, what put that thought in my head? It's very well to talk in anger, but not when it comes to the point. Just to sit down and think calmly that yer going to do it. No.'

He glanced around him furtively at the bright, sunlit air, cold and vigorous air, full of sunlight. The jingling noises of the trams, the patter of feet, the purring of human sounds made him shudder.

'Hurry,' he said to himself. 'Bill Hanrahan is a good fellow. That is a *good* man. And yet his brother has done it. Yet, who could say he is a cruel man? In self-defence. . . . How would that be? Eh? He's a blackguard, but what about her? Christ! There I am thinking again. I mustn't. No, I mustn't. No. No. No. I mustn't. I mustn't.'

He crossed the end of Grafton Street hurriedly through the traffic, and entered Suffolk Street, where he began to walk very slowly. Again he began to think of her, first tenderly, and then with a curious sensation of coldness, which soon merged into a fixed contemplation of some final act that would forever keep him with her, keep her with him, keep the two of them together, entwined, locked, inseparable.

Several people looked after him as he walked, stooping slightly, with fixed eyes.

'How?' he thought. 'How would that be, other than by what I swore I would do if he came back? So I swore I'd do it then. And if I swore I'd do it I must have it in me. Because a man told me once, who was he, a Swedish engineer, that every man is capable, he has seeds, he said, of every act capable of being done by a human being. If another man could do it, so could I. But what would be the purpose of doing it? If I could only prove to myself that it was worth doing, then that would be. . . .'

Perspiring, he realized once more that he was thinking of it. He turned about and began to walk back the way he came. But he had not gone far, when he stopped and thought:

'I wonder is anybody watching me? But why should they watch me?'

He glanced around him cautiously and saw nobody watching him. Then in order to prevent anybody who might be watching from suspecting anything, he lit a cigarette slowly and puffed at it several times, while he put on the glove he had taken off to light the cigarette. Then, twirling his stick jauntily, he went on, through slum streets, to Bill Hanrahan's tobacco shop.

CHAPTER XIV

Bill Hanrahan's tobacconist's shop had been for a number of years the meeting-ground for revolutionaries. It was situated in a very old street, surrounded with slums, where a seemingly endless stream of people passed from morning till night. All the houses in the street were little shops, curiosity shops, second-hand shops, huckster's shops and public-houses. In the thoroughfare there was a market, where women sold fruit and other commodities. Voices screamed, traffic rattled. Everything was dirty and shabby.

So that people darting into the little shop went unnoticed in this multitude.

Lately, this revolutionary activity had subsided. The people who entered the shop, other than the local customers, came sighing and talking of old times. One might see them, standing with their hands in their pockets, with cigarettes drooping from their lower lips, scowling in silence or muttering jagged sentences about something past, cursing individuals, murmuring prayers for somebody dead. There was an air of melancholy about the place. The tide of revolution had subsided, leaving the frequenters of this little shop still in a sort of stupor from which they were unable to recover. These fellows, the artificers of revolution, had become amazed at the extraordinary appearance of the tool they had fashioned. Cursing, they stepped away from it, after having attempted to destroy it.

The proprietor of the shop, Bill Hanrahan, was

not a revolutionary. He was a tall, thin man, like a monk. He had a pallid countenance, womanishly delicate hands, and grey eyes in which an immeasurable love of humanity glowed, like water in a sea-pool on which the sun is shining. No man ever saw him angry with an individual, but evil, or oppression, or ugliness of any kind made his eyes glitter. His thin, pale lips would close and little tremors passed down his hollow cheeks. Living in the midst of violent men, killers, conspirators, desperate characters, who thrust obstacles from their paths like stones, ruthlessly, men, institutions, personal ties, the traditions of centuries, this gentle man never became imbued with one single drop of this violence. Murderers told him their secrets. Fugitives left him their guns when they were hard pressed. And the pursuers of those fugitives, looking into these eyes, felt ashamed and pursued no farther.

And yet all the little children about thought him a gay fellow. And the old women who came to buy snuff bantered him, offering him their aged charms.

Mr. Gilhooley had come one night to this shop with Shemus Hanrahan, Bill's brother, and a few others, to drink some potheen that Shemus had received from the country. He met Bill and became a firm friend of his. They had many philosophical discussions. As Mr. Gilhooley became more and more depressed with his manner of living, he paid more frequent visits to the shop and he always came away refreshed, comforted, firmly determined to leave the city and start a bee-farm, a rabbit-farm, or some other project.

As he approached the shop now, he felt ashamed, just as he used to feel in his boyhood when the day approached for the monthly confession, and he would have to kneel to the old priest and tell his little sins. He was especially ashamed of the terrible temptation that was agitating him, and that he could not put away. And he was ashamed, too, of the fact that it was for some other reason he was now going to the shop; not to see Bill, but for something else.

In fact, he halted a little way down from the shop, pretending to listen to a quarrel between two old apple women, who were being moved on by a policeman. Looking at them he thought:

'When it comes to deceiving myself like this, I must be in a bad way. It's not him I want to see but his brother. And why? To get a gun, what else? Eh? So I must be thinking of it longer than I think. To get a gun. Good Christ! Is there any cannibal worse than me, to think of murdering an angel like her? An angel! Less of the angel! But an angel is someone ye love and to kill her because I can't have her! A cannibal. A bloody cannibal.'

He prodded a man who was watching the quarrel in the leg with his stick unconsciously, and moved on.

'Sorry, sir,' said the man, moving away.

'No offence, no offence,' said Mr. Gilhooley, quite loudly.

The man started, took a few paces after Mr.

Gilhooley, and stared in amazement, amazed by the strange tone of his voice.

When he entered the shop Bill Haranhan was leaning over the counter talking to a man who was walking rapidly up and down the shop, with his hands clasped under the tails of his raincoat. When this man saw Mr. Gilhooley he stared angrily and passed out without a word.

Mr. Gilhooley raised his white eyebrows and then nodded slightly. Bill Hanrahan's face brightened. Rubbing his fingers slowly down the smooth counter, he said:

'And what have you been doing since we saw you last?'

Mr. Gilhooley smiled and shook his head. Hurriedly he put his hand in his trousers pocket and said, pulling out some money:

'I want some cigarettes. I came around to . . . No! I think I'll have some cigars. A dozen. Here, put them in that case. No, damn it. I forgot the case. Give me cigarettes. Give me a hundred of those, two packets of fifty.'

Agitated, without knowing why, he had suddenly thought that he must account for his coming to the shop on this occasion in some other way than by having come on purpose to see Shemus Hanrahan. Bill Hanrahan looked at him curiously and then fetched the cigarettes. Mr. Gilhooley fumbled with the money.

'Yes,' said Bill, 'Shemus was telling me the news.'

'What news?' said Mr. Gilhooley excitedly.

'Why! Your marriage, of course,' said Bill.

'H'm,' said Mr. Gilhooley. 'A man can't turn around in this town without . . . . '

'Well, I suppose it's too late to offer congratulations,' said Bill.

Mr. Gilhooley straightened himself and looked at Hanrahan in the eyes.

'Is there any such thing as happiness?' he said.

Hanrahan looked at him cautiously for several moments. Then, fingering the coins that Mr. Gilhooley had placed on the counter, he looked out the door.

'Happiness?' he said.

Then he fingered the coins again, looked cautiously at Mr. Gilhooley, darted a sudden glance at the coins, and then slowly went to the till with them. He dropped each coin slowly in, fingering carefully, lovingly. Then he sighed and closed the till.

'Happiness,' he said again. 'That's a queer thing to say.'

'Why?'

'Just after marrying.'

'How d'ye make that out?'

'Ye should be away on yer honeymoon now, saying soft things in some quiet place, dreaming about children and all the other foolish, nice things that people do.'

'Christ!' thought Mr. Gilhooley, 'the very thing I was thinking. See that? It's like going round and round in a . . . . '

'Look here,' he said. 'I'd like to. . . . Damn it.'

'Yes,' said Bill.

Mr. Gilhooley struggled violently to open his lips and tell Hanrahan all about it. But he could not do so.

'Nothing,' he said. 'I think I began too late. So I did.'

'Not at all,' said Hanrahan. 'It's never too late. It's never too late to be happy. The funniest people on earth are happy. I've seen people come into this shop that you'd never expect to be happy. I've seen murderers that —'

'Murderers,' said Mr. Gilhooley. 'How do you mean? Murderers?'

'Well,' said Hanrahan, 'it's a manner of speaking. I call all men who kill others murderers. These men were, of course, acting under orders for somebody, let us say an army of men, acting for some ideal purpose, as you call it. But still they are murderers. During the Civil War I saw men lying in that street out there, with their rifles cocked, waiting for an enemy to show and, what do you think, two young lads they were, they were telling one another fairy stories. And I've seen one man come in here, the most awful man you could imagine, he had done everything, a cold brute, you might say. He had a cold, brutal face, you might say, and he had killed many men, both in war and in private robberies and jealousies, but he had a simple character, a very loving, gentle character. I knew him as a little boy. He was a shy little boy, and he was always praying in the chapel. He wouldn't swear or do anything naughty like the rest of us. Yet, suddenly, one day in Grafton Street, he was about sixteen at the time, he clutched my arm and he said, "I'm going to kill So-and-So." He had a terrible look in his face. "Why?' I said. "He robs his clerk," he said. "He should be killed!" '

'He should be killed,' said Mr. Gilhooley. 'Eh!'

'Just like that,' said Hanrahan. 'I paid no attention to it at the time. But six months later that boy joined a secret society which I won't name. He suddenly became a great drinker and a young blackguard, and it was always: "See that fellah? I'm goin' to kill him." Just because he had a tender soul and he couldn't bear to see anybody suffer. That's what it was. Since then, he has managed to kill most of the men he marked out. During the Civil War, he used to come in here and grin at me, twisting his lips. He'd pull out a long-nosed Smith and Wesson and say through his teeth: "One more notch, Bill. She's pretty well loaded down now. So-and-So creased.' Then he'd dash out. They never got him. But he'd cry in a corner maybe when nobody was watching him.'

He rubbed his thin fingers along the smooth counter and added:

'It's all chance. There's no such thing as a criminal.'

'Not murder, surely,' said Mr. Gilhooley indignantly. 'My dear fellow, that's rather a . . . rather a . . . well, these ideas do a lot of harm. I tell you,' he said violently, 'you don't know what harm these ideas do.'

'How do you mean?' said Hanrahan, surprised at his heat.

'Property has got its rights,' said Mr. Gilhooley, stammering slightly. 'Crime of any sort is injurious to society. It's injurious to everybody. The criminal must be stamped out. Look at me now. What do you think? Supposing I commit a murder, what happens? Who's going to pity me? I'm a man of a certain position. I've done my duty by the community. I've laboured in the vineyard as the saying is. I'm resting on my oars. I've never taken what I didn't labour for. I've paid my way. I injure no man. But suppose I commit a murder I get less sympathy than if I were a rambling, ravin' hero like that fellah. It's *not* the proper way to look at it. Now, tell me, could you commit a murder?'

'No,' said Hanrahan after a pause. 'I couldn't commit a murder. It's not in my nature, but that's not my virtue. It's chance, heredity and a few other things over which I have no control. Look at the people that crowd every morning into the chapels here. Thousands, let us say, receive Holy Communion.'

A little golden-headed girl came in with a penny, which she was sucking between her teeth. Hanrahan smiled on her and called her by name.

'I wonder did he notice anything?' thought Mr. Gilhooley. 'Why did I bring up that question? Eh? No. I'll drop it. I must get shut of him and find Shemus. But will I, though? Hadn't I better clear out back home now. . . .'

'A pennorth of sweets, May, is that what you want?' Hanrahan was saying.

'No. It's a matter of self-protection,' thought Mr. Gilhooley. 'That fellow is mad. But is it really that fellow? Isn't it a fact that I don't mean to let him have her? None of them, the bastards.'

The girl went out, looking curiously at Mr. Gilhooley. Hanrahan fondled the penny lovingly as he brought it to the till. He dropped it in slowly and listened as it rang against the other coins. Then he closed the till furtively.

'Yes,' he said, 'what was I saying? Yes. It's in the blood. Nothing can stop it if it's in the blood.'

'What?'

'The desire to kill. But there's a way to deflect it into other channels. Healthy work. Co-operation. Clear out these slums.'

'Oh, that's ranting,' said Mr. Gilhooley. 'Ye must have a working class. There'll always be one class subject to another. Sure, haven't I seen them in South America? Listen. I'm tellin' you that the only people deserving pity are . . . well, intelligent people; people that are well off, that deserve something of society . . . so to say, people that pay their way. Look at me. . . .'

'Yes. Each man has his own philosophy,' said Hanrahan. 'And each man makes his philosophy to suit his own position. But philosophy is a trivial thing. There is only one true thing in life.'

'What's that?' said Mr. Gilhooley.

'Love,' said Hanrahan.

Mr. Gilhooley started. He looked at Hanrahan suspiciously.

'He suspects something,' he thought.

He became angry.

'I don't believe you ever had a woman in your life,' he said.

'I wasn't speaking of women,' said Hanrahan softly. 'I was speaking of love.'

Mr. Gilhooley drew himself up.

'Ech! That gets ye nowhere,' he said. 'I believe in work, see. Just go yer way and take what's coming. No nonsense. It's cool, honest-to-God people who don't believe in dreams that make the world go around. But, blast it, they reap none of the benefit. It's the dreamers, the nonsense-mongers, that get the benefit. They shirk it and they get the . . . . '

'There's something on your mind,' said Hanrahan.

'What's that?' said Mr. Gilhooley. 'What would be on my mind?'

Hanrahan shook his head.

'I don't want to interfere,' he said.

'Why? What would you interfere with?'

'With your fate.'

'What the hell are you talking about?'

'You have just got married and you are talking like this, There are hollows under your eyes. Your voice is hoarse. You look with suspicion at everything. You have lost your gentle manner. You used to be tired and fed up with everything and now you are biting at ideas like a mad dog biting at lamp-posts. Woman has bitten you.'

'Christ!' said Mr. Gilhooley. 'That's a . . . that's a . . . that's a queer thing you are after saying.'

'Maybe so,' said Hanrahan, shrugging his shoulders. 'Do you think I have stood in this shop for ten years for nothing? Many men have come in here during the past few years, since the big disaster, the Civil War. And no matter what they were before that, there have been only two things biting them since. That's women and money. Those that had money wanted women, and those that had no money wanted money. It's like . . . it's like . . . well, it's like this.'

He stood erect and pressed his palms against his chest.

'Something is shut up in here for a long time, and then it bursts out. You sow hatred in your heart; you grow it there a long time, and then it bursts out.'

He shook his head and leant against the counter again.

'No,' he said sadly. 'There's no love in this country now. There's no religion. People are crowding the chapels. They say Christ has come to Ennis and that people are shouting "To hell with the politicians. Give us Christ." Publicans are kneeling in the gutter when a religious procession passes. They are hanging the picture of the Saviour in the public-house windows beside Guinness'

Brown Label. They'll probably soon have the Inquisition again. Priests are demanding the burning of atheistic books. Yet the country was never as corrupt, never so much bribery, never so much poverty, never so much sneering and shaking of heads and smiling of cynical lips. We are standing on the edge of the pit and we need some hand to pull us back, the hand of love. That's what it is.'

Mr. Gilhooley looked angrily at him.

'What's that got to do with me?' he said. 'Damn it, did I have anything to do with it? I say it's bloody idleness is the cause of it.'

'You have as much to do with it as everybody else,' said Hanrahan calmly.

'How do you make that out?' said Mr. Gilhooley.

'The man is mad,' he thought. 'Here among all these cut-throats. What made me come here?'

'You have. You have,' said Hanrahan, gazing moodily out the door. 'You are a part of the machine. You seek your own pleasure. You love yourself, not others.'

'That's bunkum,' said Mr. Gilhooley. 'It's every man for himself, provided, yes, provided ye respect the law and pay yer way. Look. It's easy for you talking. You are comfortable here. They say tailors talk a lot, sitting on their straddled legs. But I . . . ' – he struck the counter – 'twenty years in South America. Then I come back here with a bit of money. Don't I deserve . . . '

'Yes, yes,' said Hanrahan. 'You deserve what you deserve, according to your deserts. What did you come back to? To the public-houses and the kips or maybe worse.'

'That's strong language,' said Mr. Gilhooley angrily.

'Don't mind me,' said Hanrahan. 'I'm a fool. My brother says I should be plugged or creased as he says. Probably I should. We'll all be plugged for telling the truth soon. Why should I bother to speak to you? Yes. Probably you are a good man and you want something more. Wanting something more, you have taken a woman, and now you find that doesn't satisfy you. Ha. I know why you are unhappy. Taking a woman, you find . . . . '

'What?' said Mr. Gilhooley.

Hanrahan's eyes shone, and it was now obvious that he was a fanatic. Mr. Gilhooley saw it and immediately he thought of the way the coins were fingered lovingly, the way the fingers were rubbed along the smooth counter. He started violently, and he suddenly thought that everybody was mad except himself. Something began to whir in his brain. He raised his stick slightly as if to defend himself.

'All these things are signs,' said Hanrahan.

Mr. Gilhooley said nothing. He watched the fellow.

'Soon, soon,' sighed Hanrahan, 'the scourger will come with his rods. But 'twill be too late for you to be scourged. You will have scourged yourself. I don't despair. I know. I know the people will rise again. I go to the chapel on Sunday evenings and see the great crowd of poor people kneeling.

Or maybe see the procession of unemployed marching through the streets, Then I know they will rise. Then there will be love again in people's hearts.' He raised his right hand above his head and twittered the fingers.

'People will sing in the streets,' he said.

Mr. Gilhooley's face darkened. He gripped his stick, frowned and muttered:

'This is damnably insulting. I . . . . '

He uttered an oath and was about to rush out of the shop, when Hanrahan leant forward and touched him gently on the shoulder. He smiled gently.

'No, don't be angry,' he said in a low voice. 'There are so few of us, why should we quarrel? You and I are alike. We are unhappy. The others are not unhappy because they want something they can get by selling their souls. But you and I will always be unhappy . . . unless we struggle for something that cannot be bought, for love. What you have tried to buy. That's why you are unhappy. You have tried to buy love. Eh?'

'This is the devil,' said Mr. Gilhooley.

Perspiration stood out on his forehead.

'How do you know. . . . How do you know?' he said.

'Why should I blame you?' said Hanrahan. 'I too . . . In myself, there are the same lusts. And I stand here and think and think. How can we love in the midst of all this ugliness?'

'I'll kill them all,' suddenly thought Mr. Gilhooley.

The veins in his throat swelled. He gripped his stick savagely and dashed out of the shop. He hurried away down the street, feeling somebody in pursuit of him. He paused and glanced behind him. There was nobody. Then he realized that he had expected to see the man with the club.

He hurried on, muttering:

'Why did I go there? There's a curse on the place. Murderers. Madmen. Fanatics. I went because I . . . I see it now. . . . I too am a murderer. Ha, then. Let it be murder. Murder and blood. I'll have my say. I'm not going to be wiped out like a dog without striking a blow. Who cares? But I'll make them care. I'll raise such a noise that the world'll hear it. By God! I will.'

He saw a public-house in front of him and walked towards the entrance to the private bar. As he pushed open the door, there sat at the counter, with his red, bloated face staring drunkenly towards him, Shemus Hanrahan, brother of the man he had just left.

Mr. Gilhooley paused.

'Ha,' he said to himself. 'This is fate, sure enough. Well! Here goes.'

CHAPTER XV

Mr. Gilhooley had come by chance, if, indeed, his subconscious mind had not directed him thither, into a little room at the back of a public-house, where a certain band of ex-officers and soldiers had their meeting-place. When he entered the room there were five men there, including Shemus Hanrahan.

Of these groups, there are many at the present time in Dublin. But they are rapidly disappearing. Their members are dying, reverting to former unsavoury pursuits or emigrating. But the members that remain retain a sort of romantic glamour, which seems always to attach itself to the person of a mercenary soldier of fortune.

Years ago, during the Black-an'-Tan war, these men emerged from obscurity, suddenly, called up by the necessity which the community experienced of defending itself against the English invading mercenaries known as the Black-an'-Tans. The Irish community called up those among its citizens who resembled in character the monsters that had been let loose upon it. Coming from haunts and pursuits which breed lawlessness, fearlessness and vice, these men distinguished themselves in the performance of the one act for which they were useful, the act of killing Black-an'-Tans. They were, in fact, Irish Black-an'-Tans.

After the expulsion of the Black-an'-Tans, the community again used these men to make war on the Republican Volunteers. They put uniforms on their backs, gave them military titles and publicly honoured them, while they were routing the Republicans. Then, when the Republicans were routed, the mercenary gunmen were quietly dismissed. The community, again endeavouring to follow normal pursuits, to civilize itself and to reorganize the basis of its economy, found that it must rid itself of these uncouth barbarians, whom in a desperate moment it used as military heroes.

The gunmen made futile efforts to blackmail the community, but their lack of intelligence, so peculiar to mercenaries, prevented them from effecting anything. For a moment they seemed to be a menace, protected by the glamour that had lately attached itself to their heroic exploits. But soon their artificial power dwindled away. They resorted to the public-houses and carried on petty intrigues with various discontented politicians, attempting as a last resort to carry out *coups d'etat.* Shunned by the Republicans and feared by those who intrigued with them, they became mere braggarts and swashbucklers.

It was strange that Mr. Gilhooley should come come upon a group of these men, so to speak, men who, like himself, were remnants of the last generation. And indeed, it was not the first time he had intercourse with them, for during the Civil War, no man had been more enthusiastic than he in praise of these gunmen. He had subscribed liberally to their war chest, fearing that if the Republicans won the war, 'every bloody Bolshevik in the country could put his dirty claws on his money.' And now, when he felt the ordered routine of his life slipping away, when he felt himself caught in the mesh that this woman had spinned for him, it was strange that he should come here to look for help.

Hanrahan was sitting on a stool, leaning against the counter, very drunk. The other men were standing about, some with glasses in their hands, others sulkily staring at the ground with their hands in their pockets. All looked up when Mr. Gilhooley came in. Mr. Gilhooley knew nobody but Hanrahan.

Hanrahan did not recognize him for a moment. Then he uttered a guffaw, dropping to the floor a cigarette that had been suspended from his purple lip. Throwing back his head, he slid to the floor unsteadily and held out his bloated right hand.

'Larry,' he said. 'Larry, me bold Larry. Boys, know him, know . . . a friend of mine . . . know the best man . . . Larry, I always said . . . listen . . . there's no man, know what I'm going to tell ye . . . the best man . . . he's made a home. Boys, he's a home.'

He took Mr. Gilhooley's right hand and shook it violently. Mr. Gilhooley looked furtively at the other men and felt afraid. Their faces looked very cold and stern, all with faces utterly unlike Hanrahan's good-natured, weak face. Their faces were cruel.

'That's all right, Shemus,' said Mr. Gilhooley. 'Easy, now. I . . . I . . . . '

'It's no use,' he thought, 'he's drunk. I better go. No. I must have a drink, though.'

'What will ye have?' he said.

'Sure, Mike,' said Hanrahan, stretching out his left hand circularly and clearing the atmosphere with it. 'I knew it. I knew it. Look. Friends of mine. Good men. Listen. Come here. Meet my friends. What'll ye have, boys?'

'Yes,' said Mr. Gilhooley. 'Gentlemen, give it a name.'

The others looked at one another and then nodded their heads. With an air of contempt they mentioned their drinks and then tossed off the drinks they had already purchased. One man came up to Hanrahan and tipped him on the shoulder.

'Chuck it,' he said angrily. 'Put a sock in it.'

Hanrahan looked at the man mournfully and began to blubber. Then he sat down on his stool again.

Mr. Gilhooley ordered the drinks and while he waited, he listened to Hanrahan's muttering absent-mindedly.

'I'll get him away out of here,' he said, 'and have a talk to him. A meal 'ud set him up. Then I could. . . . She certainly wanted him to know the address, otherwise she wouldn't write. It's all a dodge this. . . .'

'There's no man need be afraid of me,' Hanrahan was saying, looking askance at the sour-faced man who had spoken to him. 'Larry. Take it from me. There never was a man-up – I may get tight, but – up – ye needn't be afraid of me. See that? I got a record. Better record than some people. I get bugger all for it. There's them that done jobs and jobs. But the Ginger Bloke was there every time. Every time.'

He shook Mr. Gilhooley's arm violently.

'That's right,' said Mr. Gilhooley. 'I'll just swallow it and beat it.' he thought. 'It's obvious what's she's up to. I got to watch. The whole thing, all these clothes, and yet she said she slept out three nights. Then the attempt to get into this flat. God knows! There might be something awful at the back of this. And still. . . . Supposing I asserted my dignity. Carried her off . . . eh? Played the high hand? That's what should be done. Yes, it's clear I must get one. Look at these fellahs. They get away with it. Keep in well with them. A little bit of money. It does the trick.'

The drinks were passed around. Mr. Gilhooley raised his glass, turned to the men and said:

'Here's to old times, boys. Hope they come again. We're not dead yet.'

They looked at him furtively and raised their glasses in silence. Then they glanced at one another. They winked.

'Yes,' said Hanrahan, raising his glass unsteadily. ' Then hark a cry comes o'er the plain . . . wha'? We're not dead yet. True word.'

'Shemus,' said Mr. Gilhooley, leaning over to Hanrahan. 'I'd like to have a talk to ye. Are ye busy?'

Hanrahan started and straightened himself. He

breathed heavily, tried to close his lips and glanced suspiciously at Mr. Gilhooley. He detected in Mr. Gilhooley's voice a tone that indicated something of interest.

'No,' he said. 'What is it?'

'Just a little thing,' said Mr. Gilhooley. 'Come and have a snack somewhere. I just want to have a little talk about a certain matter.'

Immediately Hanrahan slipped off his stool, tightened the belt of his raincoat and thrust out his chest.

'Back again, boys,' he said to the others. 'Come on, Larry.'

He lurched out the door, followed by Mr. Gilhooley.

'Hey, Ginger,' said one of the men, the fellow who had previously warned Hanrahan.

Hanrahan turned back. The man took him aside and whispered to him. Hanrahan began to gesticulate. Then the other man nodded. Hanrahan came out and took Mr. Gilhooley's arm. They walked off.

'Friel was telling me,' said Hanrahan. 'So ye've settled down. Well, it's a good job. There's nothing like it. I had a wife. She died . . . she died in a year. Honest to God, I have never lived since. There it is. Molly, poor Molly. That's why . . . only them as once . . . I know what it is.'

He rambled on and Mr. Gilhooley did not listen to him. He was busy trying to formulate an excuse for asking him for a revolver and ammunition.

'In here,' said Mr. Gilhooley. 'We can have a snack at the counter.'

They entered a hotel bar, where there was a luncheon counter. They sat on stools in a corner. The place was empty, except for the two barmaids. Mr. Gilhooley ordered sandwiches and stout. While the barmaid went to fetch them, he leant over and began.

'It's this,' he said. 'There's no use beating about the bush. I want to get a revolver. Can ye get me one?'

Hanrahan started. He looked quite angrily at Mr. Gilhooley.

'What happened?' he said.

'How do you mean?' said Mr. Gilhooley.

Hanrahan stooped and spat into a cuspidor beneath the counter. Then he raised his head and looked into Mr. Gilhooley's eyes.

'What d'ye want it for?' he said cunningly. .

'Listen,' said Mr. Gilhooley. 'I'd prefer to say nothing about this. You know me, don't you?'

'Still,' said Hanrahan warily. 'These are tough times. How do you make out I should have a gun? Eh?'

'Damn it,' said Mr. Gilhooley, 'don't talk so loud.'

'I'm talking in a whisper, man. What's on yer mind?'

'Easy, now, easy. It's nothing like that at all.'

'Like what?'

'What you were thinking of.'

'How do you know what I'd be thinking of? Listen. Did you come in here to ask me to do a job for ye? If you did, you came to the wrong man. No, Larry. Nothing stirring. I'm done with that. See?'

'Who's talking about a job?' said Mr. Gilhooley angrily. 'I just asked you to get me a revolver. I didn't say you had one. I'm prepared to pay the money down.'

'Well, then,' said Hanrahan, with affected stupidity, 'why don't ye go to the Civic Guards and apply for a licence? Ye can get one if you show cause same as a bank manager or a publican or anything like that, for protection of property. Eh?'

'Listen. It's a private matter,' said Mr. Gilhooley.

'A private matter?' said Hanrahan.

'Yes, a . . . . '

The maid brought the stout and the plate of sandwiches. Mr. Gilhooley paid, tipping her the change. He pushed the plate towards Hanrahan.

'Have a bite,' he said. ''Twill do ye good.'

Hanrahan picked up a sandwich slowly and bit it.

'He's too drunk,' thought Mr. Gilhooley. 'I'll touch him up.'

He took out his note case, extracted a note, closed the case and put it in his pocket. Crumpling the note in his palm, he tendered it towards Hanrahan's thigh.

'A little change,' he said softly.

Hanrahan bit another mouthful off the sandwich and then lowered his head, looking upwards gloomily at Mr. Gilhooley. He waved away the offered note, with his left hand. Silently he chewed the morsel, swallowed it and gripped Mr. Gilhooley's knee.

'Larry,' he said in a melancholy voice, 'a man like you. . . . It's not right. It's not what I'd expect. You always treated me like a friend. Like a friend. That's why I . . . My brother Bill, I says to him, "Mr. Gilhooley is straight as a die. That man is a gentleman." It's all very well for me. I'm no good. But you are a man. . . . Well! I didn't expect it of ye.'

Mr. Gilhooley flushed. Taking his glass of stout, he finished it in two gulps. He rapped the counter. The barmaid came. He ordered a double Scotch.

'Two double Scotch,' he called after her.

'It's either more or less,' he thought. 'I'll try another dose on him. I must get it.'

'Listen, Shemus,' he said. 'I always played fair with you, as you say. And take it from me, what I'm asking ye now is only — '

'Wait a minute,' said Hanrahan briskly. 'Tell me this and tell me no more. What d'ye want it for? That's what I want to know.'

'I want to defend myself from a murderer,' said Mr. Gilhooley quickly.

'It isn't anything else?' said Hanrahan.

'Honest to God,' said Mr. Gilhooley.

'God! What have I come to?' he thought. 'Mixed up with fellahs like this, that my father wouldn't touch with a shovel.'

'An' ye just after getting married,' said Hanrahan.

'It's not right,' he added. 'It's not right.'

'Very well,' said Mr. Gilhooley suddenly. 'I can get a licence if it goes to that. Fair-weather friends, that's what you people are. Gunmen! Frightened of yer own shadows. Ach!'

Then indeed Hanrahan drew himself up with pride.

'Don't say another word,' he said. 'Larry, put it there.'

He stretched out his hand. Mr. Gilhooley took it.

'Swear on yer word of honour there's nothing dirty in this,' he said.

'I don't swear oaths in public-houses,' said Mr. Gilhooley, taking away his hand. 'I asked ye to do me a favour, and if ye don't like it, cheese it.'

Hanrahan scowled. Then he looked suspiciously at Mr. Gilhooley. He was rapidly getting quite sober.

'God! Yer looking bad,' he said. 'Where have ye been this last fortnight? Ye look bloody bad.'

'Go to the devil,' said Mr. Gilhooley furiously.

The maid served the drinks. He threw down three coins and shook his hand at her. She looked at him curiously and then smiled. She moved over to the other maid and they both watched Mr. Gilhooley, whispering to one another.

Mr. Gilhooley was trembling with rage, against he knew not what. He tossed off his drink again. Then he turned to Hanrahan fiercely.

'Look here, Hanrahan,' he said. 'Will ye get me a revolver for ten pounds or will ye not? Not ten. I'll give ye twenty. I'm not a miser. Twenty pound-notes. Are you ready to do it?'

'Twenty quid,' said Hanrahan. 'I haven't got a gun.'

'That's all right then,' said Mr. Gilhooley, getting to his feet off the stool.

'Half a mo,' said Hanrahan quietly. 'I might find out . . . . '

'What?'

Hanrahan glanced at the girls. They were watching.

'Come on,' he said. 'Move out of here. Let's go outside.'

'All right,' said Mr. Gilhooley.

Hanrahan swallowed the glass of whiskey and took a sandwich with him. He ate the sandwich going out.

Night had fallen by now. They entered upon a side street in which children were playing and screaming.

'Come up this way,' said Hanrahan.

At the corner of a small alleyway they halted. Hanrahan seized Mr. Gilhooley's coat lapel.

'That's settled. Twenty for a Mark Five Webley and ten rounds. Eh?'

'Good order,' said Mr. Gilhooley in a whisper. 'No crock. Mind, I've used a gun in South America. This is not for a cod.'

'Listen. Not for another man. But see . . . I haven't got it.'

'Oh, hell!' cried Mr. Gilhooley loudly.

'Hist,' said Hanrahan. 'Easy there. It's no joke, you know. Yer not in South America now. Easy now. I know a man who — '

'Now,' said Mr. Gilhooley, brushing Hanrahan away with his hand. 'This bunkum doesn't get me. It's either a bargain or not. I don't want to be carted about from one man to another. You get me the revolver or it's finished.'

Hanrahan began to splutter.

'You can go to hell then,' he said. 'I'm not going to bother. Bugger off.'

The two men seemed about to fight. Mr. Gilhooley took a pace away. Then he turned back again. They could hardly see one another in the alleyway.

'You've got the gun yourself,' he said.

'No,' said Hanrahan. 'I got no gun.'

'Eh? Can ye get it then?'

'That may be.'

'When?'

'It all depends. Two days, maybe three.'

'How d'ye make that out?'

'Here. Ask no questions and ye'll be told no lies. Put the money down and take yer chance. That's all there's to it. Then when it's all keff ye can come an' take it. But ask no questions. D'ye see? No witnesses, no evidence. I don't want to be mixed up in anything. Eh? How the hell do I know?'

'How do you know what?'

Hanrahan came close to Mr. Gilhooley and stared

into his face. Mr. Gilhooley could smell his drunken fetid breath.

'Larry,' he said, 'pull out of it. See, with the money in me hand, I tell you pull out of it. Take it from me. I know what I'm talking about. I ask no questions, but I'm an old dog on the road. Pull out of it.'

'Listen,' said Mr. Gilhooley with great violence. 'For Christ's sake, speak. Will ye get me the gun?'

Hanrahan began to breathe heavily.

'Twenty pound-notes,' said Mr. Gilhooley in a low, tense voice, 'and ye need never go short . . . while I . . . . '

'It's not that,' said Hanrahan, and he began to scratch his head.

'Curse him,' thought Mr. Gilhooley, 'he won't get it.'

'The night after to-morrow,' said Hanrahan. 'Will that be all right?'

'You mean . . . . '

'Right here,' said Hanrahan, pointing to the gutter with his right forefinger. ''Twill be handed to ye here, let us say, by someone ye don't know. Get me?'

'I pay then, do I?'

'No, you pay now,' grumbled Hanrahan. 'We take no chances.'

'Christ!' said Mr. Gilhooley, 'ye think I was a stranger.'

'We're all strangers,' muttered Hanrahan, 'when there are guns going about.'

'But . . . my God, man,' began Mr. Gilhooley. Then he took out his wallet and began to count notes.

While he was counting them, he suddenly started, raised his head and looked about him.

'God!' he said almost aloud. 'Is this why I took the money out of the bank this morning?'

He mused. Then he almost burst into tears, as he thought with a sudden burst of maudlin tenderness:

'Curse my soul, I took it out to buy her clothes and a bracelet. God forgive me.'

Hanrahan fingered the tendered notes roughly, counting aloud.

Then he made an appointment with Mr. Gilhooley for eleven o'clock at Chancellor's corner.

'D'ye see?' he said. 'I'm going off now to see him, ye see? All squared. All keff, ye see. I can tell ye definitely. If it doesn't come off, honest to God, these'll come back into yer pocket-book.'

'Blast the money,' said Mr. Gilhooley.

Hanrahan walked away hurriedly. Mr. Gilhooley walked towards a lamp-post and examined his watch.

'Eight o'clock,' he cried in alarm. 'Is she gone already?'

He began to run towards the tramway line.

CHAPTER XVI

MR. GILHOOLEY hurried back to the flat. His nerves were so excited that his hand trembled violently giving the fare to the tram conductor. People stared at him in the tram and the woman who sat beside him moved away. He didn't notice anything, either his trembling, or the curious way in which the people watched him. In his mind now he was debating furiously whether he should kill or should not kill. Everything else was rapidly becoming unintelligible to him.

He almost ran up the street to the house, after leaving the tram. He saw Friel's car in the roadway, and halted. He paused a moment and then went on again. As he was entering the hallway, Nelly was coming out of the tobacconist's shop. She was laughing, but she stopped laughing as soon as she saw Mr. Gilhooley. He also heard laughter within the shop and then Friel came out, smiling broadly and eating sweets from a paper packet. When Friel saw Mr. Gilhooley he stopped smiling. He became serious for a moment. Then he moved his moustache and raised his right forefinger to his forehead.

'Hey, Larry,' he said confidentially. 'The very man I was looking for. Listen.'

He took Mr. Gilhooley affectionately by the shoulder, hunched his shoulders and began to whisper.

'Me cousin said to take the wife around, ye see . . . d'ye mind? She couldn't come, ye see, so she said . . . a party at her place for tea . . . something about a charity concert Monday week . . . so she said. . . .'

'Very well, very well,' said Mr. Gilhooley.

'It's only for an hour or two, d'ye mind?' said Friel.

'Good Lord,' said Mr. Gilhooley, 'why should I mind?'

'Right,' said Friel, jumping down the steps to the street. 'I'm late as it is. Ye wouldn't like to come along . . . I suppose . . . yer busy,' he added, looking over his shoulder.

'Yes, yes,' said Mr. Gilhooley. 'I'm busy.'

He began to walk up the stairs. On his way up, he heard Friel crank the motor car and he heard Nelly laughing gaily. Were they jeering at him?

'What does it matter?' he muttered.

He entered the sitting-room and strode across the floor to the divan. When he was in front of the fire he halted. He stretched out his right foot. He took off his hat slowly and held it also in front of him, held by the fingers of his left hand. He dropped his walking-stick to the floor and slowly drew his right palm across his face.

'Now,' he said aloud.

He waited without thought. The car moved away. He dropped his two hands to his sides and said in a whisper:

'This is my end. I end now. The end. Collect the tools.'

He raised his eyes to the ceiling and shuddered. He expected to see the sky there. Terrified of the white ceiling he crouched his head between his shoulders and went stooping to the divan. Pawing beneath his lowered hip with his hand he dropped gently to the divan, looking upward and trembling. He lay flat on his back and then put his hands under his head.

He closed his eyes. Immediately little red spots formed in front of his eyes. They advanced and receded regularly. He watched them for more than a minute in peace. But then he saw pictures in them. A thousand pictures came in a moment before he could sit up hurriedly and put his hands to his eyes. They were horrible pictures.

With his hands covering his eyes, crouching forward, he began to mumble:

'I confess to Almighty God, to Blessed Mary ever Virgin, to . . . . '

He stopped. Some voice had cried out afar, telling him to stop. He listened. There was no sound. He struck his temples with his clenched fists.

'Who's there?' he cried out in terror.

Jumping up, he ran to the door and called again. Nobody answered. He rushed through all the rooms and called. There was nobody. He hurried back, dragging his limbs heavily. He threw himself again on the divan, flat on his back. He closed his eyes once more. Nothing came in front of his eyes now. So he opened them again. When he opened them he could hardly see anything for a moment. A mist had formed on his eyes. He was afraid of this and he stayed motionless. But soon tears welled from his eyes. He felt them trickling down his cheeks. He sighed and brushed them away with his fingers. He could feel his fingers touching his cheeks and he thought they were as big as mountains, his fingers, so heavy that he could hardly lift them from spot to spot. Then he let out a heavy sigh. His hands dropped to his sides.

He began to think now with great rapidity. Voices called in his brain, at first with a jumbling sound of many intermingling voices; then unified they formed a single chant, unintelligible at first; then, simplified, he heard clear words uttered slowly.

'The scourger will come with his rods, but it will be too late for you to be scourged.'

He began to laugh, silently at first, then gradually his laughter became loud, until it became a jeering shout. With his mouth wide open, he stopped laughing and jumped to his feet. He closed his mouth and bit his lower lip.

Then he became very cunning.

'Heh,' he said. 'These fellows can't fool me. They're surrounding me, but they can't fool me. It's my money they want. They want to drive me mad so they'll get it. They hired her, the bastards. Heh, heh. Won't I have a laugh at them? Let me see now. Who will I begin on? Eh?'

He sat down to the table and interlaced his fingers on the board.

'I'll get her first. When? As soon as ever I get

the gun. Wait now, though. No. What am I talking about? Nelly. What do I care about her? Eh? What put that idea into my head? There's some mistake here.'

He got to his feet and paced the room, trying to think of Nelly, but it was absolutely impossible. He kept wiping his forehead with the palm of his hand. His forehead was prickly. The power of thought failed him, and even though he struggled to be violent, he sank into a comfortable stupor, as if he had taken opium.

Presently he found himself lying on his back on the divan once more, with his eyes closed and his hands under his head.

Then a thundering sound approached him from afar, not a sound of the world around him, but the despairing cry heard by all living things when the evil of death approaches with slow, silent feet. It came like the whisper of the night winds among mountains, when the mists are fallen in the valleys and the marsh beasts moan. It was a formless murmur of mighty clouds brushing their vapourish sides against stars. It was the roar of disbanded oceans spilling in great foaming cataracts through the universe. It was the cracking of the earth and the hissing of volcanoes in the sun, when the great white star becomes disembowelled and scatters its blazing members in the void. And through this wrack of sound he heard the cry of all humanity, crying out for help. Help. No help. What help?

Then high over all this chaos, he himself arose,

grown to mighty stature, a vapourish grey figure, moving rapidly with widespread legs, flying with flapping hands into the void. He flew over the sounds and his soul was exalted by the despairing cries. Everywhere he saw the wrecked universe below and everywhere there was consoling death and sorrow and cries of anguish.

Then all sound died. He passed into a state in which there was nothing. For a moment his figure paused. Then it dwindled into nothing and he himself became nothing.

He surveyed this nothingness with pleasure, and he thought with glee that he was now safe. But a brooding expression came into his face. Then it darkened with fear. His eyes roamed about. His ears were intent. He put out the tip of his tongue and licked his lower lip. He strained his muscles. Numbers of eternities passed while he sat thus motionless. The loneliness was so great that it seemed to close in on him, an endless wall of emptiness. He was choking. He moved.

With a crash everything came back, the horrifying sounds and the turmoil of the universe being wrecked again.

He jumped to his feet and then he heard the slow murmur of the city traffic. He became weak and staggered forward. He began to mumble prayers.

'God have mercy on me. Jesus, Jesus, you died for me. I say. I say. I believe. I believe. I don't want . . . I don't want to die. Help. Help. Help.

He raised his hands to the ceiling and yelled:

'Help. God blast it, help. Curse it. Help, I say. I'm being smothered.'

Exhausted, he stopped screaming and listened. Somebody was running up the stairs. He rushed out to the door and locked it. Then he waited there. Somebody knocked at the door.

'Who's there?' called Mr. Gilhooley.

'I heard screams,' said a man's voice. 'I thought I'd . . . . '

'It's not here,' said Mr. Gilhooley.

Then he thought:

'Better let him in. He'd suspect something.'

'Just a moment,' he said calmly.

He unlocked the door and passed out on to the landing. Fleming, the Government official, was standing there in the dusk.

'Sorry,' he said. 'I was just coming up the stairs and I thought I heard somebody shouting.'

'That's all right,' said Mr. Gilhooley. 'It must have been at the back there. Eh?'

'Probably,' said the man. 'I'm awfully sorry to disturb you.'

'That's all right. That's all right,' said Mr. Gilhooley. 'No offence, I'm sure.'

They said good-night and parted. As the young man went down the stairs, Mr. Gilhooley wanted to call out to him for help, but he was afraid. Instead he turned back into the room and closed the door. He looked at his watch. It was half-past ten.

'I must go at once,' he said. 'At eleven o'clock, he said. This is surely the end.'

He took his hat and stick and went out without his overcoat or his gloves. But although the night was cold he did not feel cold. He did not feel now like other people. His mind was so intensely concentrated on one idea that his body was quite numb.

He walked the whole way to O'Connell's Street, and such was his weakness that it took him half an hour to do so, although the distance was no more than half a mile. Hanrahan was not there. He waited. There were loiterers there at the corner and he stood in among them, listening to their conversation and pretending to himself that he was one of them. He felt happy in their company.

At a quarter past eleven, Hanrahan tipped him on the shoulder. He turned around. Hanrahan was standing beside him. He motioned him to follow. They turned the corner and passed down along the quays.

'To-morrow night,' said Hanrahan, when they had gone a little distance. 'Where I told ye.'

'Yes,' said Mr. Gilhooley. 'To-morrow night. What time?'

'Let's say quarter to eleven, sharp.'

'Right.'

'Ye'll find the place again.'

'Sure.'

'All right. Good-night.'

Hanrahan walked away rapidly. Mr. Gilhooley set out after him, but he was so weak that he could not catch up on him before Hanrahan disappeared into the crowd. Then he paused on the kerb and said to himself:

'What do I want that damn gun for? I'll go back and tell him I don't want it.'

He gazed into the gutter. Then a whore jostled him, whispered something and halted a little below him. He shrugged himself and walked across the street towards the O'Connell monument. When he got to the middle of the roadway he forgot whether he wanted to go forward or sideways and he stood still, swaying. A policeman came up.

'Hey, Jimmy,' he said. 'Are ye sayin' yer prayers?'

'No offence, no offence,' said Mr. Gilhooley, moving off rapidly, straight in the middle of the roadway towards Westmoreland Street. His weakness had suddenly left him, but he was not aware of being in the city and that he must walk on the pavement to avoid the traffic. The policeman ran after him, caught him and said:

'Where are ye goin'?'

Mr. Gilhooley looked at him stupidly and said:

'I'm going to the devil.'

'Well, ye better take a cab then,' said the policeman with a hoarse laugh, 'or begob ye'll get into the lock-up instead.'

'Yes, I'll take a cab,' said Mr. Gilhooley.

The policeman got him a cab and Mr. Gilhooley got into it. He gave the address to the policeman. The policeman notified the cabman. The cab began to rumble off.

'It's about time ye went out to yer bee-farm,' said

the policeman mockingly to Mr. Gilhooley in through the door of the cab.

Then he turned to a detective in plain clothes that had come up.

'Who is that?' said the detective.

'That old ram Gilhooley,' said the policeman. 'Remember the fellah came into the station one night for a drink an' he began to do an ologon about a bee-farm. Ye better keep an eye on him. Them blokes all go the one road.'

The detective spat.

'Remember Turley,' he said. 'The ole bollocks that ran off with the waitress outa the. . . ?'

'Indeed I do,' said the policeman, laughing loudly. 'Seventy-five, wasn't he?'

'More,' said the detective. 'An' he thumpin' his craw for twenty years in the chapel before that. Everybody thought he was going to enter a monastery.'

'Heh,' said the policeman. 'Move on there now,' he called out to the little crowd that had gathered.

Mr. Gilhooley fell into a doze in the cab. He had to be awakened by the cabman at the door of the flat. He got out and took the cabman by the arm.

'Let me tell you,' he said to the cabman, 'that I want to state here and now that I . . . . '

'Yes, yer honour,' said the cabman hurriedly, leading him towards the steps.

'One moment,' said Mr. Gilhooley, making an effort. 'I'm in full possession of my faculties. That's a statement.'

'So it is,' said the cabman, helping him up the steps. 'Five bob, sir.'

'Eh?' cried Mr. Gilhooley, pulling himself up with a jerk. 'Five bob, did ye say?'

'Yessir,' said the cabman, touching his tattered hat.

Mr. Gilhooley got very angry. With his lower lip protruding, he seized the jarvey by the coat lapel and shook him violently.

'Look here,' he said in a calm voice. 'You are all trying to rob me. Every damn one of you. Think I'm drunk?'

The cabman became terrified of the powerful man who was standing over him.

'Honest to God, yer honour — ' he began.

But Mr. Gilhooley interrupted him. Making a gesture with his right hand, he cried:

'That's all right. I'm not a miser. I just wanted to show ye, ye see, that I'm in possession of all my faculties. As for the money. Here.'

He took a handful of silver from his pocket and spilt the coins, one by one, into the jarvey's outstretched hand.

'That's enough, that's enough,' cried the jarvey, when he had received the five shillings.

But Mr. Gilhooley uttered a curse and threw the other coins at his hand. The jarvey let them drop on the street. Then he stooped and picked them up. Mr. Gilhooley turned to the door and began to search for his key.

'Hey, sir,' said the jarvey. 'Here's yer money ye dropped.'

'Keep it,' said Mr. Gilhooley.

'Aw, no, sir,' said the jarvey. 'It's not right. It's not right. Put it in yer pocket, for the love of God.'

Mr. Gilhooley turned to him angrily and took the coins. Then he hurled them out into the roadway. The jarvey crossed himself and ran down the steps.

Mr. Gilhooley found the key, opened the door and passed in. He went up the stairs leaving the door open behind him. He entered the flat and sat down in the sitting-room.

The electric light was still burning. He had not turned it off going out. The light hurt him. He got up and turned it off. Then he groped his way back to the divan. The room was absolutely dark, as the fire had gone out and the blinds were drawn. He felt a great comfort in moving about in the darkness. It was also very pleasant to lie on the divan, with his head propped against cushions, without thought.

It seemed to him that he was several hours sitting there when he heard a motor-car halt in the road outside. But he had really only been there half an hour. He did not move when he heard it and he took no interest in it. He heard steps on the stairs and voices whispering. That meant nothing whatsoever to him. Then the outer door opened. A voice spoke.

'Are ye there, Larry?'

It was Friel's voice. Mr. Gilhooley did not reply.

'He's not in,' said Friel in a melancholy, thick voice. He was evidently drunk.

'Who cares,' said Nelly's voice, 'whether he's bloody well in or not?'

Mr. Gilhooley started slightly but again he relapsed into a state of indifference.

She laughed drunkenly. Then he heard Friel staggering about.

'Turn on the light,' he said.

They turned on a light, evidently in the kitchen.

'Hey, Larry,' said Friel again.

'He's not in,' said Nelly. 'Come on, Mick, let's have some fun. There's a bottle here somewhere.'

'I must find him,' said Friel, in a maudlin voice and angrily. 'I must find Larry. Lemme go. Larry. Hey, Larry.'

Mr. Gilhooley did not reply. He heard Friel staggering towards the door of the sitting-room. Then the light was turned on. Friel stood in the doorway, blinked for a moment stupidly, and then saw Mr. Gilhooley. He started violently.

'Christ!' said Friel.

Mr. Gilhooley's face looked like the face of a corpse and he sat like a corpse, propped up and motionless. Friel supported himself against the wall, with his two hands.

'Hey, Larry,' he said. 'Did ye not . . . hear . . . me callin'?'

'Yes, yes,' said Mr. Gilhooley in a hollow voice. 'I heard you calling me.'

Friel shook himself loose from the wall, thrust out his right hand in a circle and said:

'Well, then, why didn't ye answer me?'

Mr. Gilhooley sat up and drew his two hands across his face. Then he stared sombrely at Friel.

'I didn't think of it,' he said calmly.

Friel began to walk slowly towards him on his bandy legs, bobbing his head and twitching his large shoulders.

'Larry,' he said. 'I've something to tell ye. Some . . . thing important.'

'So,' said Mr. Gilhooley.

Friel leaned unsteadily against the table and then came to the divan in two strides. He almost fell over Mr. Gilhooley and then swerved, falling heavily beside him on the divan. Mr. Gilhooley did not move or look at him.

'It's important,' said Friel, 'for ye to know this.'

'Where the blazes are ye gone, Mick?' came Nelly's drunken voice.

'Wait a moment,' Friel called out. 'With ye in a moment.'

But she was already in the room, walking with a swaying motion like a dancer, though unsteadily. As she came, she wiped her mouth with a little handkerchief. Mr. Gilhooley stared at her.

A shiver passed up his spine. She was so voluptuously beautiful in her drunkenness! As he looked at her, all his imaginings, all his hatred, all his murderous intentions changed into a powerful desire to possess that voluptuous slim body. Her hat was in her hand. Her golden hair shone in the light, as it had shone that night when he first saw its beauty in the supper room. Her face bore that wild bacchanalian look which it bore when she threw her arms around his neck in his lodgings and gave him her first kiss. In a clinging black dress, her limbs swayed with drunkenness, suggesting that eel-like wriggling of her body which made her embraces more maddening than the wildest dreams caused by an opiate.

Her wanton drunken smile, the glitter of her cold eyes, the kittenish bosses of her rounded jaws, the short white teeth that had bitten him in passion . . . all, all created such desire that the most sluggish stream of his heart's blood essayed to burst its vein.

He neither moved nor spoke. She stared at him and then laughed stupidly. She threw her hat on the floor. Then she tossed back her curls with her right hand.

'Well, my tame bear,' she said. 'Mick, he's my tame bear . . . one of 'em.'

Friel struggled to his feet. She advanced towards Mr. Gilhooley, breathing heavily and staring at him with a smile, half mocking, half desirous. Friel came towards her, with his hand raised.

'Go to bed, Nelly,' he said. 'I want to . . . to speak to Larry.'

'Mind yer own business now, Mick,' she said. 'It's all over. See?'

'None o' that now,' said Friel. 'Me an' Larry are ole friends. There is something I want to. . . .'

'Now, don't you be butting in,' she said. 'Out of the way, Mick. I want to hug my tame bear. He and I have made a bargain. So, as long as I'm here, ye see, I play the game.'

Friel took her in his arms to restrain her. She struggled for a moment and then laughed into his face. She struck him a blow on the cheek lightly with her hand.

'Come on, now,' said Friel. 'Into yer room. Just a moment. I'll just say a few words and then ye see . . . it'll be all right.'

She winked at him. Then she said calmly.

'Lemme go. Just one kiss. Our bargain, see.'

Friel stared at her. Then he let her loose. She came to Mr. Gilhooley, stood in front of him and then cocked her head to one side. Mr. Gilhooley did not move. Standing unsteadily on her toes, she bent down, holding up her skirts with her hands and kissed him on the bald patch at the top of his head. He trembled but he did not move.

'Right,' she said, straightening herself.

'God Almighty!' said Friel. 'Larry, why the hell don't ye say something?'

'That's all right, now,' said Nelly. 'Talk away. I'm going. I'm going. Snoozy snooze. Then we'll roam, roam, roam, far away, far away and we'll come to the isle of. . . .'

She danced towards the door, singing. Friel followed her unsteadily out of the room. Mr. Gilhooley did not move. After a minute or so Friel came back again.

'Larry,' he cried, crossing the room rapidly, 'see what ye've done to yerself. God Almighty!'

Mr. Gilhooley looked at him coldly and smiled maliciously. Friel sat down on the divan, seized Mr. Gilhooley by the shoulder and began to talk rapidly:

'I asked ye to tell me an' ye wouldn't. A friend that would just put ye right an' ye went off like a damn fool to do a thing like this. See?'

'What are you talking about?' whispered Mr. Gilhooley.

'Ye told me ye were going to get married, didn't ye? Says I, it's all right goin' to live with a woman an' ye never said a word. An' then, I bring ye in here, into a man's flat an' who d'ye bring? Eh? A bloody whore.'

'Eh?' said Mr. Gilhooley turning to him fiercely. 'What did ye say?'

'Easy now,' said Friel, gripping Mr. Gilhooley's shoulder fiercely. 'You know nothing about women.'

'Not what scoundrels like you know,' whispered Mr. Gilhooley savagely.

Friel loosed his shoulder and drew back.

'Take that back, Larry,' he muttered angrily.

Mr. Gilhooley looked at him with his upper lip raised. He smiled.

'What does it matter?' he said. 'Go ahead. I know you. You're all right. I'm no better myself. What does it matter what you say or what anybody says? Do what ye like. Say what ye like.'

'So ye know all about it, then,' said Friel.

'About what?'

'About her.'

'What about her? What are you meddling yerself with her for?'

'Listen. I was dragged into this. I'm goin' to tell ye, ye've ruined my life.'

Friel suddenly became maudlin and very angry. Mr. Gilhooley puffed out his cheeks and then shook his head, blowing out his breath slowly.

'Listen to me,' said Friel. 'I did you many a good turn and ye've ruined my life. Ye brought a bloody whore into a flat I got for ye, into a man's flat, a respectable man's flat, and then. . . .It's not that. Ye got to clear out, right now. Right away. Toute suite. Gaby. Vamoosh. Blow out of it.'

'Go an' have a runnin' jump at yerself, ye bloody drunkard,' said Mr. Gilhooley.

This insult did not irritate Friel. Instead he became restless and more deferential.

'So ye don't know anything about it, after all,' he said.

Mr. Gilhooley looked at him with curiosity for the first time.

'What have ye got up yer sleeve? Ye're wasting my time here. So say what ye have to say and beat it.'

'I'm not going to beat it,' said Friel. 'I'm responsible for this flat. But when I tell you what I'm going to tell you, you'll beat it. See? Not as an enemy, but as a friend, I'm telling ye. Man, dear, ye don't know what ye've got. Ye've got the slickest little bitch on two legs. That's what ye've got.'

'The dirt on yer tongue is only a sign of the dung on yer soul,' said Mr. Gilhooley bitterly. 'Talk away. I'm beyond that now.'

'Yer takin' an advantage of me because I'm drunk,' cried Friel.

Mr. Gilhooley sighed and leaned back against the cushions. His face took an ashen colour and his eyes became fixed.

'I imagine I know it all,' he said quietly.

'D'ye know where we were to-night, then?' said Friel.

'I don't care where ye were,' said Mr. Gilhooley.

'No, but ye should, though,' said Friel. It's a damn disgrace. Me too. I'm disgraced. Eh? Did ye ever hear of Mrs. Considine? Did she tell ye anything about her?'

Mr. Gilhooley started. Friel leaned over.

'That got him McDara,' he said, touching his forehead with his right forefinger. 'Listen. I pulled a good one on you, Larry. I'm soft, eh?'

He suddenly became jolly and opened several buttons of his waistcoat, so that his fat stomach could be seen heaving against his striped shirt.

He shook his head.

'I spotted it as soon as I came in here, to-day,' he said. 'A mile off. I can tell 'em. So, all that stuff about my cousin and a party was all bunk. I just wanted to get her going, see. Business is business. I don't want to cast a slur on my father-in-law. So

I says to myself, I'll see what's in this. He's playing a dirty trick on me. But Christ! I got more than I bargained for.'

Mr. Gilhooley sat up and began to tremble.

'You are a cur after all,' he said.

'That cuts no ice,' said Friel. 'If I didn't, somebody else would. Fleming or the bloody landlord. I've got to watch my p's and q's. Friend or no friend. But anyway, this is the toughest proposition I ever came across. When I brings her out along the road, right away ye see, there's no hedging about in a case like that, I just puts it to her straight: "What little job are *you* up to?" She tried to monkey about for a bit, but not long. So she digs me in the ribs and winks. That does it, says I to mesel'. So, here goes, anyway. It's all the same now, I thought to myself I might as well bite off the same biscuit. Looked good to me, so it did. Didn't think what I was letting myself in for. Christ!'

He straightened himself and mopped his forehead. Then he whispered with enthusiasm close to Mr. Gilhooley's ear:

'When all's said an' done, that kid is a corker, Larry.'

Mr. Gilhooley became very still and it seemed to him that something snapped in his chest.

'Ye mean to say that you . . .' he began.

Friel leered drunkenly.

'No, not me,' he said waving his hand towards Mr. Gilhooley. 'But wait till I tell ye. We'll pass over that. So I gets a jag on her. And then . . .

scarified Christ! She opens out. Not till she was well on, mind. Not a word first. As dainty as you like, only soft on the bubbies, but . . . as soon as she got a little . . . ye know . . . out at J—'s Hotel at C—, there's where I brought her, if ever ye want a good time. . . '

Mr. Gilhooley drew in a deep breath and he wanted to fall upon the fellow and crush him to death. Instead he said:

'God have mercy on me.'

He spoke in a soft whisper and Friel started.

'What's that?' he said nervously.

'Nothing at all,' said Mr. Gilhooley.

'That's the ticket,' said Friel.

Then he scratched his head and mumbled something. Mumbling to himself, he began to search in his pockets, finally bringing out a crumpled cigarette, which he put unsteadily in his mouth. He rubbed his fingers to and fro in the air, like a man striking a match. Mr. Gilhooley did not offer him one. Mr. Gilhooley was staring at the floor, motionless, his face an ashen colour. Friel shook him violently by the shoulder. Mr. Gilhooley turned his face slowly.

'Light,' said Friel. 'Light. Blast it. Look at that hand. Trembling all over. How I drove back, Christ only knows. I treat her bloody badly, that little car. She's good, though. Still . . . . Hurry with the match.'

Mr. Gilhooley contemptuously threw him a box of matches. Then instead of taking the box of matches or lighting his cigarette, Friel began to chew the cigarette, while his eyes opened wide, as if in fear; and looking fearfully at Mr. Gilhooley, he said:

'Yer not thinkin' of anything, are ye?'

'What would I be thinking of?' said Mr. Gilhooley.

Friel's eyes almost closed and he shrugged his shoulders. He spat out the mangled cigarette.

'It's sad all the same,' he said mournfully. 'And you're to blame no more than anybody else. It's damn sad. The kid is a corker an' it's not her fault. It's a whore of a story.'

'What is?'

'Amn't I after telling ye?'

'If I weren't in the state I'm in,' cried Mr. Gilhooley ferociously, 'I'd . . .'

'What would ye do?' said Friel in a whisper. 'Eh?'

Mr. Gilhooley said nothing. Friel suddenly began to laugh.

'Yes, yes, she told me all about it,' he continued irrelevantly. 'Did she tell you, though? That's what I want to know? Did ye know all this before ye came here?'

'I won't bother with him,' said Mr. Gilhooley to himself. 'What does it matter? It's all over now an' 'twill have to be done sooner than I thought.'

He looked at Friel.

'D'ye want her?' he said.

'How d'ye mean?' said Friel.

'Go ahead,' said Mr. Gilhooley, with a sneering

smile. 'Go ahead into the room. The more the merrier. I know well what yer after. Bring them all here to-morrow, in their turn, like rams at a fair. There's room for them all. Only it might be a little different by then. Now, though, is *your* time. Hit the iron while it's hot.'

Friel drew back and leaned his elbow on his knee. 'Yer thinking of something,' he said.

Mr. Gilhooley suddenly thought with great violence.

'Will I finish him too?'

'So ye know all about the Considines?' said Friel.

Mr. Gilhooley shut his eyes.

'God! Larry,' said Friel, 'this is a terrible world.' He became ruminative again and almost maudlin. 'She coughs up her guts to me, like a judy makin' her confession to a priest. All about her bloomin' Matt, his red hair and his glittering eyes. Jay! I can just make that fellah out. Didn't give a God damn as long as he got his an' she thinkin' all the time he was nuts on her. That's what she came over here after. Larry!' He struck Mr. Gilhooley on the knee violently with his clenched fist. 'What I don't know about women ain't worth knowing.'

Mr. Gilhooley felt himself becoming very weak. He was afraid that he was going to vomit. His stomach was heaving up formidably. He wanted to be alone, to contemplate what he intended doing and yet he felt comforted by the presence of Friel. 'Will he be the last?' he kept thinking.

'Yes, she told me that she told ye that part,' said

Friel. 'She told me all about the jockey too, more than she told you about the jockey. Ye see, they tell me everything. I look silly. Never mind. Sure, I said, that was a good dodge. It was all a game to get planted in here, so she could get him back.'

Mr. Gilhooley started.

'Is he coming back?' he said.

'Who?'

'Matt.'

'Not he. Listen.'

Mr. Gilhooley sighed. 'That's better,' he thought. 'I've nothing against him.'

'I told *you* a minute ago,' said Friel, 'that I know that boy's game. He just got what he wanted. He went after it while he wanted it. Then he got fed up. She follyied him. Ye see. All round. And then she thought he was follying her. They all do. Once a woman is in love with a man . . . but we needn't go into that. What I don't like is this. The way I was dragged into it. I'm known here. My old man is known . . . to these bloody people. So if they ever found out. Christ! However, I was just feeling in that state after . . . ye know what I mean, out at the hotel and . . . that's a funny thing too. Other women, afterwards ye want never to see a sight of them, but with her it's the other way about. Afterwards with her, yer just gone crazy. I had a few on me too, so I was half blind, an' I said, I'll take ye around to see him, I said to her. We'll put the wind up him.'

Mr. Gilhooley jumped to his feet suddenly.

'Is he here?' he cried in a hoarse voice. 'Quick. Tell me. Is he here?'

Friel looked up with the affected stupidity of a drunken man and waved his hand back and forth.

'He's not here,' he said. 'He's gone to Canada with his wife. Sit down.'

CHAPTER XVI

Mr. Gilhooley put his clenched fists to his temples and drew in a deep breath. Friel looked at him curiously. Mr. Gilhooley's eyes had become glassy, like the eyes of a corpse. Friel got afraid.

'God Almighty!' he said. 'Larry. Don't look like that. Yer thinking of something.'

He got to his feet and put out his hand to seize Mr. Gilhooley's arm. With a sudden movement Mr. Gilhooley seized Friel's hand and gripped it violently.

'Tell me,' he said hoarsely, ' what's between you and her? Quick or I'll . . .'

Friel's face became cold and stern. Now it seemed that he was quite sober. Suddenly the same evil desire became manifest in his face also. Unconsciously they both glanced towards the door leading to the bedroom in which she was waiting. For what?

'Mick! Come here at once.'

She called aloud, as if aware of what they were thinking. Neither noticed her call. They turned to one another again and stared.

'Clear out,' said Mr. Gilhooley, so hoarsely that his voice was almost inaudible.

Friel uttered a hoarse laugh, shook his shoulders and took a pace backwards. Meeting the edge of the divan with the calf of his leg, he staggered and fell down upon it, on his buttocks. The gleam of passion left his face and he seemed to become drunk again.

For a moment, however, a cunning look came into his face. Then the cunning look vanished and his face became stupid. Mr. Gilhooley watched him sideways. Then he went over to the divan and sat down. He took hold of Friel's knee.

'What did ye want to tell me?' he whispered. 'What were ye drivin' at?'

Friel looked at him with a slow, stupid, drunken stare.

'I declare by the Cross of Christ,' he said fervently, crossing himself, 'that I came as a friend. She said to tell you nothing of it. She made me swear. She wants to . . . now listen.' He shifted himself closer to Mr. Gilhooley. 'She wants to get some money out of you and then run off to Canada after him.' Mr. Gilhooley started. 'No. One moment. There's a plan in this. She wants me to come along with her. See? Because I'm drunk. I'm a good fellah. I don't like to see anybody suffer. So I . . . what are ye lookin' at me like that for?'

Mr. Gilhooley had closed his right eye and the corner of his upper lip was turned up.

'That's enough,' he said. 'This is all a fake. Ye concocted that in the pub because ye. . . . I see. Ye want her yerself, isn't that it?'

'Didn't I tell you I went to the house with her?' he said with a great effort, as if trying to remember something.

'What house?'

'Mrs. Considine's house out at D—y.'

'Ye told me nothing of the kind. What? What are ye drivin' at? What are ye doin' here in my house, bringing allegations against my wife?'

'Ha, ha, ha.'

They both looked up. Nelly was standing in the doorway in her dressing gown, holding on to the doorpost unsteadily. Friel got to his feet and was going towards her, when Mr. Gilhooley reached forward and caught him by the left leg. Friel staggered and fell against the edge of the table. He sprawled there and then struggled erect. Mr. Gilhooley was standing over him.

The three of them stood in silence, looking at one another. Then Nelly came from the door until she reached the table.

'What were you saying to him about me?' she said to Friel.

'Nelly,' said Mr. Gilhooley, in a hoarse whisper, 'go back to yer room.'

She turned to Mr. Gilhooley.

'I was listening at the door,' she said. 'I heard what he was saying about my trying to get money out of you, to follow him to Canada. Did you believe that?'

'What does it matter?' said Mr. Gilhooley. He seemed to be talking to himself, although he was looking at her. 'What does it matter what he says?'

'It's a lie, uncle,' she said in a maudlin voice. 'It's a lie. He told you a lie. He made me drunk and then he made love to me and then he brought me to see Mrs. Considine and he kicked up a row there, broke the furniture in the drawing room and. . . .'

'I'll wring yer bloody neck,' cried Friel. 'Ye lying bitch.'

'Shut up, you scoundrel,' cried Mr. Gilhooley.

'I'm not a lying bitch,' cried Nelly. 'Believe me, Larry, sooner than ye'd believe. . . . I know what he wants. The double-faced cur.'

Friel moved around to the other side of the table and cried:

'Now, I'm going to tell him all about you and see what ye get. He's a friend of mine. You're going out into the road now. D'ye hear? I took pity on ye, ye little bitch.'

Nelly caught up a flower vase from the table but Mr. Gilhooley rushed over and seized her.

'Come on, come on,' he said. 'Into your room. I'll see to him. Get in now.'

He took her up in his arms and walked to the door with her.

'Uncle, uncle,' she sobbed drunkenly in his arms. 'I'm afraid. Don't hurt me. Sure ye won't let anybody hurt me. Speak to me, uncle. Say something nice. I'm all alone and I know nobody. Say something nice to me. . . .'

She babbled all the way into the bedroom. He laid her on the bed, pulled back the clothes and put her under them. She lay in the bed flabbily, mumbling and looking up at him with the eyes of a beaten cur, just as she had looked that first night when he met her. He stared at her with glassy eyes and the same feeling of pity overcame him, as on that first night. This feeling of pity seemed to strike against his forehead. But there was another immovable feeling within in his brain that made his eyes glassy. He did not speak. He retreated three paces from the bed, staring at her right arm, that lay limp and white and soft over the bedclothes.

'Uncle,' she mumbled. 'You've been so kind to me until now. Why do you look at me like that? I have nobody . . . nobody . . . say something nice to me."

Turning suddenly, he left the room. He closed the door. He entered the sitting-room. He met Friel just inside the door. Friel had in his hand the flower vase that Nelly had picked up. Seeing Mr. Gilhooley, he made an attempt to hide it behind his back and then dropped it to the floor.

'Can ye get us a drink, Larry?' he said, stuttering.

His head was quivering after the manner of a man who has been disturbed in the contemplation of a violent act.

'Yes, that's the easiest way to get rid of him,' thought Mr. Gilhooley cunningly. 'I'm too weak for anything else.'

'Sure,' he said quietly. 'I've got a drink. Come in here. Follow me.'

He brought Friel with him into the kitchen, making him walk in front all the way. Friel dropped to a chair by the stove and leaned his head on his arm. Mr. Gilhooley got the bottle of whiskey which had been purchased for the previous night's carousal, but which had remained unopened. He couldn't find a corkscrew and knocked the head off it. He got two glasses from a shelf.

'Come on, now,' he said, 'back into the other room.'

Friel shook himself and got to his feet. He glared at Mr. Gilhooley. Then he said:

'I'm bloody hungry. Any grub?'

He searched around. In a cupboard he got a plate of cold meat. He brought this plate with him, together with a loaf of bread. They entered the sitting-room. Mr. Gilhooley entered last and left the door wide open. Then he sat down facing the door, at an angle that gave him a view of the outer door. He was afraid she might go out quietly.

Friel began to eat ravenously, tearing the loaf with his fingers and then biting the piece of meat and tearing at it. Again Mr. Gilhooley felt sick, looking at him.

'Here, drink this,' he said, handing him a glass of whiskey.

Friel stopped eating and came over.

'Bring a chair over here,' said Mr. Gilhooley. 'I want to talk to ye.'

Friel brought a chair. He accepted the drink and swallowed it immediately.

'Now, tell me,' said Mr. Gilhooley quietly. 'Did she say when she was going?'

'To-morrow,' mumbled Friel. 'She's clearing out to-morrow. I'll clear her out of here. Leave it to me, Larry.'

He seemed to have altogether forgotten what he was saying before. He was swaying about, breathing heavily and unbuttoning the remaining buttons of his waistcoat.

'The man is an idiot,' thought Mr. Gilhooley.

'You clear out now, though,' mumbled Friel. 'Right here. I'll flop here for the night. Just a moment. I'll take you around in the car to the — Hotel, and then come back. Must look after the flat. I'm responsible.'

'I see,' said Mr. Gilhooley, winking his right eye. He did not look at Friel, but suddenly, he felt that somebody was standing behind him at a distance, brandishing something and he became very cunning.

Friel stretched out his glass for more whiskey. Mr. Gilhooley filled the glass. Instead of raising the glass to his lips, Friel let the hand holding the glass go limp. The glass tilted over and the liquid spilt slowly, tremulously, to the floor.

'I love that kid,' said Friel. 'Larry, I love her. I had her in me arms. God forgive me, I have a wife, the best little woman and two peaches, but I love that kid. The way she cuddles around ye. Then there's no harm in her. I love that kid, Larry, an' I'm going to let no man do her harm. I'll stand by her.'

He made a gesture with the hand holding the glass and then put it to his lips. It was almost empty, but he drained the remaining drops down his full brown throat and sucked at the rim, smacking his lips and gurgling.

Then he dropped the glass to the floor, heavily, as if it were a great weight. He looked at Mr. Gilhooley ferociously.

'She got the wind up about you last night,' he said. 'So she wired to him, Matt Considine, otherwise Frank, a Trinity medical that was. Ted Reddington knows him. Heard him talk about him. He's buggered off, though. That's why she wired this morning. She's got the wind up about you. She said to me, I'm all alone and I'm. . . . What the hell did she say? So I do horrid things. Can you blame me? That's what she said. I raised hell. Broke all the furniture. Look.'

He bared his right arm to the elbow and showed a long thin red scar.

'Met the corner of some bloody glass thing in the drawing-room. They'll be sure to tell the old man. What do I care? My life is ruined. I love her. Same way I got into a row before over Molly Dalton and her bloody kid. Not mine. I swear to Christ it wasn't. But. . . . Ye got to clear out. Ye've got something in yer mind.'

'Have another drink,' said Mr. Gilhooley tremulously.

He was beginning to lose control of himself. Would he use the bottle?

'No,' said Friel heavily. 'I'll not have another drink. Ye want to make me drunk. Ye got something in yer mind. Yer not a Dublin man. Yer a country bastard. A South American whore master. I'm a Dublin man. Every Dublin man is a gentleman. We play the game. We got a heart in us. Ye got to clear outa here, here an' now.'

'All right,' said Mr. Gilhooley, in a whisper. 'Don't talk so loudly. Have another drink and we'll go.'

Mr. Gilhooley filled his own glass and offered it to Friel. Friel, almost senseless with intoxication, stared with blurred eyes and then put the glass to his lips. He emptied the glass, and then he struggled to his feet.

'You clear out now,' he said, holding out his right hand with the fingers spread. 'I'm going in . . . in to her. The little kid. She's mine . . . at least to-night. She belongs to me. If ye don't think so, I'll fight ye for her. Here an' now.'

Mr. Gilhooley stood up, gripping the bottle firmly by the neck. There was silence for a moment. Friel took a step towards the door. Mr. Gilhooley was about to move forward behind him, when the flat door-bell rang violently and continuously. Both men became rigid. The bell kept ringing. Then voices were heard shouting in the street below.

'Who the hell is that?' muttered Friel.

Mr. Gilhooley began to tremble.

'Go to the window and look out,' he said.

'No, you go,' said Friel.

Neither moved, however. The bell stopped ringing and then after a few moments it began again.

'Go down and see who it is,' said Mr. Gilhooley.

'I'm staying here,' said Friel.

Suddenly losing control over himself, he collapsed on to the floor, face downwards. For a few moments he mumbled something. Then he began to breathe loudly. The bell stopped ringing again.

'Let it ring away,' thought Mr. Gilhooley, 'now is my time.'

He stepped forward and raised the bottle. He drew in a deep breath. Then he paused and began to smile sardonically. He walked as rapidly as his trembling legs would permit him over to the window and raising the blind, he peered through the panes of glass. He could see nothing. Then he raised the window and leaned out. Two men were standing down at the door. He could not recognize them.

'Who's there?' he called out in a loud whisper.

One of them looked up.

'Is that you, Larry?' came Culbertson's harsh voice.

'Yes,' said Mr. Gilhooley.

'Open, in the King's name,' said Culbertson. 'A debt of honour, to be paid as promised.'

'What's that?' said Mr. Gilhooley.

'Item, one treasury note, value twenty shillings,' said Culbertson, 'due first o' the month. Couldn't be delivered owing to the secrecy of your movements. Open in the King's name.'

'Go home, for God's sake,' said Mr. Gilhooley. 'I'm in bed.'

The other man now moved out from the door and

looked up. Immediately, Mr. Gilhooley recognized Macaward. He could also hear his low laugh.

'He's in bed,' said Macaward, 'the connubial couch. Let's break open the door and disgrace him.'

'Come down and open,' cried Culbertson angrily. 'We want a drink too. Have you got a drink?'

'Can't you see I'm in bed,' cried Mr. Gilhooley desperately. 'It's . . . . it's after one o'clock.'

'Half-past,' said Culbertson. 'Time to get up. Arise and shine. Open the door. Tell that to the marines. I recognize Friel's car. Come along. Sound the advance.'

'All right, blast and curse it,' said Mr. Gilhooley.

He pulled his head into the room. Friel had moved. He was trying to drag himself up into a sitting posture.

'Who's there?' he muttered.

Mr. Gilhooley walked past him hurriedly without answering him. He ran out of the flat and down the stairs. Half way down he paused and said excitedly: 'That's the ticket. Right!' He ran on down. He opened the door and admitted them. They stumbled into the hall and immediately began to do a dance about him, laughing and talking excitedly. They also were intoxicated, enjoying Culbertson's allowance, which was paid on the first of each month.

Mr. Gilhooley closed the door and caught hold of Culbertson's shoulder.

'Come, make no noise,' he said. 'I want to get

Friel out of the house. He's dead drunk and kicking up a row. I didn't want to wake the people. Take him away. Follow me quickly. You stay here, Macaward. I don't want you upstairs.'

Culbertson said:

'This sounds queer. What's the idea?'

'Come on, quickly,' said Mr. Gilhooley. 'It's important.'

Culbertson did not move.

'This ain't Gilhooley,' he said quietly. 'It's a damn ghost. Exorcise him, Sean. Holy . . .'

'I've put my foot in it,' thought Mr. Gilhooley.

His head became dizzy and he wanted to lie down. But he made a great effort and laughed. He said:

'Come, come, Culbertson, you're a gentleman. Do me a favour. My wife is not very well. He's disgusting. For God sake, take him away. Don't let me have to call a policeman. Come on.'

'Sir,' said Culbertson after a pause. 'At your service.'

The two of them moved towards the stairs. Macaward thrust forward the crook of his stick and hooked Mr. Gilhooley by the thigh. Mr. Gilhooley turned around, became furiously angry and dealt Macaward a savage blow.

'You disreputable hound,' he said, 'take that.'

Macaward, struck in the chest, reeled back. The two men went upstairs hurriedly. When they were passing Fleming's landing they heard somebody moving about within and voices talking.

'Don't make any noise,' said Mr. Gilhooley.

They reached the outer door of the flat.

'Nelly, where are you, where are you?' Friel was saying.

Mr. Gilhooley dashed in and collided with Friel, who was groping about with his hands outstretched, trying to reach the bedroom door. Mr. Gilhooley seized him. Friel immediately collapsed, either feigning helplessness or overcome once more by his drunkenness, into Mr. Gilhooley's arms. Mr. Gilhooley staggered with him to the sitting-room door and then pushed him violently inwards. Friel fell to the floor.

Culbertson stood with his hands in his overcoat pockets, laughing quietly.

'May I come in ?' he said in his harsh voice. 'It looks like a feast.'

Mr. Gilhooley, standing over Friel, turned around slowly and looked into Culbertson's cynical eyes. Culbertson started. Mr. Gilhooley's eyes were glassy, like the eyes of a corpse. Culbertson stared and then lowered his eyes. For a moment a serious look passed across his face and it appeared that he was going to stretch out his hand and say something serious and personal to Mr. Gilhooley. But immediately the cynical, careless expression returned and he continued to laugh, as he pointed to the floor with his finger.

'Item, bottle, neck off, decapitated. Item, flower vase, may or may not have been intended as a missile, floorward fallen. Item, glass, empty, on floor. General environment; strained relations between two gentlemen. Suggestion of lady in the background. Good. However. Here.'

He tipped Mr. Gilhooley on the chest and then putting his hand in his hip-pocket, he said:

'My debt, with thanks.'

'Who's that?' said Friel, trying to get to his feet. 'Who's that? I know him.'

'Keep the money,' said Mr. Gilhooley, in a loud thin voice. 'I don't want it. I want to go to bed. Take this fellow away.'

'Who's that?' said Friel again.

'Hullo, Friel,' said Culbertson. 'Be of good cheer. You're among friends. How's the body?'

'Who's that?' said Friel, standing up with the assistance of the back of a chair. 'What name?'

'Culbertson,' said Culbertson. 'Culbertson, gentleman, of no visible occupation.'

'Visi . . . visibedamned,' said Friel. 'You're a friend o' mine. Listen. This is important.'

'Here's the debt, Gilhooley,' said Culbertson, handing him a pound-note.

Mr. Gilhooley had been standing slack, with his left shoulder raised, his eyes watching the doorway. He suddenly stiffened himself and cried out loudly as before, in a thin, strained voice:

'Take him away at once and keep the money.'

'Not on your tintop,' cried Friel, staggering towards Culbertson. 'Just in time. He has something in his mind. You . . . Culbertson . . . see to this.'

Mr. Gilhooley began to make signs to Culbertson, suggesting that he take Friel out at once. But Culbertson was either too intoxicated to understand correctly, or else he was amused at the situation and wanted to prolong it. He laughed aloud, thrust the pound-note into the hand Mr. Gilhooley was gesturing with, closed the fingers carefully over the note and then said:

'Anything left in that bottle?'

'Bottle,' said Friel, gripping Culbertson violently around the body. 'Listen to me. Bottle. There's a . . . he's got a . . . he's got something in his mind. Ye mustn't, ye see. . . . It's up to me . . . for God sake . . . ye . . . don't leave me alone . . . Culbertson . . . ye can look . . . he's got something. . . .'

'One moment now,' said Culbertson, 'we must drink to clarify our minds.'

'No time, no time,' cried Friel.

He made a supreme effort to continue, reaching out his right hand with the fingers outstretched and failed. Culbertson was pushing him away, either too stupidly intoxicated to understand that Friel was in earnest, or else too cynical to pay any heed even to the most pressing warning.

Mr. Gilhooley was swaying forward, listening eagerly to what Friel was trying to say and it seemed to him that he was trying to help Friel enunciate the words, instead of trying to prevent him.

Suddenly they heard a great shouting on the stairs. Somebody was coming up, banging something on the wall and yelling. Mr. Gilhooley and Culbertson rushed out on to the landing to see. At the same time Nelly began to cry out in the bedroom: 'Uncle, uncle, protect me.'

It was Macaward who was coming up, waving his stick and threatening to kill Mr. Gilhooley. He was frothing at the mouth, possessed of one of the fits of frenzy to which he was addicted.

'He struck me,' he yelled, 'the voluptuary. He struck me. I'll make his marrow freeze.'

'Go back, you fool,' shouted Culbertson, 'don't wake the house.'

'Where is the voluptuary?' shouted Macaward.

Mr. Gilhooley, beside himself, caught up a wooden stand, used for holding walking-sticks and umbrellas and stooped forward to hurl it down. Culbertson caught him. Friel staggered out of the sitting-room:

'Nelly, Nelly, are ye callin' me? I'll not deser-t ye.'

Mr. Gilhooley turned back and tried to hurl the stand at Friel. Friel suddenly stiffened, hunched up his shoulders and hurtled forward with a wild shout. He went crashing out against the banisters, the banisters gave way and he fell on to the stairway beyond, head over heels. He lay quite still for a moment. Then he began to shout again.

Immediately there was a wild medley of sound. Culbertson rushed down crying:

'Are you hurt?'

Macaward was still coming up, yelling:

'The voluptuary struck me.'

Fleming, the official, rushed out of his flat on the floor below and dashing down the stairs, began to cry out: 'Police, police.'

The three men, Culbertson, Friel and Macaward, met on the stairway and attacked one another. Macaward, in his frenzy, attacked the first man he met. Friel, struggling up, put his strong arms around Culbertson and threw himself down the stairs with him on top of Macaward. They all fell at the little landing made by the turn of the stairs and began to tussle about, shouting.

Mr. Gilhooley rushed into the flat, closed the door and stood within it listening. Nelly was still crying in a low, terrified voice:

'Uncle, uncle, uncle. . . . Don't let anybody touch me. . . . Be kind to me, uncle. . . .'

Mr. Gilhooley, holding the door handle with both hands, became weak and almost lost consciousness. He lay limply against the door, with his eyes closed. It seemed to him that a great river was flowing turbulently around him, carrying him down with it to the sea.

Then he recovered again and listened stupidly to the sounds. He made an effort to remember what was happening and could not. He heard his name being called.

'Yes,' he said.

Opening the door, he went out on to the landing and, walking straight in front of him, he almost fell through the hole in the banister. He drew back just in time and listened. There was a buzzing sound in his ears and he just heard, as it were, at a great distance:

'Do you want to make any statement?'

He started and looked to his right. A policeman was standing there in the gloom.

'What has happened?' said Mr. Gilhooley to himself.

Then he suddenly remembered. Drawing himself up very stiffly, he coughed.

'Take him away,' he said calmly. 'I don't want any trouble. He's made a disgusting. . . .'

'Constable,' cried Friel. 'I want to make a . . . he has something . . . in his. . . .'

Mr. Gilhooley looked down over the banisters. He could see the figure of another policeman there, holding Friel by the arms.

'Mr. Laurence Gilhooley, that right?' said the policeman, writing in his note-book.

'Right,' said Mr. Gilhooley. 'I don't want any trouble. Not really. This is rather dreadful . . . vulgar . . . he burst in upon me. . . . . My wife is not feeling very well . . . it's dreadful.'

There was now a violent hubbub again on the stairs and Friel was making a desperate attempt to say something. Macaward was also shouting. But Mr. Gilhooley, although everything was blurred and at a great distance, listened avidly for what Friel was trying to say. As before, it seemed that he was trying to help Friel to say this. But at the same time, he moved over cautiously to the policeman by his side and pressed the pound-note, which he still held in his fist, against the policeman's chest. The policeman put up his hand, touched the note and then rejected it silently.

'Heh!' he said hoarsely. 'Wan moment.'

He went down the stairs, called the other policeman, whispered something and then came back again.

'I'll just take a look around,' he said, moving to the door behind Mr. Gilhooley.

'With pleasure,' said Mr. Gilhooley.

The policeman entered into the lighted sitting-room, looked around suspiciously and came out again. Mr. Gilhooley did not enter. He did not want to look into the policeman's face, or let the policeman see his face. Supporting himself against the doorpost, he waited. Friel was still mumbling, becoming more and more maudlin and unintelligible; and yet more determined to make some sort of warning statement.

'Who's in here?' said the policeman, knocking at the bedroom door.

'My wife,' said Mr. Gilhooley turning around suddenly. 'Don't disturb her.'

The policeman paused a moment. Then he called out:

'All right in there?'

'Yes,' came Nelly's voice. 'I'm all right.'

The policeman came out, said good-night to Mr. Gilhooley and passed down the stairs. Mr. Gilhooley did not reply. He felt that the effort to say another word aloud would make him vomit.

Again there was a babel of voices.

At last, however, the voice of the policeman who had been talking to Mr. Gilhooley rose high over the other voices:

'Oh! Come on,' he said. 'He's balmy. Come along. Tell that to the station-sergeant.'

Friel shouted out:

'He's got something in his mind. Lemme go.'

'You got the rats,' laughed the policeman gruffly. 'Haul 'im off.'

They seized Friel and then . . . they all went off together . . . away down . . . slow sounds . . . Mr. Gilhooley thought . . . wave sounds . . . gently falling . . . nothing.

CHAPTER XVIII

WALKING on tiptoe, Mr. Gilhooley stepped within the door of the flat, closed the door, and then put his back to it, leaning against her coat, that hung on an iron crook at its back. He waited, straining to catch the dying sounds of departing feet. They rose again, the sounds, as the hall door banged, away, far away. And then, through the window of the sitting-room, they came to him afresh, different sounds, mingled with the crooning of the night wind, the sound of rising wind and of human voices purified by the wind:

'God blast you, lemme go,' Friel yelled. 'He's got something in his mind.'

'Have I?' mumbled Mr. Gilhooley, setting his teeth.

He shook himself and smelt, sniffing, three times, her scent from the coat behind him. Then he heard her voice sobbing, mumbling something. The voices in the roadway jumbled. The car started. A man began to sing as the wheels whirred and the engine throbbed:

> '*I wish I were in Banagher, sitting on the grass,*
> *A bottle o' wine were in my hand and by my side*
> *a lass. . . .*'

'Are they gone?' she cried out.

The sounds ended in a soft, whirring, hooting, ringing sound. The wind moaned clearly, slowly, undisturbed by human sound. She cried again:

'Mr. Gilhooley.'

'Eh?' he said, but he made no sound.

He leaned forward. Then she went into hysterics. He heard her and raised his shoulder.

'Larry, uncle, what's going to happen? Quick, quick. God have mercy on me.'

'Silence,' he cried, making a sound which he himself heard, loud, thin and harsh.

He heard her feet thud on the floor. He looked. Her bedroom door was slightly ajar and there was a thin parallel shaft of light showing from her room beyond the darkness of the oblong hallway passage. He raised his hands in front of his body. She did not come. A lid was raised. Her trunk? She rummaged. Then he heard the bed creak and the sighs of her sobbing. He opened his mouth wide and closed it again. Then he opened it again, afraid of lockjaw. Then he closed it again softly, joining the lips, not the teeth. He felt cold.

'Will I go in?' he said in a whisper.

'No,' he thought. 'Not yet. I'm cold.'

Leaning his head wearily against his right shoulder, he stumbled into the sitting-room and turned off the light. Then groping in the darkness, he sought the window, bending forward, opening his lips to receive the inflow of the rising night wind, that flapped the hanging pale yellow blind. He caught the blind, swayed with its flapping and then jerked it. Up it went and finished rolling on its rod with a sharp bang. He started. He began to shiver so violently that he had to hold his knees. Then he drew in a deep, deep breath of the rising night wind and afraid of the wind, he seized the window fiercely and pulled it down. It descended creaking, slowly, until it met the sash. Then all was still. Again he pulled the cord of the blind and the pale-yellow blind descended softly. Then all was dark.

With his feet he touched the leg of a chair. He caught it and sat down. Putting his head in his hands he began to shed tears.

He felt the tears trickling on the palms of his hands, which he held against his eyes. He held out his hands and tried to see the palms. He saw nothing. He thought the moisture was blood and he gaped at the hands which he could not see in the darkness, sniffing to smell the blood. He licked the right palm and touched his palate with his tongue. It was a salty taste, not blood. Then he became aware of his love that could not be satisfied. And it was such anguish that he raised his head and threw it back and spread out his hands, appealing with his mind to some power for the boon of instant annihilation. But nothing fell upon him. Instead his mind grew clear and light, so light that he could feel the movements of his brain. He thought he felt. He thought he heard it move. He thought he heard it trying to form some thought, a message. But it formed nothing. And there was nothing within his brain. Nothing fell on him. He could think of nothing. There was nothing but a formless dark cavity in which he was placed immovable.

He rose, swaying, drawing in a deep breath, so deep that it would fill the emptiness and prevent him moving towards her whom he loved and whom he could not cherish. As he stood, his limbs seemed to him big and uncouth. He drew his hand across his face and felt its disfigurement. He felt, with his hand, the ugliness which all of them had seen that day, the face of a ghoul. But with his lips he tried to form some words in denial. He wanted to cry out that he loved, that he meant no evil, but good. Not a sound.

Thrusting out his chest and drawing his hands down stiffly by his sides, he stood erect. He set his lips firmly together. He raised his eyebrows languidly. And lo! he felt calm. But there was a feeling within his chest, as of a fire burning there. He walked steadily to the door, rounded the door-post, passed the open door of the kitchen, in which no light was burning, and put his hand against the door-post of her door that stood slightly ajar. Then he snorted and entered rapidly, thrusting the door wide open.

He saw her at once. She had sat up in bed, against the pillow, frightened by the sound of his approach. One hand was clutching the coverlet and the other was hiding something under the pillow, thrusting it in furtively. Her eyes were wild, looking at him, and her lips moved tremulously. The look of fear in her face caused an extreme revulsion of feeling in him. He wanted to respond to it, to counter it by some look in his face that would dispel it. He made a great effort and he tried to smile. But instead of smiling he burst into tears, making a mumbling sound that made him feel terribly afraid. For the sound to him, of loud weeping, coming from himself, was ghoulish. An unaccustomed, long-forgotten sound, sound of childhood woes, of a mother's absence, of a harsh, fatherly word, a strange, unmanlike sound, symbol of despair.

'Mother,' she said in a low, timid voice, lifting her hand suddenly from the coverlet and putting it to her lips.

He stretched out his hands towards her and, coming forward with jerky, uncertain steps, he began to speak:

'Nelly, Nelly, my only love . . . why, why are you afraid of me . . . my . . . my . . . let me touch you. . . .'

Going on his knees beside the bed, he let himself fall slowly against her covered body and then hid his face between his arms, moving his hands over her limbs, feeling the trembling of her body, exalted by the ecstasy of his love.

'Protect me,' he heard her whisper, not to him.

The words were almost inaudible and they were uttered with the calm certitude with which human beings, in despair, address an infinite, supernatural power.

He raised his head and fixed his glassy eyes on her. He cried excitedly:

'I won't lose you. I won't let you go. I love you.'

She stared into his eyes coldly. Then her terrified eyes grew soft. He thought his eyes also grew soft, looking into her soft eyes. Slowly, she took her hand from near her mouth, stretched it out slowly, with the twitching movements of a helpless child, and touched his forehead with the tips of her fingers.

'You love me?' she whispered.

'Kill me,' he murmured with his lips, hardly making a sound.

Then they stared again each into the other's eyes. A strange light came into her eyes. She turned away her eyes a little and opened her lips. She seemed to listen. He moved his right hand and pressed the palm against her left breast. She started and said in a whisper:

'I lost him.'

'You have lost him,' he said.

His two hands gently touched her, moving, touching; every vein was throbbing.

'Isn't he coming yet?' she said.

Again their eyes met. He stretched his head upwards towards her, striving to reach her face and touch her lips with his lips. When his face was near hers, he said thickly:

'Give me a last kiss, Nelly. Kiss me once and then . . . I'll remember it for ever. Touch me with your lips. Touch me. Call me by my name, so that I'll know you know me. You I love, so queer, so queer, that I don't know myself. Forever then I'll know you by that one kiss. I touch you . . . softly . . . look . . . I see you. Oh! My love. . . .'

He gasped and then he tried to say, 'Bend down your face,' but his lips would not utter the words.

She was looking at his face. Her eyes wandered over it, but there was no sense in her eyes. Then she smiled faintly and said like a child:

'You never saw his face. His face is beautiful. I lost him.'

He drew back his head and sighed wearily. His hands fell back too, slowly touching and fondling her body.

'You gave me . . . ' she cried suddenly, in a childish voice, 'all gave me. . . . I see . . . but wait . . . I'll give him to you . . . . I'll give him . . . what have I to give? . . . nothing but him . . . I gave him to her . . . because I love her . . . like a queen . . . a big proud cat. See?'

'Speak to me, Nelly,' he whispered.

His lips were dry and he could feel his face becoming ghoulish again. The skin went taut on his face. He struggled violently, but the ghoulish feeling invaded his limbs and they too became rigid. Still he spoke again in a tender voice:

'Say you know me. Say I was kind to you. Say I loved you.'

'I never knew my mother,' she said softly. 'That's why I love her. Maybe she is my mother. Wait, wait . . . don't touch me,' she gasped.

He had raised himself against the side of the bed, leaning on his clenched fists. The terror had returned to her eyes, but they were still senseless. In a hoarse voice he mumbled:

'Can't you see I'm going mad?'

'No, no,' she said, 'you can't. He'll protect me.'

She doubled up her left arm behind her and snatched something from under the pillow. He made a little movement and then stopped, seeing what she drew forth. She held it in front of her breast, gripping the sides fiercely with her fingers. He gazed at it. It was a photograph. He leaned forward and peered at it, closer, closer, until he saw a short, slim man smiling coldly at him from the photograph. He knew who it was. He thrust forward his hand and grasped the thing, tore it from her and threw it violently to the floor.

'Mother . . . mother,' she whispered. 'I love . . . I love.'

He uttered a low cry and grasped his throat. His head swam round and round and round. He felt himself falling down, down, down into a bottomless abyss. And behind there came at an immeasurable speed a strange man brandishing a club.

Jumping forward, he heard her low, soft voice say wearily:

'I love . . . I love . . . .'

Then he lost consciousness of what he was doing. And yet . . . he was aware of a great mass surrounding him, pressing inwards, crushing, crushing slowly and then there was a snap, a gasp and complete silence.

The universe had re-formed. There was order everywhere. But there was no sound. All life had passed away. The sun, stars, moon, earth, all stood motionless, waiting, contemplating a brilliant light.

What light?

He raised his head. It was the light in the room. Blinking, he shook his head several times. Then he struck the pit of his stomach with his left hand and dashed his face against the bedclothes. He must not see. His forehead pressed against a motionless limb, a leg, her leg. He drew it back. Then he became aware of his hands. They felt so heavy and lifeless. What had they done?

He tried to hide his hands, to put them away, to separate them from his body. He tried moving his body without moving his hands. But they followed him. Slipping from the bedside, he sank to the floor and his horrible hands fell with him. One after the other, flabby, supine, heavy, they fell upon his body and then tumbled about, stiff and distended, ghoulish members of his being, clinging to him.

Slowly his senses gathered. He opened his eyes and looked at himself. And he knew himself. He knew his hands, his feet, the contours of his body. He felt his head resting on his thick, strong neck. He knew he had not died. He knew he must still suffer and remember everything. He knew he must not hide from it.

But that light! The devilish light?

He rose lightly and ran on tiptoe to the door. He pawed about. The switch was not there. Was it by the bed? He was going to look, but he covered his face with his hands and rushed out on tiptoe into the little oblong hallway. There he exposed his eyes and looked, but in horror he covered them again.

The light streamed from the room. Shielding his eyes with his left hand, he moved in slowly, caught the door handle and pulled out the door. He closed it gently.

Then he sighed and turned to move away. But immediately, he felt a violent longing to go in and touch it once more . . . just one last touch . . . to speak to it . . . to lie down beside it and clasp it in his arms . . . and . . . and lie there beside it forever . . . so that nobody could steal it from him.

Yet he could not move to go towards it because the light was in there, shining upon it and shouting at him.

Then he covered his face again with his hands. Uttering a loud groan he took two paces forward and then struck his head against the door. He struck his head against her coat that was hanging on a crook in the door. The faint perfume of her coat reached his senses. He knew it was hers, her coat, the perfume she had used on her body. Tenderly he seized it with both hands. He became weak and sinking down he dragged it with him, violently tearing it from the crook, until he fell helplessly and supine at the door's base, hugging it in his arms. He kissed it many times slowly, murmuring, wetting it with his tears. And then murmuring, he rubbed it over his face, back and forth, back and forth endlessly.

CHAPTER XIX

DAY dawned while he lay by the door, clutching the overcoat. The morning light came through the kitchen window and through the blind-covered window of the sitting-room. He watched the light making things visible about him, and he recognized each object that became exposed, with wonder.

But when the first human sound reached him he started. It was the sound of footsteps, moving slowly in the distance. He got to his feet, moving carefully, lest he should be heard, either by what was in the bedroom or by what moved in the street outside. Walking on tiptoe, he entered the sitting-room and found his overcoat, his hat, his walking-stick and his gloves. He put on his coat, his hat and his gloves, took his stick and then moved again on tiptoe to the door. He went out and down the stairs, walking on tiptoe. He opened the hall door slowly, and then, suddenly trembling, he rushed down the steps, leaving the door open behind him. He paused on the pavement, wondering in what direction he should go. Failing to decide, he walked across the street until he reached the opposite pavement and found with alarm that he was standing uncertainly there also. There was nobody in the street, but there was a rumbling sound afar off, where a cart was moving. And the day was dark, with an angry wind blowing.

He moved off to the left away from the sound. He thought he was walking slowly, at his ease, but really his legs were trembling and he was continually breaking into a trot. He was not thinking. The activity of his brain was concentrated on listening to the sounds that reached him, counting them, discovering their origin and measuring the danger they might cause. He did not recognize the streets through which he walked, but even the slightest sound was familiar to him.

At last he saw a human being and stood stock still, with staring eyes, in fear. It was a man walking towards him at a distance, with downcast head, with his hands muffled in his sleeves, with shuffling gait. The man was shuddering, and he moved his head spasmodically. Mr. Gilhooley stepped into the doorway of a shop and intently watched the man approach on the opposite side of the street. He gripped his walking-stick fiercely and his body became rigid.

The man went past, with lowered head, shuddering and jerking his head, a homeless wretch. Having night-walked, he was going now to an almshouse for a meal. Mr. Gilhooley watched him pass, and he did not see in him a homeless, powerless wretch, but a terrible menace. A human being. An enemy.

He sighed when the man had gone past. The man had not looked into his face. He was still unseen. For although he was not thinking, he felt sure there was something in his face which they would all recognize. He went on.

His fear increased rapidly as the sounds multiplied and it was no longer possible to count them.

Several human beings came into view, coming towards him, approaching from behind, hurrying, going past in milkcarts behind trotting horses. He imitated their movements, walking with hurried steps, with downcast head, striving to hide his identity by pretending that he also was doing what they were doing, hastening to work.

But still he did not recognize the streets or know where he was going, since he was afraid to think or to recognize the streets. His mind was now concentrated on an endeavour to prevent the people who passed from seeing his face.

Nobody had yet seen his face.

Then suddenly he himself saw his face in a shop window. In the dim morning light the face was indistinct, and yet the reflection was horrible. When he saw the reflection he did not realize that it was the reflection of his face for several moments. He had taken several steps past the shop window before he knew that the reflection was the reflection of his face. He stood still and looked around him slowly. Now he recognized the streets. The shock had awakened his mind fully. And before he could persuade himself to go forward, he recollected all that had happened during the night. Each movement of his body during the night was acted in his mind slowly. And he could now feel the room where it lay on the bed. If he stretched out his hand he could feel it.

He moved on, walking slowly. Seeing a bench by the roadside he approached it and sat down. He was exhausted. Staring into the roadway he sat perfectly still. He began to commune with himself, talking hurriedly without making any sound or moving his lips. He spoke at random, but what he said was unintelligible. He had no interest in what he was saying. But he repeated all the words which he could remember in order to prevent thought.

After a while, however, his words found voice and he began to mumble, moving his lips and jerking his shoulders.

Now there was busy trafficking of human beings upon the roadway where he sat on a bench. Tram-cars went past. Shops were opened. Milkmen rattled their measures on the railings of houses. Postmen knocked, dropped letters into doorslits and moving to another house, dropped and knocked and knocked and dropped. All were calm, moving hurriedly, busy human beings, not knowing what he suffered, babbling on his seat.

Now he was not aware of them and he did not care who looked at him, for a new fear possessed him. He was struggling to keep his mind from thought, babbling ceaselessly to prevent it thinking of what lay in the room, in the bed, under the dazzling light.

The wind became louder. The sky was rapidly filling with black clouds.. The black clouds overlapped the dun wall of vapour that had covered the sky overnight. The sun was sinking out of sight.

Suddenly Mr. Gilhooley became aware that a child was staring at him. Looking up, he saw a small ragged boy standing in front of him. The little boy was picking at his nostrils with his right forefinger. His big blue eyes stared in wonder and his forehead was wrinkled. When Mr. Gilhooley looked up, the boy's mouth opened wide and an expression of pity came into his face. Then he raised his eyebrows, was seized with fright and bolted towards a shop that stood on the far side of the road.

Mr. Gilhooley immediately jumped to his feet and pulling his hat down over his forehead he walked off, at what he thought was a fast walk. But he really moved very slowly. He went in the direction of a side street to the left. He wanted to go down that way off the thoroughfare. Amazed, after walking for more than a minute, that he had not yet reached the turning, he turned about excitedly, thinking somebody was holding on to his coat tail. He saw the boy standing on one leg in front of the shop door on the far side, with his hand outstretched. The boy was pointing him out to a fat man. The man, wearing a dirty apron, in which he was wiping his hands, was stooping over the boy and looking.

'Ha,' said Mr. Gilhooley.

Immediately his limbs, which had hitherto refused to obey his will, became supple and obedient once more. He began to run quickly and rounded the corner. A woman was just coming around the corner, and he collided with her. His weight thrust her aside. Without looking to see whether he had knocked her down or not, he dashed on, turned into another street, broke into a walk and then, at the next turning, entered a dark laneway.

He halted at the mouth of the lane and for the first time, the fear of capture possessed him.

'I must hide,' he thought.

He moved down the lane until he came to a green-painted door. He touched it with his hand. It resisted, but weakly. He pushed violently. The door bent inwards at the top. He could see it was fastened with a string. Putting in his hand through the aperture he had made, he tore at the string until he burst it. Then he pushed open the door and entered cautiously.

He was in a little kitchen garden, at the rear of a tall house. The garden was desolate. The earth had in part been freshly dug and, in part, it was still covered with weeds. In the corner, within the door to the right, there was a wooden shed, with its door ajar. He walked towards it hurriedly and stooping low, he entered. He tried to shut the door, but his body was so large that he could not let the door close upon him in the small space. So he sat down among the tools. He began to smell the earth and putting down his right hand he touched a spade that was clotted with earth. He rubbed off the earth and taking some in his palms he wiped his hands with it. It was a comforting smell.

Then suddenly he closed his eyes. His head fell forward on his chest. He sank into a thoughtless, senseless stupor. He was not asleep and he was aware that he was alive, smelling earth, but he was at peace. There was a sharp pain in his forehead, but it appeared that his body had no relation to it and there was a fresh smell in his nostrils which gave him peace.

Hour after hour passed and he still sat thoughtlessly among the tools. He sat thus for six hours, and night again began to darken the earth.

Then a dog entered from the lane, ran a little way into the garden, smelt the air, took fright and darted out again into the lane, barking. Mr. Gilhooley sat up and opened his eyes.

'What's that?' he said aloud.

Hearing his own voice, he jumped to his feet and made a loud noise, knocking the tools about. He plunged out into the garden, tearing his overcoat against a nail. He looked at it, saw it torn, and immediately pulled it off.

'Hold on there,' cried an angry voice.

Mr. Gilhooley looked. A little red-haired man was running towards him down the garden path. Mr. Gilhooley dropped the coat, threw his walking-stick at the man and ran out into the lane. The man ran out after him, shouting. Mr. Gilhooley emerged from the lane and turned to the left. He ran on until he found another turning. He turned to the left again and saw a railed-in square in front of him. He walked rapidly until he reached the far side of the square and then halted. He turned around. The little man, in his shirt sleeves, was standing at the far side, gesticulating. Mr. Gilhooley crossed the road and entered a side street. When he had entered it, he started and put his hands to his face. It was becoming dark again. The wind was howling and the sky was pitch black.

He ran on. The short street twisted a little to the left and then he saw an open space in front of him. There was a high bank at first and then when he came closer, over this bank he saw a canal. It was getting dark, dark.

'God!' he cried out. 'Where am I? Where have I been? Night is falling.'

He passed under an iron chain, which barred the end of the street from the high mud bank of the canal. His feet floundered in the slippery mud. He climbed to the top and then looked around. On either side the darkening city stretched. On either side there was a thundering mass of sound and through the mass, human voices were distinct.

'Stop Press! Stop Press!' he heard.

He moved forward, shuddering at this cry. He halted under the shelter of a crooked tree that grew beside the horse path on the canal brink. He listened and then his mind began to think violently.

In terrible agony he searched the heavens for a God, and finding none he sought devils to destroy the universe and make a void. And finding nothing to heed the desire of his imagination he was forced back to earth again out of the universal emptiness, to contemplate his kind that pursued him. And he knew them now as he had never known them, not as beings with names and personalities, but as living parts of himself, each with a face like his own.

And he addressed them all, appealing with craven submissiveness for their mercy. And his mind saw no face soften in pity. But in all faces he saw his own face, horrible with the mark of guilt. In all faces he saw the ugliness of his own face. His mind knew that he had brought it to their faces. And then . . . he heard again:

'Woman Strangled in City Flat. Stop Press!'

Hearing that cry, he grew limp and moved away from the tree. He saw her, moving in front of him, dressed in white. And he tried to hasten in order to catch her, but he could not. He tried to cry out, but her name babbled on his voiceless lips. He followed her until he reached an arch that spanned the canal, and there she vanished. He halted under the arch. He looked slowly to his right and saw the slowly heaving water, heaving with the movement of some distant barge. It filled with phantoms. He stretched out his hands towards the phantoms, but they mocked him and vanished. Then he felt weary. His legs began to give way under the weight of his body.

With an effort he straightened himself. He remembered . . . he heard the cries of the people and the thundering sound of the city and he began to smile. Then he laughed raucously.

'I defy them,' he muttered. 'I defy everything. There is nothing. Nothing, you devils, nothing.'

His eyes gleamed and he looked into the water again, smiling maliciously. Again he laughed and said, almost joyously:

'There is nothing. Nothing at all.'

Suddenly the clouds burst and rain began to fall in a slanting shower, carried by the wind. He stretched out his hands and leaned forward on the bank. The water heaved more and more. Again it filled with phantoms, and smiling, he covered his face with his hands. Turning around he fell in backwards. There was a dull sound.

The sound was immediately silenced by the city's roar and the moaning of the wind. And the fleeing clouds spewed their water wantonly on the spot where he had fallen.

He rose once, flapped his hands and sank again. He rose again and sank and rose again. Then his body vaulted and sank slowly.

The rain pattered on the heaving surface of the canal. A horse, dragging a barge, tinkled, tinkled, with his steel-shod hoofs, coming up the archway.

And the dark, wind-driven clouds, spewing their water on the earth, fled before the howling wind.

Whither? Whence?